THE CONTEST

Other Great Fiction from Islandport Press

Strangers on the Beach
by Josh Pahigian

Stealing History
by William D. Andrews

Breaking Ground
by William D. Andrews

Contentment Cove
by Mirian Colwell

Mercy
by Sarah L. Thomson

Silas Crockett
by Mary Ellen Chase

There and other books are available at:
www.islandportpress.com

Islandport Press is a dynamic, award-winning publisher dedicated to stories rooted in the essence and sensibilities of New England. We strive to capture and explore the grit, beauty, and infectious spirit of the regional by telling tales, real and imagined, that can be appreciated in many forms by readers, dreamers, and adventurers everywhere.

THE CONTEST

JAMES HURLEY

ISLANDPORT PRESS

Islandport Press
PO Box 10
247 Portland Street
Yarmouth, Maine 04096
www.islandportpress.com
books@islandportpress.com

ISBN: 978-1-939017-10-9
Library of Congress Card Number: 2013930189

Dean L. Lunt, Publisher
Book jacket design by Karen F. Hoots / Hoots Design
Book design by Michelle A. Lunt / Islandport Press
Cover photo by Dean L. Lunt

Prologue

IT'S NOT DIFFICULT to understand why individuals with a mutual interest have a desire to assemble in an honest attempt to share in that pleasure. The camaraderie and common cause create friendships that might not—very often, could not—function on any other level or in any other world. However, the diverse personalities that can be charmed by the same pursuit can sometimes be the root cause of a certain amount of ... I guess what would most accurately be described as tension within that group.

What could possibly motivate Jack, an attorney and local, conservative councilman; Mike, a liberal, high school math teacher; Dave, an auto mechanic; Mark, a chef at one of the area's most unique restaurants; Wilson, a VP at a local bank; Dan, a teller at the bank across the street from Wilson's bank; Rick, a musician; Andy, the owner of a general store; Bill, the owner of the Crossing House; and me, Benedict Salem (or simply BS, as I'm better known around here), to come together in an effort to bond over a shared activity?

For those involved here, there is only one answer to that question: fly fishing. Fly fishing is the "common cause" that allows these varied personalities to function together in the same room. This conclave convenes regularly at the Crossing House—most of the locals call it "Bill's place," but it was the Crossing House for a hundred years before Bill and Sarah moved up from the city and bought it, so the Crossing House it has remained. Old Bill is no fool.

Bill doesn't fish as much anymore, but he still enjoys selling booze, so his good business sense allows him to make his back room available for the scheduled meetings of the Samuel Tippett Fly Fishers, or, as we formally refer to ourselves, the STIFFS (Samuel TIppett Fly FisherS).

It is said, and certainly believed by the members here, that fly fishing has magical qualities. Maybe it's some of that spirit which allows this bunch of fly casters to come together in relative harmony the vast majority of the time. Stories are told, and the acceptance of their content carries no consequences, so even outright lies are tolerated, as a rule. Now, stories are stories, and lies are lies, and exaggeration is part of most anglers' lives, but the sincere attraction we all feel for our usually pastoral pastime can create a rather combustible atmosphere when one's beliefs and personal truths are challenged.

It must be understood that a person does not arrive at his station in fly-fishing philosophy with a casual indifference. It is a journey fraught with trial and error, success and failure, cold and rain and bright sunshine, and, of course, wet and dry. It takes years—a relative lifetime—to establish what the uninitiated may perceive as insignificant and unapparent truths. However, these dogmas are the creed we take with us each time we go to the river, and their denigration carries with it an implied charge of heresy.

What follows is the story of how our little band of dedicated, and dare I say opinionated, fly casters became entangled in a quest to determine the perfect trout fly. The resolution of this arguably absurd notion found its expression in the form of a contest. It wasn't planned—it just happened. Ultimately, however, I believe it's safe to say that the Contest affected the lives of everyone involved. As Bill, the sage of the Crossing House, would say: "Funny how things happen."

But I'm getting ahead of myself. Let me step out of the river here and tell this story of men and fish and beautiful water and the pursuit of perfection . . . a tale of life.

Chapter 1

THIS IS A STORY of trout and troutmen, and not of a specific place and what happened there. Nonetheless, a little history may be helpful in understanding the affection some have for the river and the property through which it flows, because unlike a lot of other places in this world, our river is a much better place now than it was in the not-so-distant past.

When the disputes with Massachusetts over the independent claims of this northern territory were settled in 1820, as part of the Missouri Compromise, Maine entered the Union as the twenty-third state. Fast-paced economic growth soon followed. From the mid-1800s until almost the dawn of the twentieth century, a score of mills and factories stood along this river like a battalion of wooden soldiers. Everything from sawmills, textile mills, and even leather tanneries dumped their unwanted leftovers beside and into the stream.

Construction of the original Crossing House was completed sometime before the Civil War, the exact year shrouded in the many stories that make up local history. It served as a place for farmers and merchants, buyers and sellers, traders and tourists, to rest and relax on the road to success. It derived its name from what, at the time it was built, was the intersection of two major routes through the mountains. These roads shuttled the folks who were coming and going from all directions, allowing them to discover the possibilities of this vast new wilderness. However, the social and economic base that sustained the area's growth slowed as nearby urban centers, which boasted the power potential of much larger rivers, siphoned away a large portion of business. Through the late 1800s the mills and factories would, one by one, become idle. Despite all the misfortune that came crashing down around it, the Crossing House did manage to survive, continuing to serve as a haven into the early 1900s.

As it rested unoccupied, it was struck by lightning in 1917. It was only slightly damaged by the ensuing fire, although no one is quite sure why. Some of the older residents tell of divine intervention in the form of an unusually heavy rain that accompanied the storm.

The history of the building and its surroundings took an interesting turn—imperative to this tale, anyway—during the early 1920s when the Crossing House became the private residence of a reclusive gentleman by the name of Samuel Tippett. His money was believed by some to have come from the liquor business, which at the time of Prohibition was extremely profitable, but that assumption was never validated. It has been proposed by others (and also unproven) that real estate and the stock market might have been the source of Mr. Tippett's accumulated wealth. What is certain is that while he lived at the Crossing House, Samuel appeared to do very little work, spending most of his early years there enjoying nature, writing, painting, puttering around his estate, and fishing. None of these activities ever brought him fame or fortune, but apparently he never sought either. His purpose seemed to be pursuing the things that made him happy, and I must say, that's pretty close to my vision of a contented man.

Years after the departure of Mr. Tippett, some of his artwork was discovered in the secluded attic area of his home. Those paintings now grace the walls of the Crossing House. Samuel's love of nature and fishing can be seen not only in his paintings, but may also be inferred from the lovely room he added to the back of his home when he undertook the extensive reclaiming of the property. The space was open and airy and allowed him a beautiful vista that looked over the meadow to the young, riverside trees and beyond to the still-struggling but recovering river. I have no doubt this was his studio, and I believe he would be pleased to know that this very room now hosts the meetings of the club that honors him, the Samuel Tippett Fly Fishers.

The ultimate demise of the local economy was the best thing that could have happened to the river. The death of the mills breathed life into the stream and the surrounding ecology. The natural recovery of the river from the abuse and neglect of the mid- to late 1800s was already many decades old when Sam, for his own edification and pleasure, stocked the waters with trout—brook trout first, and then, a few years later, browns. This is all documented because along with his artwork, two of Samuel Tippett's personal journals were found; much of the river's story is told in these volumes, in his own hand.

He must have reasoned that it was his land and his river, to do with what he wished; after all, he was king of his domain. As far as I have been able to discover, old Sam never received permission to stock the fish. German brown trout had been imported into New York and New England as far back as the mid-1880s, but due to the fear of disrupting and doing damage to the native—and, after the 1880s, the augmented—brook trout population, most of the brown trout plantings were curtailed through the first couple of decades of the twentieth century. But trout, both brooks and browns, were easily obtained from any of a number of small, private hatcheries, a fact of which Sam must have been well aware. With his money, desire, and resources, Sam Tippett became an unwitting savior.

This is all rather significant because when the Crossing House was built, the river was of no importance as a fishery, a consequence of its earlier history. Before contact with the Europeans the native Abenaki surely took some pretty large trout from the stream, but with the years of misuse the river had earned a well-deserved reputation as a troutless waterway. Its slow road to recovery had remained hidden to all except the wealthy idler, Samuel Tippett.

Another boost to the river's recovery was the fact that the two roads which intersected at the Crossing House, those two major conveyers of humanity, were now merely country lanes. The isolation also appeared to be one of the key ingredients in uniting the property with the stream's first and foremost benefactor, the secretive Mr. Tippett, who stayed on through the 1920s and into the '30s. The river, still hidden from public light, grew stronger and healthier as it played through the meadows and trees of his property. The same cannot be said for Sam's fortunes, which began to dwindle even as the trout population prospered under his protective care.

There may be a connection between the apparent melting away of Sam's money and the approaching end of Prohibition, because they both happened at about the same time. It should be noted that this was also not long after the stock market crash of 1929 and the beginning of the Great Depression. I will withhold personal judgment and opinion on the erosion of Sam's wealth; it is of no matter here. What is certain is that his money slowly disintegrated. All the while, the now-aging Samuel Tippett seemed content to fish and paint and write in his journals as his money went down the river, so to speak. The Tippett estate would be lost, only to become the Crossing House once again, years later.

It is important to point out here what is truly central to this story, to these trout that we now angle for in our river; what Sam was to others is "as useless as breast on a woodcock," as Bill would say. What is important is that his passion was the single dominating factor that saved the river. With his selfish hedonism, he unintentionally left this wonderful legacy for the rest of us. We can only hope that our passions will create something equally as enduring.

With the Tippett fortune virtually gone, the estate, its trout stream in the early stages of convalescence, got just what it needed: nothing.

Sam Tippett headed to warmer weather, "for his health" (the reason given to the few who had the opportunity to know him). The river— its reputation as a lousy trout stream still intact, despite its growing, stabilizing trout population—reveled in the solitude. Now, it would prosper in the neglect.

The building that was the Tippett mansion was purchased by people, oddly enough, from "out west." It was enthusiastically refurbished and expanded, and for many years the new Crossing House struggled to survive once again as an inn and restaurant. It is also of some consequence that the new owners were people who knew little of angling and could not have cared less about it—another fortunate stroke of luck for the river and its residents.

When Bill and Sarah happened upon the Crossing House while honeymooning in the mountains, Bill said that he wasn't really aware that he'd been looking for a way out of the city. Sarah lovingly told Bill that she never believed that.

I'm with Sarah on this one.

Chapter 2

Bill took the long way home from World War II, seeing as he was required to stop for a little R&R at a US Army hospital. He eventually returned to the States with a hole in his leg, thanks to a run-in with the German Army, and a different outlook on life, thanks to that same late-night encounter.

Whatever else had changed in Bill's life, Sarah remained the calm in the storm, the constant he could—and would—always rely on. Soon after his return from Europe, William Christopher Cahill married his high school sweetheart, Sarah Margaret Kaddison. For the rest of his life Bill would say it was the only big decision he'd ever made that he didn't have second thoughts about. Sarah was Bill's perfect complement. Bill got lucky and he knew it.

I'm not going to relate a lot of ancient history that has little to do with the Contest, but Bill and the Crossing House are major influences in this story, so I'm taking a moment to give a sense of how all this came to pass. After all, if Bill had not purchased the Crossing House, none of this would have taken place, something that has crossed my mind on more than a few occasions.

Long before Bill discovered the Crossing House, he had become quite familiar with the mountains and waters of western Maine. For as far back as he could remember, the Cahill clan had taken almost all of their summer vacations in northern New England. Bill's father would take him and his brother, Jonathan, fishing just about every day, while his mother settled in at the cabin and contented herself with reading and knitting Christmas gifts for the upcoming holidays.

As they grew older, the brothers would float the lake in the ubiquitous, old wooden rowboat that always seemed to come with whatever cabin they stayed at, searching for rainbows and browns, casting lures to the shoreline or trolling spoons and spinners deep along the drop-offs. What Bill enjoyed most, however, was exploring the brooks and rivers with garden worms, teasing the native brookies out from under the banks or from behind logs and rocks. He became quite adept at this technique and would, in short order, be more successful at it than either Jon or his father. Duping the brilliantly colored speckled trout, wherever his family happened to journey that summer, became his specialty.

Cars and jobs and Sarah and a world war chipped away at Bill's interest in fishing for several years leading up to his marriage, but the slight limp that was now a permanent part of his gait would constantly remind him of the importance of enjoying life. So, after a traditional wedding, the new Mrs. Cahill was happy to go touring the Maine countryside with her husband as he attempted to reacquaint himself with what he said he thought about more than anything while he was confined to that army hospital bed. Those little brook trout brought a smile to his face; remembering those times on the water with his brother and father made things far less painful. (Bill didn't have to tell Sarah that he'd really thought about her more than anything else during the war, and Sarah didn't need to hear it; she just knew.)

Among the new adventures Bill promised himself he'd experience in those days was to learn to fly-fish. Although a high school diploma marked the end of his formal education, because of his mother's influence, he had become an avid reader. He would read the great stories of fly-fishing literature. He would become exposed to the beauty of fur and feathers, and how that bent piece of metal used to impale worms could be transformed into the guts for delicate mayflies and caddis flies and even little fish. It was no accident that Bill went to Maine on his honeymoon and learned to cast a fly.

He shared with Sarah the lakes and streams he'd visited as a child and as a young man. While they were places of visual beauty for both he and Sarah, for Bill they were emotionally stimulating as well. He learned to float a dry fly over the brookies in some of the streams where he and Jon used to guide worms, weighted with split shot, down and around the boulders. But Bill and Sarah were not Bill and Jon, or Bill and his father. They deserved something new—a place of their own.

One twilit June evening during the final days of their honeymoon, Bill and Sarah were wending their way down to Lake Coventry. As they rounded a curve on the country road, the Crossing House appeared out of the mountains like a fairy-tale castle. As the crow flies, the Crossing House is about twenty miles or so north of Lake Coventry, but if the crow had to walk, he would have to travel twenty-five or thirty twisting miles through the mountains to reach the shores of the lake. The lake and a ski area just to its south were major tourist meccas. One had to travel a distance north, past the Crossing House, to reach the next ski resort and other popular waterways.

The Crossing House is nestled in the hills, and all the most traveled routes ushered the traffic around this pocket. The highways brought people to Lake Coventry for all manner of water sports. Its reputation as a fishing lake was excellent and well-deserved. The Coventry River, which flowed into the south end of the lake, was a famous provider of large brown trout, and big rainbows ran the river during the early spring.

Just to the west of the Coventry was another considerable body of water, Pine Lake. Although the fishing was not as good, water activities of the boating kind were just as popular. These lakes and several other rivers, in addition to the Coventry, mandated the presence of a multitude of inns and motels, a couple of hotels, and even a small resort, to accommodate the legions of seasonal travelers.

This left the Crossing House on its own most of the year. Unless you were out exploring, as Bill and Sarah were, or you were returning as a guest, or seeking out the inn because someone who'd stayed there had recommended it, the chance of stumbling upon the big white house was remote. I must point out here that this isolation was an attractive element to most of the people who became regulars at the inn, both locals and tourists alike. It's also true that the Crossing House restaurant's reputation as a high-quality eatery kept the doors open even though the guest list was often rather slim.

Getting a room on a Wednesday night was no problem, and the best one in the house, the Samuel Tippett Suite, was available. Innkeeper Dan Taylor escorted Bill and Sarah to their room. Large windows filled the room with a welcoming, late-day glow. A small balcony provided views down to the river and a set of stairs leading to the lawn. An old bamboo rod that may have been one of Sam's hung over the fireplace, which was made of local river stone. A watercolor of the sun setting over the river, signed s. TIPPETT in the lower right corner, adorned one of the soothing green walls of the simple, homey space.

Bill told Dan that they were only going to stay one night, finishing their trek to Lake Coventry the next day. He knew of a nice little inn near the lake, very close to the cottage where his family had vacationed several times during their summer sojourns. He wanted to share a picnic on the river there with Sarah.

Bill and Sarah stepped out on the balcony with Dan. Bill could see the river across the meadow, and asked if it might be home to some trout.

"Some local guys fish it," Dan replied. "A few of my guests come up here and fish quite a bit, too. I hear there are some nice trout to be caught, but most folks head down to the Coventry. Some real lunkers there, I'm told. I don't fish myself, but a lot of folks love it," he continued, noticing the fishing equipment in Bill's possession and wanting to play the pleasant host. "I'd rather golf myself—that is, when I have a little free time. A place like this can hold a person hostage if he's not careful." He forced a weary laugh. "Been here for about ten or eleven years now, me and the missus. The older we get, the more attractive the warmer weather sounds, especially during the winter. It's real nice here now, though. . . . Well, I'll get out of your way and let the two of you settle in. Hope to see you in the dining room. Enjoy your stay."

Bill returned to the balcony after seeing Dan to the door. It was a beautiful June evening. Pink sparkles of fading light danced on the river. He vowed to get up early and make a few casts before they left in the morning.

Chapter 3

The next morning Bill awoke at first light, the river at the end of the meadow acting as a silent alarm clock in his head. As he readied for fishing, he tried very hard not to disturb Sarah's sleep. They had traveled a lot of miles this past week and a half, and he felt she was probably as weary as the old Ford. He whispered to her that he wouldn't be long, certainly back in time for breakfast. He quietly closed the balcony door behind him and headed down the back stairs to the lawn that sloped past the inn's gardens.

Bill made his way rather hastily through the damp field grass and quietly approached the water he could hear tumbling near the tree line. The river was even more beautiful than he had envisioned. Along the far bank the water pushed gently against the ledge that supported a small, boulder-strewn hill. Caddis flies were scooting to the surface, erratically launching themselves from the perfect wavelets into the warm, morning air—at least, those fortunate enough to get airborne, having avoided the trout almost playfully splashing at them.

Bill told me about this first experience on the river years later. We were sitting alone late one winter evening in the inn's small library, sipping Chivas Regal while the wind whipped the snow into a Maine blizzard. The scotch was perfect encouragement for the story mill, and we kept the fireplace stoked until the early-morning hours. With affection, Bill recounted his first morning on the river behind what would eventually become his home. I believed I could have been look-ing into the face and reflective gaze of Sam Tippett.

Bill was still a rank novice after spending only ten days trying to fulfill his promise to himself, to learn to fly-fish. It was actually just parts of ten days; he was, after all, on his honeymoon. He laughed as he recalled his inability to make consistently good casts that would float drag-free in the tricky currents that wiggled along the ledge. Eventually that morning, with a bit of perseverance, he was able to place some good casts among the not-so-good, and the fly tied to his leader would bounce down the riffles and reckless browns would rise to eat the bug—if an aggressive brookie didn't whack it first. He told me of releasing a half-dozen wild brook trout and several fat browns, at least one over sixteen inches. He also told me that he'd never enjoyed a morning on a river more, and may not have enjoyed one as much since.

He sipped the last of the scotch from his glass. "You know," he said with a smile, "if I had slept late that morning, I might never have come back to make my life here. I might have become a wealthy con-tractor somewhere in Massachusetts. Maybe someone else would be telling you fish stories right now. . . . Funny how things happen."

Bill was late getting back to Sarah that June morning, but she didn't mind. He knew she wouldn't.

All the way to the lake that day, Bill talked about the river behind the Crossing House. Later that afternoon, Bill and Sarah had their picnic along the Coventry, and Bill caught trout on cream-colored Mayfly patterns in the evening. He would show each fish to Sarah and each time comment that the trout was not as bright as any of those he'd caught that morning.

They stayed at the little inn Bill remembered from childhood, just down the road from the cottage his family had vacationed at. Dur-ing dinner Sarah patiently listened to Bill talk of the river and the lovely trout behind the Crossing House. While they relaxed with an after-dinner coffee, Sarah took Bill's hand and asked why they were at the Coventry Inn and not at the Crossing House. She reminded him that in a couple days they would be starting life away from the mountains and the rivers. There were no trout in the city.

Bill was up early the next morning—not to go fishing, but to pack the car for the short jaunt back north a little way, to the river behind the Crossing House. Bill and Sarah had found their corner of the world.

Funny how things happen . . . Bill's words, in a matter-of-fact way, sum up the next year of his life. He and I have killed enough bottles of scotch together to allow me to feel comfortable relating a quick—and, I believe, accurate—account of that year.

Bill had a few options for jobs upon returning home, politely refusing the opportunity to work with Sarah's father, building houses, and instead settling in at his family's business, Cahill & Sons Custom Woodworking. Bill did have some concerns that once he became involved in the family business, his favorite job—working with his hands—would soon be replaced by selling and managing and doing paperwork, and he was right. Although he worked well with both Jon and his father, being groomed as a future owner and boss bored him. By contrast, his brother Jon not only enjoyed the work but was also much better at it.

Bill often questioned what would have happened if he had gone to work for Kaddison Construction, building houses, a booming trade after World War II. He would have been in the field with tools in hand, doing what he liked while learning a new trade. He imagined combining the knowledge Sarah's father might have provided with the skills he already possessed from working in his father's business since he was a kid, and becoming a rich man by the time he was forty.

As winter slowly ground its way forward, Bill tried to settle in, but sitting behind a desk in his office, he would see the caddis behind the Crossing House fluttering into the streaks of June sun. He could picture the trout chasing them around the river. He became more restless. Jon told him to take some time off. His father offered him a raise, "for nothing," Bill later suggested, feeling he was not doing a very good job in the first place.

Sarah understood her husband's discontent, for she was also feeling unfulfilled, with just housework and reading and what she felt was merely busywork, helping out part-time at her father's office.

When Bill was not thinking of trout, there was that haunting vision of diamonds dancing on the river, visible from the balcony of the Samuel Tippett Suite. He never forgot Dan Taylor's forced laugh as he'd told Bill and Sarah that after ten years, he sometimes felt like he was being held hostage, and that he and his wife desired a warmer climate.

And so, in the early spring, after a rather severe New England winter and multiple family discussions, and ultimately with the support of both families, Bill and Sarah decided to make an offer and pay the ransom to free the Taylors. With some financial help from the owners of Cahill & Sons Custom Woodworking and Kaddison Construction, the remains of winter still on the lawn of the Crossing House, Bill and Sarah offered themselves up as fresh hostages to the Crossing House.

Funny how things happen.

Chapter 4

My description of the events leading up to Bill and Sarah's eventual purchase of the Crossing House seems uncomplicated, and Bill would have people believe just that. In most discussions of what might have been, or in accepting the conditions of the way things are, Bill could strip any philosophy to the quick with the following rationale: "If a frog had wings, he wouldn't bump his ass every time he jumped." This phrase became such a reasoning ploy for Bill that his friends created a winged frog from a stuffed animal, presenting it to him as a birthday gift. That frog and similar replicas have functioned as Crossing House mascots for years.

Bill doesn't spend much time talking about how he and Sarah wound up at the Crossing House. He has no desire to carry on a conversation in response to a question to which there is no knowable answer. But occasionally during our late-night powwows—usually in the dead of winter, when he's feeling a bit isolated and melancholy—Bill will reveal to me the magnitude of such a move, made by two people who were young and naive about what they were getting themselves into. He talks about overcoming the fear and apprehension that they both experienced at leaving the security of their home and families, the surety of good jobs and what they felt could be the loss of friends to distance and time. "Too young and stupid to know any better," he says, then smiles and adds, "but we had each other."

The decision to move to Maine would prove to be a fine choice for the young, enthusiastic couple; they were perfectly suited for this lifestyle, both in ability and temperament. In the early years Bill spent most of his time working on the inn. Although the Taylors had invested a fair amount of money in upgrades, Dan Taylor wasn't a handyman, and he and his wife had mostly just kept up the cosmetic appearance of the Crossing House. Bill knew how to repair what the Taylors' many seasons of patchwork renovation had left in their wake, and he enjoyed it; after all, this was the kind of thing he'd wanted to spend his life doing back in Massachusetts. Any misgivings about their decision melted away as he and Sarah adjusted to their new life.

Resident chef Michael Martin, known around the kitchen as Mickey, was the person responsible for the Crossing House's stellar reputation as a fine place to dine. Mickey enjoyed the company of the new owners, and with Sarah's blessing he was given creative liberty, Sarah reasoning that he knew best about the food and the restaurant, and what people came to eat. Mickey relished the new freedom and the fresh start away from the watchful eyes of Dan and Laura Taylor. The restaurant at the inn, soon to be known as the Castle Lawn, became even more popular as the menu began to reflect Chef Martin's epicurean imagination.

It was apparent that Sarah was a people person. Handling much of the scheduling at Kaddison Construction, greeting and dealing with the myriad personalities that constituted the client list at her father's company, had prepared her well for her new job as mistress of the Crossing House. In the evenings, Sarah would warmly greet the guests while Bill, with good humor, a friendly ear, and his famous witty and entertaining "Billisms," would pour drinks in the intimate tavern, later renamed the Winged Frog. They both capably tended to the minor nightly disasters.

During the day, Sarah lovingly cared for the gardens, and with an ease not usually found in a woman so young, headed the small inn staff, soon turning the personnel into more of a family than mere employees. Everyone that had worked for the Taylors stayed on after the transition. People liked working for Sarah; she was understanding and patient, and she knew how to listen. Bill told me how some of the women, especially the younger girls, would come into work early just to have coffee and talk with Sarah, often staying late just because they liked being there, going out of their way to do a good job.

Bill's handiwork was evident from the very beginning. He truly was a master carpenter, and turned much of what was ordinary in the Crossing House into exceptional, one-of-a-kind features. Two of Bill's more striking alterations to the inn were the restaurant dining room and his pet project, the studio, with the adjacent library. Sam Tippett's old studio was used for small functions, private meetings like those held by the STIFFS, and for a little intimate conversation if the Winged Frog was crowded and you told Bill you wanted a bit more privacy.

The restaurant was transformed into something truly unique. Thanks to Sam Tippett, a fireplace was prominent, focusing attention on the far wall as one entered the dining room. The room was enhanced by the warm glow of natural oak and the soft green shade on the walls. In the corner of the room near the fireplace, along the back wall and about a quarter of the way up, was what Bill called the Castle terrace. Four steps made of rock slabs led to a small indoor terrace, which held only three tables. The facade of the elevated area was fashioned of stone and textured concrete and resembled the top of a castle tower. Ornate wrought-iron bars lined the top of the stone wall and separated the tables from the rest of the room. A heavy wood and hammered-metal chandelier hung low over the space, and along with candles on each table, dimly lit the area. Most people who came to dine at the Crossing House wanted to be seated in the Castle terrace.

In the rest of the dining room, featured artwork included Maine landscapes and sailing ships. Why? Because Bill and Sarah liked

Maine landscapes and sailing ships. The green seat fabric, the complementary forest-green tablecloths under the candles, and fresh flowers filled the room with the ambience of spring even in the dead of winter. Early on, Sarah had Bill construct a small greenhouse so Mickey would never be without fresh herbs and the dining room would always have fresh flowers.

The studio remained the bright, open room that it had always been. French doors were installed to open out onto the patio deck that Bill had added along the studio, which meant that breakfast and afternoon tea could be served there in nice weather. Stairs extended off the deck to the manicured lawn and the paths that laced through the grounds and Sarah's gardens, which flourished under her attentive care.

Inside the studio, potted trees and flowering plants thrived in the light of an artist's world. A short walk through a side door and down a short hall would take guests to the library, Bill's favorite place in the inn. Again, a Sam Tippett fireplace was a warming feature. A trout carved of wood sat atop a low table set between two big, overstuffed chairs, one green, one brown. The room itself was not very large, and I imagine that when Bill first started to tinker there, it was rather barren and ordinary. He would turn it into a welcoming, comfortably cluttered space, with floor-to-ceiling bookshelves and two locked barrister bookcases near the big chairs.

The wall shelves held mostly books on fly fishing, enhanced by volumes on birds and nature and Maine history. Among the ever-growing number of fly-fishing books were newer copies and reprints of most of the first editions that remained locked in the barrister cases— Bill's personal collection, amassed during a lifetime of searching. These books were not for public reading; they were pieces of angling history. Nestled rather inconspicuously between a 1960 first edition of *Trout Madness* by Robert Traver and a like-new original copy of Jack Atherton's *The Fly and the Fish* were the two Samuel Tippett journals.

Tippett watercolors of trout streams and an early pen-and-ink sketch of the old homestead were highlights on the dark walnut walls.

This would become my favorite place at the inn.

All the work kept Bill pretty close to home. Sometimes the river at the end of the meadow seemed like it was a hundred miles away. Bill would often joke that in the early years of owning the inn, he would have fished the river more if he had stayed in Massachusetts and just vacationed at the Crossing House—not far from the truth. He would suffer a severe case of cabin fever each spring, and early in the season, even though the stream was usually high, he would cast streamers and Woolly Buggers and big nymphs in the discolored water. This time of year, some of the biggest trout would recklessly make fatal mistakes in the roiled river.

Later, when it warmed, he always managed to fish some of the Hendrickson hatch. At other times the cream-colored light cahills, sulphurs, or the pale morning and evening duns would be there. He could always cast an Adams with confidence, and caddis flies would be around most anytime he managed to get to the stream.

Unlike Sam, however, most of Bill's time at the Crossing House was not played out on the water. Often during stretches of nice weather, when the inn kept him from the river, Bill would get a bit cantankerous.

"So help me, if you don't get out of my sight," Sarah would threaten with whatever was at hand. She would then give her husband one of her discerning little stares, trying to keep from smiling, and head out to the garden.

Bill would grin, grab his gear, and go fishing.

Chapter 5

One of the things Bill didn't realize until after he'd been in Maine for a while, and had had the opportunity to do a little exploring, was just how isolated his part of the river really was. Roads crossed the stream above and below the Crossing House, but at points over a mile from the inn. At these easy-access areas the river received a fair amount of fishing pressure. However, a riverside often thick with brush, a healthy tree line, and several steep hillsides littered with boulders and ledges made the tract of wilderness along the Crossing House stretch seem unworthy of the effort. As a result, the direct descendants of some of Sam's fish that decided to live in this neighborhood grew quite large and smart. These trout only came into contact with a few local fishermen, a handful of adventurous anglers, those guests who knew of the river's bounty, and Bill.

But this isolation led to a paradox: Bill reasoned that because the trout here had grown wary of intruders, aliens throwing hardware or whipping flies at them could make them difficult, easily spooked, and often very selective. And yet at other times, this same lack of human contact seemed to make them fearless and unaware of the potential threat people posed. The fish would slash at any artificial lure that managed to make its way to the water, no matter how poorly it was presented.

Certainly, Bill relished catching trout as much as anyone, especially during the periods when his time was limited. But he also enjoyed a challenge, and much preferred the days when the trout were not so easy to fool. The intimacy that developed between Bill and the river, and his growing respect for the trout that lived in his backyard, were the result of the path Bill traveled to secure his empirically discovered, personal truths—his fly-fishing philosophy.

Over the years, Bill consistently found ways to understand and outwit the most persnickety trout. He would become a fly tier, mostly out of necessity. Two specific incidents involving the killing of a large brown and a large brook trout from his river would annoy and sadden him, forcing him to rethink his attitude toward his trout. He would happen upon the Sam Tippett journals and spend many evenings entranced by their words. And Bill would become somewhat surprised, disillusioned, and very troubled by the fact that as the years went by, he aged. His arthritis hurt him more, and his wounded leg slowed him down.

It may seem presumptuous of me to isolate a few impressions from an era that spanned decades, but it's simply my perception of what's important to this story. If you could ask Bill or any of the other participants in the Contest, you most certainly would get a different version. However, I'm afraid you're stuck with my interpretation . . . I'm being as true as I can be.

My relationship with Bill soon grew into a friendship, and I know he looked forward to our "time wasters," as he would often call our prolonged evening discussions on fly casting and trout and beautiful rivers and life. One of Bill's favorite and most insightful tales of fishing his river involved a particular incident on a late-spring evening. Trout were gulping large, cream-colored mayflies, and they would eagerly take a similar imitation if it was at the end of a drag-free float. That evening he caught and released several big fish, a couple of fifteen- or sixteen-inchers, and one pushing eighteen. They were fat, powerful native browns—Sam Tippett's fish. The biggest trout became most active the later it got.

He hustled through work the next day. Visions of large, active trout helped push him through his daytime activities so he would have time to get to the river before sunset. That evening as he quietly approached the stream, big mayflies were hovering low over the water. He could see trout slurping the bugs. Despite perfect cast after perfect cast, his fly floated untouched through the rings on the surface. Mostly out of desperation, but relying on his belief that a trout would react to what it knew, as darkness descended upon the water he made a last fly change to a Rusty Spinner. He dropped the spentwing (he recollects a rather large size 12) into the feeding lane of one of those fussy browns. One cast, and one fussy fish sipped at the silhouette it recognized. Bill quickly went from student to scholar as he applied the lessons taught him by Sam's trout and his Crossing House river.

There were definite seasons at the Crossing House, and they were often in conflict with the seasonal fly hatches and the activity of the trout. Each year the inn experienced a couple of predictably slow times. Fortunately, they offered the best chances at the biggest fish of the year. One of those times was during mud season in early spring, when the fishing could be either very good or marginal at best. The other time Bill would manage to extend his river hours was during the fall, after the autumn leaves had faded and fallen to earth and the leaf-peepers had vanished. But all too soon he would be required to prepare the Crossing House for winter, chopping wood and tightening up the house for cold winds and snow. No fishing then, the best days of the fair-weather hatches just memories.

There were those anticipated busy times when Bill didn't have time to fish—the winter ski season, summer vacation, and, of course, the wonders of fall foliage, one of the busiest times of all. Bill often couldn't fish the Trico hatches of midsummer, the inn and its guests demanding that he be constantly available. The spring Hendrickson hatch was the easiest for him to attend. Even though the inn always needed attention after the winter, and the active summer season was never far off, there was a lack of urgency around the place in the spring. Bill knew the same could not be said for the Hendricksons. This was an acceptable rationale after the waters had finally been freed from winter's grasp, and the melting snow no longer quickened and roiled the river's current.

I'm only mentioning all of this because even though the river was just across the meadow, Bill couldn't always go fishing whenever he pleased. Those times when he was able to get to the water, he never seemed to have what he wanted—what he needed. His access to flies was limited. He could get streamers and Woolly Worms and some rather poorly tied, garden-variety, often nondescript wet flies, a few miles away at McDonald's General Store, but Bill most enjoyed angling for the surface feeders. He'd soon depleted the supply of dry flies he'd brought with him from Massachusetts, as well as the ones Jon sent him from home.

So out of necessity, during the first winter he and Sarah spent in Maine, Bill, isolated from his river, learned to tie flies. The attention to detail he expressed in his woodworking, his patience and love for beauty and quality, combined to make Bill a very competent tier. It is safe to say that it wasn't long before he became a master tier. Proof of that is evident in a shadowbox that contains Bill's favorite Crossing House flies. It holds a special place on the library wall, and beautifully complements Sam's watercolors. In the truest sense, Bill became an artist every bit as talented as Sam.

For a while, in his enthusiasm, he would promote the excellent trout fishing in his ads for the inn: *Quiet, comfortable rooms, tucked away in the mountains. Superb food, great trout fishing . . .* What more could a person want? However, Bill stopped that line of advertising before he could discover whether vacationers could be persuaded to frequent the Crossing House rather than the Lake Coventry area because of two little books and two big trout.

People who stayed at the Crossing House and wanted to "wet a line" were generally pointed toward the river. Would-be anglers were urged to release the trout after catching them, and discouraged from using live bait. Bill encouraged guests to fish with artificial lures, the barbs pinched down. There were no laws to mandate such actions—Bill just wanted it that way, even early on. Very rarely was one of the larger, wiser trout duped by the inn's neophytes, and Bill philosophically speculated that those occasional confrontations would make the fish even more wary and harder to catch.

However, one brown of eighteen inches foolishly fell victim to a gold spoon wobbling through the chocolate current on a rainy April morning. There were few guests at the time, and there were even fewer congratulations—none from Bill—as the crowing guest displayed his catch. A spectacular sixteen-inch brook trout, one of the largest Bill had ever seen there (or anywhere else, for that matter), was also paraded around the Crossing House by another patron, who'd promised Bill he'd practice catch-and-release.

Although he would occasionally keep a trout or two for a supper with Sarah, the taking of these two trout had a major impact on Bill's attitude. The feelings he experienced at those times were new to him. He had taken big trout and displayed them to friends and family as trophies, much as his guests had, and he'd received the expected ego-boosting laurels. But somehow, this was not the same. It became obvious to him that he did not like strangers killing his fish. He battled with what he thought were selfish sentiments, but after he discovered and read Sam's two journals, he became more comfortable with his emotions. The lure of great trout fishing was omitted from all future ads for the Crossing House; Lake Coventry and the surrounding streams could have that business.

Because of their effect and impression on this story, the Sam Tippett journals, Bill's physical condition and mental attitude, and a couple of other major events deserve more than a passing mention. I will attempt to relate and connect their influences on this tale as we approach the Contest.

Chapter 6

This morning I returned to the property formally known as the Crossing House. Yesterday I toured the house itself and assessed its potential to meet my needs. As important as the house is, it is the property upon which it rests that most intrigues me. I crossed the meadow to the river. When I approached I saw a doe and her fawn drinking at the water's edge. Many different birds were chasing flies over the river, but strangely, there were no signs of fish anywhere.

Several days ago I visited a large house bordering the Coventry River some distance south of here—a lovely stream with some very large trout, I'm told. Unfortunately, I had no time to fish for them that day, to see if the stories were true . . . Work demanded the remainder of my day.

Somehow I seem drawn back to this property with the grand, stately, weatherworn house and the river that I am told no longer holds trout. Maybe it's the isolation and the apparent solitude that attracts me. The Coventry house has far too many neighbors and much more activity than I care to confront on a daily basis. This river here seems to me an orphan child. I can't help but question—if deer drink the water, and birds nest in the streamside trees to feed on the river's insects, and flowers bloom on the riverbank, then why are there not trout swimming in the stream? I truly believe that a river without the beauty of a trout is no river at all.

May 25, 1921

Today I became the new owner of the former Crossing House and its orphan river.

With these first two entries in his personal journals, Sam Tippett began his odyssey—his exploration of the river behind the Crossing House. From this point on I will use Sam's musings from his journals to help tell parts of this story. Learning more about the river's early history through the words of the man responsible for its very existence as a trout stream is a rare treat, indeed.

I am also going to tell the remainder of this tale in the manner in which I am most comfortable. At times I'll refer to the journals out of their chronological order, and I won't always relate the entire entry, but for my purposes it will help to keep the story more clearly in focus. It will also allow me to keep confidential what I believe Sam would have considered intimate information; after all, these were personal journals, not for public revelation.

As I stated earlier, these journals had an influence on both Bill and me because they really go beyond the mere history of the river. They were truly journals and not diaries; entries were not made on a daily basis, but rather only when Sam thought something was important enough to record. Through Sam's meditations on the river and its trout, we see a philosopher—a man who was committed to something that he felt passionate about. The keeping of a journal, intended to be confidential and private, permitted Sam to say, and be, what he could not say or be to others. The journals removed any pretense from the man—the shadows, if you will—to reveal his private expressions, as would painting, or making music, or making love. A journal is not a place to be dishonest; it's too personal. It would be lying to yourself. It would defeat the purpose of keeping it in the first place.

If one listened to the idle chatter of the generations that followed his departure, one would never guess that Sam could be the author of these journals. He didn't need to share with others the emotions he revealed in his writing; he was a subtle philosopher, complicated and private. Although his language was often flowery and at times sentimental, I believe it reveals exactly the way he felt at the time.

I should also mention here that I was one of the few people Bill allowed to read the journals—and that was only after we had established our friendship. They became as important to him as the rare books he so cherished in his private collection. I wondered, after the first time I read them, if maybe old Sam had been uncommonly introspective, or possibly even a bit mad, but I've read them many times since, and I am convinced both of his sincerity and his sanity. The absolute virtue of his deeds is undeniable. That's all that truly matters.

Sam does not go into a lot of detail about the actual procedure of the first trout stocking, only to say that brook trout were purchased from a small nearby hatchery and released into the stream in May of 1922. Much of the physical happenings are related as just facts. His emotional investment in the endeavor seems to be what Sam was intent on saving and recording in his journals.

May 28, 1922

I purchased one hundred brook trout earlier this week. The trout were released into the river in late morning. I waited until now to be sure the water and temperature would be the most beneficial for the fish, and to be sure that the practical threat of flooding was past. This was the first of what will be several releases.

June 1, 1922

I walked to the river today to paint, but I spent more time scanning the water for fish. The painting was merely started, and poorly so. I saw no fish.

June 2, 1922

I again went to the river in an honest attempt to complete the watercolor I started yesterday. The light was different, under an overcast sky. I was relieved at the lack of light . . . it gave me a guiltless excuse to look for my trout, which I was far more intent on doing. There were none to be seen.

June 3, 1922

A steady light rain kept me in my studio today.

June 4, 1922

In a hazy sunshine I walked to the river at mid-morning. I approached slowly, hoping not to startle any fish that might be there. I carried just a sketchbook to draw the ledge that defines the far bank. And along that ledge, as if by magic, I saw them . . . first one, then another, and then a third . . . almost in a row, rings dissipating as they floated downstream. My trout were there. This morning the river truly came alive for me, for the first time.

I refrained from going back and returning to fish. I want the trout to live in the river awhile, to become wilder by the day . . . although I know in my heart that these first fish will remain tame by nature. But every day here is a day removed from human interference. I will suppress my urge to cast a fly to them for some time longer. I can only hope that they will become less civilized simply by their existence here. I watched for fish to rise until well past lunch.

No one will understand the way I feel this evening as I make this entry. I have given a second chance to a place that had no chance at all. I believe my new home is a far better place now. The presence of a trout makes any place more beautiful. I only wish Elizabeth was here to share my excitement. Still, I will have very pleasant dreams tonight.

June 6, 1922

This morning I caught my first trout on the river. A more beautiful fish there probably never was. A speckled trout of about eight inches took my wet fly as it started to swing through the Ledge Pool. Spots and scribbles of yellowish hue made brighter by the dark grays and greens and blues, grading some lighter along her flanks. Large orange spots outlined in blue, brighter than a spring afternoon. Snow-white streaks traced her fins. I unhooked her and watched her rest in the shallows at my feet . . . and slowly at first, then with a rush, she disappeared into the dark water. I fished no more this day, but I did not leave for quite some time. Now, I really do have a beautiful river at my feet.

Upon rereading those passages, I was impressed by several things that I'd simply scanned through the first time. The mention of Elizabeth was not one of them. As a matter of fact, I may have missed other things because her mention was what I remembered most.

The fly Sam was using was not identified in the entry. That's interesting to us fly fishermen, because in a fisherman's log, this is considered important information. This underscored my belief that Sam was most concerned about recording his emotions in his journals.

I also found it intriguing that he gave the stretch of water at the end of the meadow a name, referring to it as the "Ledge Pool," capitalizing the first letters. I have always viewed the naming of favorite runs as a sign of respect and appreciation, signifying a personal attachment to the place. Also rather revealing was his detailed description of the trout—an artist's interpretation for sure. And Sam's several references to keeping his trout in a wild state, away from the influences of the civilized world . . . I still wonder if Sam was attempting to create a world for his fish—a world in which he wished to exist.

I have on many occasions tried to imagine what it must have felt like for Sam to catch that first brook trout. He could have pinched himself, a reality check, and that fish would still have been there, struggling at the end of his leader, and he still would have been standing knee-deep in his own paradise. The ability to touch that particular fish and release it back into his world to become "wilder," as Sam wrote, is a heightened pleasure most of us may never have the chance to experience. To Sam Tippett, this was not just any trout, and he wasn't standing in just any river. I continue to search for such moments in my own life.

There is a lot to be learned from these journals: facts stated, experiences related, and emotions displayed. However, for all the obvious information, there are also a lot of things that are missing—things that I will carefully infer or speculate upon, because, as I said, these are private musings and not intended for our eyes.

For example, some of the entries give the sense that, like Bill, Sam did not become an accomplished fly fisherman and fly tier until after he had come to live at the Crossing House. He mentions "practicing casting on the back lawn so when I'm on the river I won't drive the trout to the next county." He talks of how he "enjoys the excitement of trout rising to my floating flies," and how he needs to do much more work, both in creating them and in presenting them to the fish, in order to make them look like the real ones, noting: "Mine are obvious by their unnatural appearance and movement."

He writes of carrying a small net to the river to catch and collect some of the insects, for the purpose of identification: "The trout gorge themselves, while I fool not a single fish." As part of one entry, written in July of 1922, he wrote, "I enjoy learning on the river; a more inspiring classroom could not be found."

Sam was an artist and drew flies that were "of most interest to the trout." These often-detailed sketches, found on the back pages of both of his journals, were accompanied by descriptions of size and color, and the time of year they appeared. This is one of the few parts of the journals that dealt purely with facts and observations.

So why did a gentleman who was, I'd guess, in his fifties or sixties, move to this rather secluded countryside and become so deeply involved in an activity at which he was apparently a novice, and a lifestyle to which he was unaccustomed? If you'll pardon me, I'm going to offer a few well-intentioned, long-considered thoughts on just that.

Sam certainly had a respect and love for the beauty of the trout's environs; his words and his watercolors are proof of that, beautiful, sensitive interpretations of trees, rivers, and mountains, and riversides alive with wildflowers. But I get the impression that Sam needed a physical involvement in nature, not just an aesthetic overview. He desired to feel it in his hands, as well as his heart. He needed to see nature through the eyes of a participant, and not merely those of an observer.

It also might be that Sam had a certain desire to escape—to move away from something he found unfulfilling, and immerse himself in something entirely new. Maybe he had finally positioned himself in life so that he could live the way he'd always secretly dreamed of living. I can imagine a young Sam toiling away at his chosen profession, whatever it was, in a city environment, playing the games of others, always maintaining a desire to be elsewhere burning warmly inside, painting nature scenes from pictures or getting a taste of wilderness on weekends or vacations, and then going back to concrete and glass and crowds, to make money to finance his dream. I don't know if any of these scenarios are true, but I believe they could be. Such a need, or maybe, more accurately, a desire, could have easily led Sam to the Crossing House.

I would also suggest that this was a well-thought-out decision, because it's a fact that Sam was not a young man when he moved to Maine. He was well past those "midlife crisis" years. If taking up fly fishing with an uncommon passion, and adopting and dedicating himself to saving and nurturing a river and its trout population, seems to some rather odd, or even eccentric—so be it. There must have been an emotional attachment, some driving force within Sam, or he would have purchased any one of a dozen other properties with a house that didn't need fixing and that already had a river full of trout. His decision to live in a house that needed so much work and a river that had only the potential to be a trout stream seems very significant to me. It may simply have been a selfish desire to leave something behind, something grander than himself—a living memorial to his own existence.

Of course, there is also the possibility that Sam needed a place to live and a distraction to reflect on; perhaps it was simply an attempt to replace the loss of Elizabeth. A romantic notion, I admit, but I believe a valid one for a man of such passion.

I know that all this information and my speculation on the life and times of Sam Tippett may not seem like an integral part of the Contest, but it should not be forgotten that the river and the fish exist today because of Sam's philosophy. I also admit a spiritual attraction to the journals, and I confess to believing in the substance of Sam's words. I feel good about keeping his philosophy alive and breathing.

Ultimately, our contest became a quest that embraced much of Samuel's wisdom. It was an unfortunate reality that, at the beginning, the participants were unable to recognize this kind of insight.

Chapter 7

Before I get much more involved with the Contest and my relationship with Bill, I suppose I should do the polite thing and introduce myself.

My name is Benedict Salem, and I was born on the first day of spring. As I mentioned earlier, I'm known as BS to those who call me a friend (although some who know me well may believe that BS stands for something else). Who I am is not really that important to this story, but what I am may make some difference. I am now a writer. I have been other things—of most note, a teacher—and I will no doubt go on to become other things at a later time. But for the moment, I am a storyteller. I am also an avid fly fisherman and fly tier, a student of nature, and, much to my dismay, merely a dabbler in music and art, and all too often, in life. But that's a story for another day; this one is not about me.

I've been a rather responsible soul for most of my adult life. I even tried to settle down a few times, although a failed marriage and a couple of unsuccessful relationships might seem to suggest otherwise. I was, however, unsettled when I happened upon the Crossing House early one warm Sunday afternoon in September, on my way home from the Sycamore River. It was just there—the big, sprawling, white building with the green shutters and inviting front porch. I was hungry and tired, having gotten little sleep the night before. I had been up since 4:30 that morning, it being my last day to fish, and the ham

sandwich remaining in my cooler possessed little appeal, especially if I
had the chance to score a real meal and an ice-cold beer.

When I stepped inside I felt instantly at home. Pictures of trout
hung behind the front desk, and antique bamboo rods stretched across
one wall. A tall gentleman with graying hair and mustache, a few extra
pounds around his gut, and a slight but noticeable limp greeted me
with a firm handshake.

"Bill Cahill," he said with a smile. "What can I do for you?"

"Ben Salem . . . and if a bite to eat and a cold beer are a possibility,
then you can do a lot for me," I responded. I knew he could see the
hope in my eyes.

"I'm sure we can chase up something in the kitchen," he assured
me. "Follow me into the Frog and I'll get you that beer you're needing
. . . then I'll see what Mark can shoot down for lunch."

I trailed Bill out the side door into the tavern and plunked myself
down on the end stool of the small bar.

"What's your pleasure?" he asked.

"Something cold," I replied. I scanned the shelf that displayed
bottles of the surprisingly extensive collection of available beers. "How
about a bottle of . . . Harp. That would be perfect."

"A fine choice. Harp it is." Bill poured the beer into a chilled mug
and the foam head hugged the rim. "I'll see what we need to get rid of
in the kitchen," Bill said, laughing.

I drank half my beer in a few thirsty swallows. A well-lit rainbow
trout nearly two feet long hung conspicuously on the wall behind the
bar, and original paintings of mountains and rivers made it an easy
place to relax. Bill returned in a few minutes with an overstuffed roast
beef on wheat, to this day one of the finest sandwiches I've ever had.
He reached for another Harp and a fresh mug while he asked me if
I wanted a refill. He had noticed, as a good bartender tends to do,
that my mug was a sip away from being dry. I used all the willpower

I could muster not to tear into that roast beef masterpiece in front of me because I needed to know about that rainbow staring back at me.

"A decoy," Bill replied with a wry smile.

"It's not real?"

"Oh, it's real, all right," he confessed, "but it was caught down on the Coventry. Our little stream here has only brooks and browns. So when people ask me 'How's the fishing?,' I point to this fish and tell them that in less than an hour they can be rigged up and casting to twenty-inch rainbows. Heck, I'll draw maps and give precise directions to some of the better pools and runs on the river. I've even been known to offer up a complimentary fly or two that's sure to fool the most discerning of Coventry trout. Just another of our friendly, courteous services here at the Crossing House."

"I was told that the river here was an excellent piece of water," I teased—but it was the truth.

"Oh?" Bill responded with interest. "And where did you hear such a thing?"

"I was up scouting around the Sycamore this spring, and I ran into a real nice older gent. We swapped a few tales and a favorite fly or two while we were waiting out a shower—we happened to be using the same tree for an umbrella. I don't know it very well, but it's a pretty drive getting there. The fish aren't as big as those in the Coventry, but they do seem a little smarter. Hell, everything's a trade-off; there are a lot fewer people on the Sycamore, and it does have some nice caddis hatches, some active browns, and some fair-sized brookies."

"God didn't make a more beautiful creature than the brook trout, did He?" Bill asked. "Yeah, I go up to the Sycamore, too, when I can get away. Once in a while I even test a few of the pools on the Coventry that I direct my guests to—but there are too many worm dunkers and hardware slingers around there for me. Hell, yeah, I'm with you. I'll take the solitude every time."

Bill then launched into a ten-minute dissertation on the virtues of the Sycamore, punctuated with personal anecdotes and accounts of fish both caught and lost, most of them worthy of stardom, I might add. His obvious ignoring of my comment about his home river and his Sycamore River smokescreen was tacit acknowledgment of what surely must be some pretty fair angling in his own backyard. I had to admire Bill's style.

For the next hour and a half we talked fishing—fly patterns, new innovations in fly tying, materials and equipment, graphite versus bamboo, trout . . . We talked a lot about trout. Mostly trout we knew personally, some big, some not, all with stories that made them unique. We talked of trout we dreamed about in New Zealand and Alaska and Montana. Yes, we talked a lot about trout.

Bill showed me the library at the inn, but only after I'd mentioned to him that I had in my possession a first edition of *The Eastern Brook Trout* by Bob Elliot, which I'd stumbled upon in a small used-book shop while I was up here this week. It seemed he needed to know I would appreciate his books before he showed them to me. My meager collection paled by comparison.

"My wife is the only thing I care about more than these books—and maybe a day on the river," he added with a wink. "Sarah's out and about somewhere. If you don't get a chance to meet her, maybe the next time you're up this way, you can—"

Before he could finish his sentence, almost as if on cue, a figure whisked past the open doorway. "Sarah," Bill called out.

As I now recall, an angelic face reappeared in the doorway, smiling back over arms piled with laundry, nearly to her chin.

"Hon, I want you to say hello to Ben Salem," said Bill. "We've been talking fishing, and I told him that if he was lucky, he'd get to meet the person who keeps this little inn here afloat."

"Hello, Ben. If you've got my husband talking fishing, you might as well consider the rest of your day accounted for. As for me, someone's got to keep this place going." She smiled and adjusted the bed linens stacked in her arms. "If talking fishing was a job, Bill would be the hardest-working innkeeper in Maine—and the happiest." She blew her husband a kiss. "It was nice to meet you. Will you be staying with us tonight?"

"I wish that was the case," I said. "But unfortunately, I didn't allow for such a pleasure on this trip."

"That's too bad. I hope you'll return to us soon. Now, if you'll excuse me, I must get the beds made. Late guests will be arriving shortly."

"Do you need a hand with the—" Bill started to ask as he rose from his chair.

"No, hon, I'm fine," she said, adding in a cheery voice, "I'll leave you men to your important work."

I only had the time to respond with the cliché, "It was my pleasure to meet you, Sarah," and she was gone. I remember the feeling of warmth in the exchange, not only for me, but between the two of them. I thought at the time how pleasant it would be to sit and talk with Bill and Sarah some evening.

I could have spent the rest of the day talking fishing with Bill, but I had a good four hours or more of road time ahead of me before I would reach home in western Massachusetts, and work demanded my attention on Monday.

It's difficult to identify with much certainty what draws people together. There are those undeniable ties that connect souls and personalities. It's not just the fishing; I know a lot of fishermen I don't particularly care for. It's not a couple of beers and pleasant conversation; I can get that at most watering holes I frequent, and these people rarely become my friends. By the time I'd left, late that afternoon, I genuinely liked Bill. We shook hands on the porch, and I thanked him for his hospitality and the tour of his library. I think he appreciated that.

"The next time you're up to the Sycamore or the Coventry, be sure to stop in and say hello."

"The next time I'm up this way, I may just stop by and try out your river, behind the Crossing House here," I said slyly, watching for Bill's reaction.

"You do that," Bill said with a chuckle, then turned and disappeared back into the Crossing House.

Chapter 8

Snow and sleet and days when it's freezing even when the sun shines can make me wish for other things. There were days that winter when all I thought about was the Crossing House and the river I had never fished. Sometimes I wondered about those streams in New Zealand or Montana that Bill and I had talked of on that September afternoon in the Frog, but it was mostly a little stream in Maine that was the focus of my affectionate daydreams. I thought of sending Bill and Sarah a Christmas card, but I didn't. Instead, I vowed that come spring, I would get up that way and renew our acquaintance early on—maybe for the Hendrickson hatch.

I envied Bill and his situation; the good fortune of being able to share it with the woman he loved, and who loved him, was no small part of that. I had failed at that part of my life and been unable to discover the key to its success. His world revolved around a job he obviously enjoyed and excelled at, in a home that he had crafted to be a reflection of himself and what he loved. He could fish a friendly trout creek anytime his schedule allowed. His life seemed perfect. He lived in Eden. He later told me that he'd always known that, even when he wasn't quite sure he believed it.

My life at that time was not being lived in paradise. Let me take a moment to set the stage for my return to the Crossing House. I'll do my best to keep it brief.

The term *midlife crisis* has always confounded me. First of all, I hoped I was too young for such an occurrence. Second, I really don't know what it means; my life had been (and continues to be) a series of crises to varying degrees. I was experiencing one—in reality, several—in the spring of that year, though I still don't know how close to midlife it was. Maybe that's one of the major reasons I so envied Bill's position. I found myself in an impossible situation with the love of my life. We were moving in different directions, our common ideals not enough to nurture, sustain, and support a healthy relationship. We had simply grown apart.

To this day I don't know if one had anything to do with the other, whether it was because of or in spite of my relationship issues, but I also felt like a teacher who couldn't teach. Trying to enlighten the teenage mind to the importance of understanding history's lessons was becoming far more frustrating than I wanted it to be. What I needed to say often seemed trite and unimportant, even to me, and I had run out of new ways to say it, even if someone had cared to listen. I lost focus. I didn't seem to know what I truly wanted in life, or how to go about obtaining what little I did consider important enough to desire.

In looking back, there was one glaring indicator that I had dragged the burden of the need to change my life for far too long. The only constant passion in my life was my love of fly fishing and all that went with it. I coveted the escape I could find sitting at my vise for hours, tying deceitful little flies. I loved to be in the world where trout lived—the rivers and mountains and forests and meadows, away from people and the demands and requirements that created stress in my life. I loved the game of stealing as close as possible to a rising trout and with the silence of an owl's wings in flight, laying out a perfect cast—presenting the fly like a breath of air to kiss the top of the river, just above the widening surface rings. The anticipation as the fly floated in natural rhythm with the current, the splash as the trout foolishly mistook my bug for a real one, feeling the power of the fish as it fought against the fragile leader, not able to break free from the unforgiving arc of the rod. When each little adventure was over, I was aware of the adrenaline recharging my system, and, as strange as it may seem to the uninitiated, I cherished the feeling of respect and admiration that the encounter afforded me—the opportunity to sense nature on a personal and essential level, and the appreciation I experienced as the magnificent fish, after a mock battle for his life, swam away.

There was a time that spring when I lost touch with all that. My lousy casts were more frequent, and they maddened me. I became frustrated when I had trouble tying on a fly in the fading light of evening. Not getting a feeding trout to take my offering didn't inspire any of the usual admiration for my adversary, and it was not the same challenge to a friendly competition it had always been. It was an affront to my ability. The once-reliable, constant passion in my life wasn't much fun anymore. The purpose it had served—that of renewing my spirit—was gone.

I couldn't afford the luxury, financially or time-wise, of tramping off to some far corner of the world to find myself; and besides, wherever I might have gone, I wouldn't have truly been there. My life was void of passion. I have since learned that in order to be passionate about something, or someone, you have to make yourself available to feel that passion.

Sam Tippett wrote in one of his journal entries: "I cast to my trout today and neither caught nor fooled even one. I saw them and their telltale circles on the water. It was as if they knew what I desired, and like a flirtatious woman, and with childlike determination, they were steadfast in their resolve not to please me. It makes me desire them all the more . . . it heightens the need for the pleasure they give me."

My spirit needed to find that desire once again. I needed to rediscover my love for the lore of the trout.

Time and daylight worked their therapeutic magic over the next few months, and I felt less burdened with the job of living and less hindered by my passionless state. But unlike other times, I still felt disquieted. Rather than embrace my daily routines, I was uncomfortable, almost desensitized by them.

I mucked my way through the end of the school year and into summer, mowing the lawn, reading, trying to relax. In August I decided to take two weeks to see if the meaning of life might be hidden in the cool, clear water of one of my favorite streams, the key to its discovery concealed in the mystery of the Trico hatch. At least I knew I could rely on those little bugs to supply some diversion, and despite the time of year, surely there would be caddis dancing all day long—a sure tonic for what ailed me.

When I got there, the Trico hatches were uncharacteristically thin and the caddis were more sporadic than reliable. It also didn't help that my attitude was not on the same planet as I was. I wanted something easy, something fun. It seemed to take hundreds of casts to hook a fish, and in the summer heat, there was a good chance that it would be under eight inches. My casts were getting lazy and sloppy, a fatal affliction if you are striving to present a size 22 spentwing to a finicky brown. Any erratic, fouled backcast—and they seemed to come more and more frequently as the days wore on—was summarily snapped from its perch with but a token attempt at retrieving the fly. Days of rain dispersed among the sun and clouds kept me damp and in my tent far too often for August. Nine days into what was the lousiest stretch of fishing I had ever encountered, I discovered something about myself: Nine days of lousy fishing is all it takes to completely discourage me.

On the tenth day I decided that for the sake of my mental health, I would abandon fishing for a few days and rummage around Maine's back roads; after all, I still had a few days left to find some enjoyment and the secret of life. I believe to this very day, on some unconscious level, I knew that all roads led to the Crossing House. Eventually, after a couple of nomadic days, I pulled up to the big, white house. It looked as homey and inviting as I remembered. It was about two in the afternoon, and although I was famished, I was hoping to wait until a beer or two had been consumed before inquiring whether Mark might have some roast beef left over from last night's menu.

Up the steps and onto the porch. The big front door creaked lightly as it swung open, and I stepped into the parlor. There were the rods on the wall; I felt better already. Bill came through the door behind the front desk to greet me, just as I'd pictured he would. I wanted to open the conversation to eliminate any awkwardness, mostly for myself.

"Hello, again—remember me? Benedict Salem. I stopped by for a quick bite and a beer, last year, in September."

"Sure I do," Bill responded.

I didn't quite believe him. He seemed pleasant, but a little distant.

"I'm hoping you still have some ice-cold Harp in the Frog?"

"I have, indeed. You know the way; I'll follow you in."

Bill moved slowly, his limp more noticeable than I recalled. "Up to the Sycamore?" he asked, as he reached for the beer and the frosted mug. He couldn't have said anything that would have pleased me more. He did remember who I was.

"I just deserted the toughest damn fishing I think I've ever run into . . . low water, spooky fish, light hatches. To answer your question, though, I thought I might hit the Sycamore, or even the Coventry. They couldn't possibly be as slow as what I just escaped from."

Bill came around the bar and sat on the stool next to me.

"Have one on me," I offered.

"I'll take a rain check," he said. "A little early for me, with so much work left to do."

"I see you still have your decoy," I jested, motioning my head in the direction of the stuffed rainbow. I had waited a long time to tease Bill about his river. "You know, I crossed this river a mile or so down the road from here, and it looks like it's held its flow pretty well. Looks like it might have some nice runs in it. If I was a betting man, I'd wager that it holds some pretty decent fish, as well. By the way— how's the fishing been this year out behind the Crossing House?"

Bill didn't answer right away. He was taking all the fun out of this. It was almost as if he wasn't paying attention to anything I was saying.

"I honestly don't know," he finally responded, staring straight ahead. Then he looked at me, his eyes a little glassy. "I haven't been to the river yet this year. You see . . . I lost Sarah this spring."

Chapter 9

For the story's sake, let me tell you briefly how and why I ultimately ended up in Maine, and a little about my early relationship with Bill—maybe because a friendship like ours is not an easy thing to come by. In fact, it's as rare as stumbling onto a riverkeeper's journals.

I can recall that summer afternoon with Bill like it happened yesterday, and that's because it changed my life. I've never been able to put my finger on exactly why I was so personally touched by Sarah's death. She had entered and departed my life in a couple of minutes. And my relationship with Bill, whatever it was at the time, had covered a span of a mere two hours that had taken place nearly a year before.

We talked at the bar for quite some time that afternoon. He even cashed in his rain check and had a couple of beers. I guess his work that day was not as important as he'd thought. Bill did most of the talking; I listened. He asked me what I did for a living, a question that made no difference when we'd first met. Then, we were just fellow anglers. When I told him I was a teacher, it seemed odd to me that he never asked, "Of what?" He simply went on to tell me that the only small regret Sarah had ever expressed to him was that she might have liked to try teaching.

"Youngsters," Bill said. "She was great with kids, and they loved her, too. Everybody loved her. She never once said she was sorry that we couldn't have kids of our own—just that she might have liked to teach them. God, she would have been great. I told her to go back to school and become a teacher if she really wanted. She said I was just trying to get rid of her, and besides, if she'd left the inn to me, I'd have run it into the ground in no time. She was probably right about that. The world sure did miss out, though."

I also told Bill, probably because of his love of books, that what I really enjoyed doing most—other than fishing, of course—was writing, and that I'd had a few minor things published, mostly articles on fly fishing. I explained that I'd been working on a novel for years, but I hadn't been able to get very far with it, my current frame of mind being what it was. And while I was telling him this, I got a funny feeling in the pit of my stomach. Here I was, mired in self-pity, and over what? A bad cast? A snubbing by a trout that was obviously wiser than me; a little rain when I would have preferred sunshine; the inability to put a thought down on paper? I was talking to a man who had just lost the most important thing in his life—his reason for living. I felt ashamed.

Bill seemed genuinely impressed with my ability to sell some angling articles and stories. "That's terrific," he said. "I only made it through high school. I always wished I could write—I mean, the way I love books. Sarah always encouraged me. I said to her, 'Can you imagine—me trying to write instead of repairing something?' Always kind of wished I had at least given it a token shot."

"You can still do it now," I said. "Age is no barrier to being a writer. Your writing would no doubt be even better now. You're older and you have more to say—a different and certainly far wiser perspective on things, to be sure."

Bill smiled a tired smile. "Well, most certainly I am older, but I'm not sure I have a whole lot to say that's worth the paper it would be written on. You know," he added, "it's difficult to accept that there comes a time when you can't do anything about making your life what you wanted it to be. It's tough to realize that it won't get any better."

I can honestly say that nothing has ever been said to me that has had a more significant influence than these words.

That afternoon, Bill and I talked a lot about life and death, but mostly about living, and why we weren't doing more of it. We talked of trout only in passing, even though we both knew that for us, trout and rivers made life infinitely better.

I asked if there was a room available that night. He said that he'd virtually shut down the Crossing House early in the season, after Sarah died, and it was just starting to recover; nearly all the rooms were empty. At his suggestion I took the Samuel Tippett Suite in the back corner of the inn. Bill said he was sure I would enjoy the view from the balcony.

Leaving the pub, Bill asked if I was going to wet a line that evening. I said I thought I might—no jesting about the river this time. He took me aside and spoke softly, as if he was relaying some top-secret information. He told me to go down the path toward the river, and when I was about ten feet from the water, to look for a side path that ducked under the tree branches. "It's probably mostly grown over, since I haven't used it yet this year," he said.

The path, if I could find it, would lead to the lower end of the Ledge Pool. Just upstream there would be a rock, really part of the ledge, jutting slightly into the water, "maybe a foot or so," he continued, describing the approach.

"Near dusk, step into the shallows opposite that rock," Bill said. "Wade very quietly into position to make a cast that will land about a foot above the rock and against the ledge, so that your fly will float naturally past that point. Stand motionless in position for a few minutes before you cast. You may see a fish there off the rock; you may not. I'm sure you'll see fish in the tailout, and up along the ledge. Ignore them; you can wait. They will be there later.

"Put on a size fourteen brown Caddis," Bill continued. "When you think you've waited long enough, wait a little longer . . . then cast. Try to make the first one count. I'll see you later in the Frog."

I thanked Bill for his advice. I knew that when he took me aside I was getting privileged information.

Trying to leave myself a little time to look around, shortly after six I made my way down the path and found the cutoff. In August, like most Eastern, freestone trout streams, the water was low and revealing. Boulders created pockets, and trees fashioned shady cover in a couple of places. The river was not unlike the stream that had frustrated me and led me back to the Crossing House in the first place.

As the sun lowered to the treetops, I followed Bill's instructions to the letter. It was a beautiful, peaceful place. Sycamores stood tall along the banks, and hemlocks rode the low ledges. I could see caddis and mayflies hatching in the early evening light. Deer tracks imprinted the soft ground at the water's edge. As I would come to know from his journals, like Samuel Tippett, I enjoy seeing deer tracks by the river; somehow, it gives a place a lived-in feel.

Fish dimpled the surface, and it was difficult for me not to choose one and make a cast. I cautiously waded into position and tied on a size 14 brown Caddis. With a splash, a fish rose within six or seven feet of me—chasing caddis, I thought. The minutes dragged, but I waited . . . and waited a little more, just as Bill had tutored me to do. Quietly I pulled some line from my reel and began to false-cast toward the rock. I stripped more line as I continued to calculate the distance, measuring in graceful sweeps. I was ready. I powered my last cast slightly and stopped the line dead in midair so it would fall gently to the water with enough slack to allow the fly to drift naturally past the rock.

"Damn," I found myself saying out loud, as my fly touched down a foot short of the ledge. "What a crappy cast." Not enough practice in the last few days, I rationalized. It was also true, however, that I was a little anxious about what was going to happen. Anticipation can do that.

The fly was carried innocently past the rock, too far from the ledge to fulfill Bill's instructions. I let it float downstream, just past the intended target. Relieved that a small brookie hadn't rushed to gobble it up, I hastily lifted my bug out of harm's way for another try. This time the fly landed perfectly, within an inch of the ledge, curling naturally into the quickening current where it started to slide past Bill's rock. The caddis bumped the edge of the jutting piece of ledge as it danced by, and in an almost undetectable swirl, the bug disappeared.

I lifted the tip of my rod. It stopped and was jerked forward as the fish raced upstream. He turned and bore down into the deep water along the ledge. Several surges stripped line from my reel in pulsing rhythms. I could see the line arcing in the current, and I feared the fly might pull free or the light leader might snap. I stepped toward the trout as I lowered the rod parallel to the river and behind his upstream movement, and coaxed him toward shallower water on my side of the river. I still had not seen the fish. The reel purred as he turned and bolted across the pool and downstream. Again, with even pressure, I urged the fish back the other way. Eventually, I ushered an exhausted sixteen-inch brown closer to shore and he allowed me to slip the net under him. My heart was racing and my hands were shaking as I unhooked the tiny Caddis just barely pricking the trout's upper jaw. There was that rush; my spirit, my system, being recharged. I patiently and reverently revived Sam's fish and watched him slowly move back to the shadowy depths of the Ledge Pool.

That day, after listening to Bill's take on life—"There comes a time when you can't do anything about making your life what you wanted it to be"—and catching that sixteen-inch Sam Tippett trout, I made some major decisions. I'll make this short and to the point: I had saved a little money. I had some equity built up in my home, so I could sell it, find a place in Maine, and try writing seriously . . . give it a chance, even if it was just for a short while. There would most likely be enough cash left over to buy a little time. What else was money for? I could always go back to teaching, I reasoned. After a hiatus I might even learn to enjoy it again.

And so, a few weeks later my home was on the market. Naturally, it would take some time to sell—winter would be in the air in just a few months—but I didn't care. I had to make the change right then. I had made up my mind to never reach the point where I felt helpless about making my life what I wanted it to be.

Chapter 10

I have often been accused of having a fascination for what others might consider the vague insinuations of life. I don't believe in premonitions or predestination. I have no proof of a divine plan, although one certainly may exist.

I am, however, willing to accept the wondrous, serendipitous quality of life, for it is undeniable. What I know is that a few days of poor fishing was a fortuitous stroke of well-camouflaged good luck. A frustrating disappointment literally drove me to the Crossing House when Bill was in need of a friend. Well, maybe that's not really accurate, because Bill had many friends. What Bill needed at that time in his life was me. Don't ask me why, for that answer is unknowable. Call it serendipity.

In turn, Bill in his grief was what I needed to make me see how urgently I needed to get on with my life. If I had experienced a few less days of rain; if great hatches had been on in the mornings; if I had caught a few good fish . . . I might still be in Massachusetts, no doubt bemoaning my state of affairs. But as Bill would have said, "If a frog had wings, he wouldn't whack his ass every time he jumped."

What was, was. Bill and I were what each other needed at a critical time in both of our lives. Part of a divine plan? I doubt it. It seems like there would be too many more-important things for a divine planner to be concerned with. Serendipity? Undeniable.

I also accept, without question, the fateful result of having gone back to visit Bill and do some fishing in the early fall of that year.

My house was up for sale, and Bill was aware that a small cabin nearby was about to come on the market. It was situated on twelve acres, more or less (it seems that all property in Maine is on acreage that is more or less than the advertised amount), with eight hundred feet of river frontage, just over a mile or so upstream from the Crossing House. The cabin had served as the summer retreat of a writer from New York who Bill had gotten to know quite well over time. He would routinely stop by the Crossing House when writer's block got the best of him. Bill laughed when he told me about this, because it had seemed to become a permanent affliction for this writer during the past few years, and was quite possibly the reason for his permanent return to the city. Bill suggested that I give the property some thoughtful consideration if I was really serious about my Maine intentions.

The river there was only slightly narrower, the pools and pockets around the boulders and along the ledges were not quite as deep, and I would have to admit that the trout were just a bit smaller, as well, but it still seemed perfect to me. Any fear of being required to make a trade-off when it came to changing my lifestyle was abandoned. I worked out some creative financing that allowed me to gain possession of the place immediately. Finally, with my house in Massachusetts sold, I moved to Maine the following spring.

Bill had surrounded himself—or should I say that Sarah had surrounded him—with a devoted and competent staff. Adele Logan, one of the ladies who had been hired by Sarah and had worked at the inn ever since, became a manager of sorts after Sarah's death. Bill trusted her implicitly, and relied on her efficiency and unquestionable loyalty to make the Crossing House a viable enterprise, affording Bill the luxury of slipping away for a few hours whenever he felt like doing so.

Bill needed little excuse to spend several hours, several times a week, up the road at my place. With a friend like Bill, whose carpentry skills surpassed even his talent as an innkeeper, my little three-season cabin soon became a comfortable, four-season home on the river.

Since Bill refused to take anything but a few flies I'd tied for helping me remodel my cabin, I would, for very little money (and often none at all), spend a couple of nights a week tending bar at the Winged Frog. I also offered my help for any two-man projects Bill might have at the inn.

Over the next few years, I watched with growing concern as Bill tried to deal with the changes in his life. This story really contains a tale of two Bills. There was the one who, with his wife Sarah, had bought, lovingly refurbished, and operated the Crossing House, making a perfect life for them in paradise. And then there was the Bill who, after losing Sarah, struggled to find purpose in the day-to-day routine of running the memory-filled inn. Having talked with Bill into the wee hours more times than I can count, I know how truly dramatic the change was.

When I first moved up the road from him, Bill would seek me out to "chase down a few trout." This was often in the evening, after Bill had spent several hours working on my little house. It was as if he didn't want to spend much time at the Crossing House; too many memories, I assumed.

Bill was a wonder to watch on the stream. He knew the pulse of the river, especially the water behind the Crossing House, as well as the trout did. He would wade in silently, reminding me of a heron, never a splash or commotion or sudden movement. When in position to cast, he would hunch over in a low profile, like a pounce-poised cat, and with effortless grace, deliver cast after perfect cast to the unsuspecting trout, which honestly stood no chance. Bill would gently suspend each fish he caught in the quiet water, talking to it and patiently waiting for it to regain its strength.

"I never apologize to the trout," he told me. "I just reassure them that no harm will come their way as long as they live in my yard . . . and, of course, I thank them. It pays to have respect."

But things did not stay that way. Eventually, Bill no longer cherished his time on the river for the pleasures it afforded. It had become, instead, a diversion—something to do to escape the sadness and pain of losing Sarah. Because he lost his love and passion for the lore of the trout—because it was not the reason he ventured to the stream—with the passing of time and the burden of being left alone, Bill virtually stopped going to the river. This didn't happen overnight; I don't want to oversimplify a complex, personal conflict, because there were several other contributing factors. However, choosing to not take the path to the river soon became the rule rather than the exception.

Passions die hard. Whether they are snatched away in an instant or slowly smothered by indifference, the passing is not easy to explain, or accept.

Shortly after Sarah's death, Bill had left the inn to stay with his brother Jon for a couple of weeks. He told me that when he'd returned, the Crossing House did not feel the same, and understandably, it hasn't felt the same to him since. It didn't feel like his home anymore; it was just a place to be.

Sam Tippett made a comment late in his journals, in reference to his move to Maine years earlier: "With Elizabeth gone, I would not, I could not, stay within the walls we had shared. I needed a place that was new and solely mine—unshared and virgin."

Bill said he sympathized with Sam. Although he was clearly burdened with the abundance of memories at the Crossing House, "Sarah would never want me to leave our home," he said wistfully, one late night.

I don't mean to imply that Bill thought himself a prisoner of the past, or that he was a gloomy, self-pitying soul after Sarah's death. It was most often quite the opposite; after all, he had an inn to run, even though he was able to routinely delegate many of the responsibilities to Adele and Mark and the rest of his dedicated staff. He would, at times, overcompensate for a lamentable mood and be more outgoing than usual. But as I got to know him better, I learned that this was just a surface veneer; he knew it, and told me so. He said that others, strangers and guests, didn't care about his personal problems, and he didn't care to involve them in his life. Unfortunately, this attitude also alienated some of his less-understanding "old friends."

I noticed the changes in Bill as time went on. Whereas he used to enjoy telling stories of the river and its trout, it soon became obvious that the longer he resided at Crossing House, the less frequently he told stories to guests. I regretted this; one of the truly simple pleasures in my life was listening to him talk of his adopted home water. I'm sure Sam would have enjoyed Bill's enthusiasm and reverence for the stream and its inhabitants as much as I did.

Early on, Bill and I fished together several times a week. Sometimes we would take a day trip to the Coventry or the Sycamore, or other local waters like the Black, and even Day Brook on occasion. We even ventured to my favorite river in the southern part of Maine a few times in those first years. Bill joked: "Those damn trout could take all the fun out of fishing—too cursed finicky. Now I understand why you came up here to fish."

However, as Bill got older, the arthritis in his hands became more than an annoyance on some days, and tying knots was a growing problem. Bill's war wound would never get any better, and when the arthritis attacked his knees, the limp from the bullet—a long-accepted gait for Bill—was exaggerated by the pain. The routine of donning waders and spending the day in a cool river became a troublesome endeavor. It stopped being fun for Bill. His eyes became a concern, unreliable in the evening light. Bill didn't trust them when wading unfamiliar water.

When I could get him to the stream, we were usually found in the Crossing House stretch; he was comfortable there, and always seemed to enjoy himself. I would often move upstream and just sit, hidden, watching. Bill's skills were only slightly diminished by the years, and on that piece of water he still had no equal. It took him longer to tie on a fly, and with the aid of a wading stick, longer to move into a casting position, but the trout, as had been the case for decades, still stood no chance.

One evening, the first winter after I had moved to Maine, we sat by the fire in his library, talking through a sleet storm. Bill said that one secret wish he'd always had was that when he got older, he would grow gracefully into the role of the "old man of the river"—the fisherman that all the other anglers knew about, and spoke of with respect and reverence. The old man who had intimate knowledge of the pockets and pools, always knew the best fly to use, and understood the secrets of "his" river, the idiosyncrasies of "his" trout.

Without any formal acknowledgment, Bill had become what he'd secretly hoped for, albeit sooner than he might have wished. As romantic a notion as it may be, no one truly wants to be considered "old." I never asked him about it, and he never mentioned it again.

Chapter 11

Shortly after I arrived here, I came within a chapter or two of finishing the novel that had been so important to me back in Massachusetts. Between the fishing and making my cabin a home, I was awash in waves of inspiration and creativity. However, I could never finish the book by way of my original motivation because I was not the same person I'd been when I started writing it. I had changed. Somewhere between my exodus from Massachusetts and halfway through the renovations on my new cabin in Maine, I had become less frustrated . . . less discontented . . . more willing to just let it be.

Thinking back, I may have thought it was all just a piece of crap. Regardless, I'm the only person who has ever read the nearly finished novel. I do keep a copy of it tucked away, and I even dig it out once a year or so to read it. Sometimes I even enjoy it, because despite my change in lifestyle and attitude (both for the better), I still feel some of the disquiet within me that was the genesis of the story in the first place.

I did continue to write. With a little perseverance, using references in the form of my published articles and stories, and an initial introductory, bargain price, I was able to secure a job writing a monthly column for a small, Maine sporting paper. I had the freedom to write pretty much anything I wanted, which almost always concerned fly fishing.

While tending bar at the Winged Frog, I met John Phillips, a Crossing House regular and the editor and publisher of a local, monthly news guide that targets the tourist trade for our Maine mountains. I persuaded him to pay me to write about the area streams and tell fish stories about this part of the state. I also convinced him that during the winter, fishermen needed to hear fish tales as much, or even more, than they did during fishing season, if only to keep their hopes up. This was not just a sales pitch spoken by a man who needed to pick up a few, cold-weather dollars; it was the truth. I assured Mr. Phillips that anticipation was a winter fly fisherman's tonic, just as a downhill skier dreams of snow in his face while eating hot dogs at a Fourth of July picnic. John didn't fish much, but he was an avid skier. Thus, I wrote about fly fishing in the winter editions.

I continued to work on freelance articles and essays for magazines, and was fortunate enough to sell a few. At times I moved away from angling and wrote of other things. My fascination with the history of our fourteenth state inspired the completion of a historical novel set in the independent Republic of Vermont during the time of the American Revolution. For me, rediscovering, or maybe resurrecting, my dormant interest in history felt a bit like absolution for abandoning my teaching position.

I even made a few dollars, which I shared equally with my coauthor, William Cahill, when we sold a story about the history of the Crossing House to a New England history magazine. Bill had accomplished a goal that he was sure would have made Sarah just as proud as he was: He had become a published writer. (We made sure we didn't mention anything about the angling opportunities in the river that flowed through the property.)

Being immersed in the fly-fishing tradition, I established a reputation of sorts as a pretty decent fly tier, and sold flies on a small scale to local casters and even a few stores that catered to fly fishers—including McDonald's General Store. It was, I felt, an honest way to earn a little beer money. Anyway, I was able to augment what was left of my savings and live comfortably. I had all I needed, or wanted.

If I was pressured with a deadline or frustrated at not being able to find the right words for a story, or rediscovering that I was not always the most pleasant person to be around, I could always tolerate myself on the river. At that point, I would simply go fishing. I liked me there. When I returned from the stream, I would manage to meet the deadlines and eventually find the right words. There's no question that the deadlines were less stressful here, the right words easier to come by, because I didn't have to work by a clock. There was no nine to five unless I wanted it that way. I could work twenty hours straight if so moved, or twenty minutes. I developed a preference for getting the actual writing, the indoor stuff, done on weekends when all the tourists and flatlanders (I no longer considered myself part of this crowd) were around. I usually avoided the river then, preferring to have the water pretty much to myself on weekdays.

Over time, I found that bartending at the Winged Frog brought me into contact with most people in the area, both prominent and not so. Some I tolerated, some I disliked, and some I got to know very well. Some even became friends. As a matter of fact, I met all the folks that eventually made up the membership of the STIFFS at the Crossing House tavern, either pouring a drink or consuming one. When I moved to Maine there were no Sam Tippett Fly Fishers. I must take the lion's share of the credit, or the blame, for initiating the club. I stop at claiming full responsibility, however, because Mark had a hand in it as well.

Mark Scott was the latest in a succession of Crossing House chefs, after Michael Martin, and he became Bill's favorite. (Bill insisted this was not simply because Mark had expressed an interest in becoming a fly fisherman early on.) We became good friends, and he would often join Bill and me for a morning's fishing. His kitchen duties kept him busy during most of the evening hatches. He was a novice, but was enthusiastic and greedy to learn. He was easy to be around, and I appreciated his dry sense of humor. It was fun having him along on our trips, and on his day off we would sometimes hit the river together.

Mark and I would routinely have a drink together after he finished working for the night. We had a lot in common besides fly fishing. One thing we both shared was a genuine concern for Bill and our friend's apparent loss of appetite for life on the river. It was late one night over a cold beer when I first suggested that we start a fly-fishing club. My intentions were noble. We agreed that it might help get Bill back to the river and hopefully allow him to reconnect with the true passion for angling he'd once possessed.

It's also true that Sam Tippett had more than a little to do with all this, in part because of this rambling and rather revealing journal entry:

July 8, 1925

Nothing is more enjoyable to me than a day alone on the river, with the quiet, the light, the trout, and the music of the water. I must confess that I lost that feeling for a while, but since I've been here, solitude on the river has become a way of life for me. It is what I love.

I don't know why I chose this way of life, for it truly was a choice. I found myself searching for answers, and it was eroding my contentment. No one else lived as I did. Was I thought a fool? I still may not comprehend why I chose this path in life, but I've come to believe that simply to do what I love is sufficient knowledge. Like my painting, I do not have to justify its worth. My life should be the same.

I have no doubts when I am on my river, but there are those days when, sitting in the afternoon shade, the river at my feet, I miss the comfort of a good companion. Someone who is familiar with the fly I used to catch a big brook trout, and who understands the delight in the victory of the catch—someone with whom I can discuss the stubbornness of a brown trout when I cannot tease him to my fly. On occasion, my journal notes and silent conversations with myself seem empty and leave me feeling lonely. Nevertheless, I can say without reservation that I would still choose to live this way.

Sam's flowery prose on his passion for the river and the trout may seem foolish to most people, but it's not my place to judge. I was then, and am now, a believer in Sam's sentiment; so, too, was Bill.

Certainly, Bill's situation was not the same, Mark suggested; they couldn't be compared. After all, Bill had plenty of friends with whom he could go fishing anytime he chose. Sam had been alone by choice.

I felt Mark was missing the point. It was not as simple as just choosing to be alone or wanting someone around once in a while. It was a question of understanding why. Bill was, I offered, spending more and more time alone, withdrawn from others. Although Sam's choice was to spend time alone on the river, Bill, for whatever reason, was increasingly isolating himself from the river and spending his time alone with all the busywork he'd created at the inn—work he designed to fill his time. Bill's place was on the river, especially at this juncture of his life; I was convinced of that.

Mark and I would routinely walk into the library at the Crossing House and persuade Bill to mark his page and join us for a nightcap. He didn't really talk about Sarah and fishing like he used to; it was as if he was saving all those pleasant memories for himself. But when we could get him to talk about the river and casting to his trout, I could see his eyes become young again, not unlike when he would talk about Sarah and the old days. Often it was not what Bill actually said in our late-night powwows that made them memorable, but rather his eyes and his smile and his honest laughter. I truly believed he needed to be reminded of what, for all his life, had made him happy, and what he was missing by not being on his river.

So, in an honest attempt to rekindle the fire that I was sure still remained in Bill's heart, I suggested a fishing club.

Chapter 12

When Bill and I went to the river, Mark was not the only other person to join us. Over the decades Bill had cultivated many friendships, more than a handful nurtured on fly fishing. (I was still the new kid in town.) My favorite of these folks was Andrew McDonald, owner and proprietor of McDonald's General Store. He was a jovial soul, a little older than Bill—the kind of person my grandmother would have described as "just full of heck." A large man, he's what I envision Santa Claus would look like without his beard. Andy kept his snowy mane on the long side, and wore it with pride. Like many converts from years of spin fishing, he would, on occasion, fish with night crawlers in the roiled spring water, but he would never consider such sacrilege in Bill's presence.

Andy was a competent caster, and astute when it came to difficult fish; only Bill was more knowledgeable about our intended quarry. He enjoyed a good laugh as much as anyone I'd ever met. His sense of humor was good tonic for Bill during his somber times. Andy could laugh at himself as readily as he could make you the object of his good-natured teasing (probably one of the main reasons he stayed so youthful). I liked fishing with Andy, and we often fished the stream together when Bill was otherwise occupied.

There was also Wilson Davis, a bank president. I think I liked him mostly because Bill and Andy did. He was only a fair fly caster, and a little too serious for me. Although I thought of him as a friend, and he no doubt returned the favor, without Bill and Andy, I believe we probably would have considered ourselves acquaintances rather than true friends. I felt he was a bit distant, and even though I never said anything to Andy, I did discuss Wilson with Bill one evening. Bill wrote off his friend's aloofness as a personality quirk, and talked of how supportive Wilson had been, especially with some financial help when things were slow at the Crossing House during a couple of the lean years. That was good enough for me; Wilson could be in the club.

I was able to get to know a couple of the regulars at the Crossing House well enough to honestly call them friends. Rick Meade was a sixties rock musician who had mellowed with age and essentially dropped out—"Not unlike yourself," he would constantly remind me. He performed a solo act that consisted of some singing and playing guitar and keyboard. A versatile musician, he was really very talented; earlier in his career he'd actually made several recordings with his own band, as well as others. Rick would do an occasional weekend at the Crossing House, which is how I got to know him. He had paying gigs most of the time, playing the Lake Coventry area in the summer and the ski areas in the winter. He lived on a small farmstead with his girlfriend of many years, and enjoyed being as self-sufficient as possible. We became good friends, and when Mark was able to join in, the three of us spent some very entertaining times together, both on the river and at the Frog.

The other person I got to know and appreciate was Mike Hartland, a math teacher at the regional high school in the next town over. He was quiet and unassuming, likable from the first time you met him. During the school year he occasionally came to the Castle Lawn for dinner on a weekend, with his just-as-likable wife Annie, and during school vacations he would make it a point to drop in a few nights for a couple of beers and some fish talk. I knew he appreciated having the sympathetic ear of a former teacher with whom he could discuss the pleasures and perils of high school academia.

During the summer, Mike and I would get together as often as
we could to harass the fish. He was a very good fly fisherman, and
had been doing it for more than twenty-five years. He had moved to
Maine to get away from the city and the urban school systems some
ten years before I'd arrived, wanting to raise his kids in a rural environment. "Kids belong in the country," he told me. "The city is for
working and shopping. The country is for living."

Mike had an obvious gift for teaching, turning down several
administrative job offers from other school systems, as well as his own,
to continue doing what he loved—a dedication I admired. He guided
me on many of the other rivers in the area, and I gained a lot of local
fishing knowledge from his years of exploring the region with fly rod
in hand. Annie encouraged his time on the river, joking that he was
always much easier to live with when he got back from fishing. (Perhaps this valuable insight came from Sarah, since the two women had
been close friends.)

Mark and I first approached Andy, Wilson, Rick, and Mike with
the concept of a fly-fishing club, and it was warmly received. Everyone, to a man, said that while they'd often thought about it, they'd
never shared the idea with anyone else. Mark and I didn't mention our
ulterior motive, which was getting Bill back to the river.

I say that these were the first people we approached with the club
idea, but in truth, Bill was actually the first. Like me, Bill was not a
particularly fraternal kind of guy. A day on the river alone or with a
single friend was all he needed to enjoy the experience. I didn't want
to create a situation that Bill was not in favor of without at least a
semblance of enthusiasm. He was quietly accepting of the notion
when I mentioned it over a late-night beer, and he became more
receptive the longer we talked. When I brought up the passage from
Sam's journal—the one that talks about missing "the comfort of a
good companion"—Bill nodded knowingly; we'd discussed it at length
in the past. Those particular talks often departed from fishing and

71

became a philosophical discussion of friends and their importance in a person's life. Anyway, in the end, with no prompting, Bill offered the studio as a meeting place, even though he said he might, on occasion, be too busy to be present for an entire meeting, a disclaimer that Mark and I were willing to accept for the time being.

The other original members of the STIFFS were Jack Windermere, a local attorney; Dave Whitkowski, a garage owner, lifelong resident of the area, and the one person we all relied on at one time or another to keep our vehicles in running condition; and Daniel Sunderland, a quiet young man, relatively new to the area and a teller at one of the local banks' branch offices.

Jack was our local councilman and a loud, pompous, self-righteous, self-appointed intellect. I didn't trust him as far as I could throw a Maine moose. As a matter of fact, I voted for his opponent in the last election. He was only a fair fly fisherman at best. I could tolerate him most of the time, and honestly found him quite amusing, even when he wasn't trying to be funny. Our paths crossed a few times on the river, where his behavior was quite different than when he was in a room full of people. After he praised God for the beautiful weather, we would exchange pleasantries and comment on the hatches, making available to each other any information we thought might be of use. I found Jack less disagreeable on the river; it was just the two of us there, and he knew that I was far more knowledgeable than he when it came to angling. But in the Winged Frog, with an audience, he was always on. Two things I deduced from this: One, a Bible-thumping politician should be avoided when encountered in a confined area; and two, fly fishing makes a person much more tolerable. I'm convinced both theories are true.

Dave . . . What can I say about good ol' boy Dave Whitkowski? Built like a beer truck, great mechanic, average fly fisherman. By his own admission, cow shit ran in his veins. He was pure country. Sober, he had the personality of a sack full of hammers; slightly under the influence, he could be a very entertaining fellow. Dave's idea of a good time was a couple pitchers of beer and a bucket of ribs. If the fish became too difficult for him on a fly, he had the habit of hooking on a night crawler even with his fly rod in hand. Dave was not a slave to tradition.

The last of our charter members was Daniel Sunderland III. Just out of college, he had taken a bank-teller job while he waited for an opportunity in his chosen field of high finance. A business major at Yale, ski bum at heart, and not overburdened with ambition, he positioned himself to take advantage of either an opening at a Maine bank or a sudden winter snowstorm that would improve the skiing. He was from a wealthy Connecticut family and not exactly chomping at the bit to enter the competitive world of business. He had skied, played tennis, and fly-fished most of his life. He (or should I say, his family) probably had more money than all the rest of us STIFFS put together. But, aside from his Saab Turbo, his logo-laden clothes, and his top-of-the-line Orvis rod, he was a down-to-earth young man—conscientious, and really, one of us. Dan was also a very competent fly caster. He may not have been the best angler of our gang, but he probably looked the best doing it. I also found it interesting that fly fishing allowed Dan to completely erase any real-world disparity between Wilson, a bank president, and himself, a lowly bank teller—or, as Dan would jokingly say, "a financial officer in training." Within the confines of the STIFFS, Dan may have been the true superior. Fly fishing can do that.

And so it came to be: Andy, Wilson, Rick, Mike, Jack, Dan, Dave, Mark, and Bill . . . and me, Benedict Salem . . . the charter members of the STIFFS.

Chapter 13

There was no reason for this group of people to come together except that we were all charmed, to varying degrees, by the same activity. We were just a bunch of guys who loved fly fishing and enjoyed a few drinks and thought that it might be fun to waste a handful of hours every couple of weeks in a witting endeavor to raise the art of fabrication to a higher level. Mark and I were the only members with a grander motive for the club. As a group, we were just an assemblage of self-serving bullshitters.

The idea was first proposed and casually discussed in late spring, but mainly due to the fishing season and everyone's immersion in it, the club never got started until late fall. So, every first and third Thursday, starting in November, the STIFFS congregated in Bill's back room, the studio at the Crossing House. Our first meetings—and I use that term loosely—basically consisted of drinking, arguing, and doing what we do best: overstating our position in the world.

The need for some structure rapidly became evident. Because the club was perceived by the others as our brainchild, Mark and I found ourselves serving as its "officers." I believe a lot of it had to do with the other members' lack of initiative, and their desire to not subject themselves to the possibility of excessive work or commitment. As Mark was usually occupied with inn duties when our group was called to order (and the completion of his required tasks was a nightly

75

unknown), I took the ceremonial seat at the head of the table with as little formality as possible.

Of all the proposals, only the name of the club was solely my doing. It was important to me to have Sam Tippett be a part of our group, if only spiritually. I wasn't sure how many of our members were aware of Sam's influence on the river, so I made it a point to educate everyone—reaffirming that I had not lost my belief in the importance of history, after all. Thus informed, the vote was unanimous to have Sam Tippett's name grace our club. It would be one of the few unanimous votes that ever took place within our little organization.

We decided on few restrictions, and in another historic vote, agreed that paying some form of dues was a good idea—money set aside to "do something with." No one had a clue as to what that something might be, but twenty dollars a head put an instant two hundred bucks into our coffers. Other rules and regulations were proposed, usually by Jack, the attorney in our midst, and although many were not bad ideas, most were rejected as just too damn formal. It seemed we feared they would remove the fun and interfere with the intended purpose of the group—even though no one could quite put his finger on what that actually was.

Each meeting, after concluding our "official business" (which usually didn't take very long), we pursued our favorite activity, and bullshit the evening away (some of us had limited responsibilities until Friday morning). At some point during each session, both in small fringe groups and en masse, we'd discuss subjects other than trout, rivers, flies, or entomology. These discussions often made clear our inherent differences when it came to the pursuit of happiness away from the river. The range of subjects covered was limited only by the lack of an ear to hear what someone had to say. In other words, we talked about pretty much anything that happened to cross our minds, as long as there was an audience.

Though we missed the World Series, we held meetings during the Super Bowl, hockey, and basketball seasons. There were wars around the world and murders in the first degree, and social injustice was to be found everywhere (at times, more evident to some than others). We discussed taxes that continued to cost all of us, as they always had, their intent usually appearing unfair. There were natural disasters on a worldwide scale, and a very tough winter on a local scale. There was concern expressed over the fires that continued to turn the rain forests into ash, but far more concern over a fire that had destroyed the world of a family just down the road from the Crossing House.

When Bill was in the market for a new truck, that became the topic of heated discussion, with advice a cheap commodity (and Bill's final decision questioned by some). There was illness and there were personal conflicts. We were Republicans, Democrats, and Independents—liberals and conservatives. We all had work-related stories of interest, at least to the one telling the story. We even argued over which of the latest fashion trends from Paris looked the most ridiculous, and why anyone with a thinking brain gave a flying rat's ass about the celebrity of celebrities, and what exactly made most of them worthy of fame in the first place.

Differences were not as significant in the beginning because of the common cause and the enthusiasm of our new endeavor. Familiarity does, however, breed a certain amount of, if not contempt, then at least some disdain. Opinions lubricated with alcohol became more or less tolerable, depending on your acceptance of the premise and of the person presenting it. Few of these opinions were rarely as important, or as absurd, as they seemed to be at the time of discussion. But allowing for the booze, the personality conflicts, and the philosophical differences, we managed to get along surprisingly well, and our shared love of fly fishing allowed us to remain civil with each other most of the time.

It's only human to gravitate toward the people with whom you have the most in common. Friends and fly-fishing philosophy certainly tended to polarize our group. It was not strange to me that the people I seemed to like best were most attuned to my approach to angling, and the people with whom I had some differences in piscatorial philosophy were those I was most apt to call amiable adversaries.

Although our perceived purpose in the beginning may have been the storytelling and the camaraderie, continued meetings and contact with each other in the confines of Bill's studio seemed to demand from us a higher goal, or purpose for being. In February, after three months of drinking, hypercritical discussions, and hyperbolized fish tales, we agreed to ante up five bucks, the first meeting of each month, and do something good for a river, whether it was ours or another one nearby. A little money and our collective manpower seemed to add up to a positive number. We were proud of ourselves. We finally agreed on something of substance—something of value. Come spring, a worthwhile project would be sought out.

During that first winter, Bill's attitude toward the club warmed. He especially enjoyed the nights when Wilson and Andy stayed late and the "old goats" could reminisce. The way life often just plodded along, that kind of conversation rarely took place before the STIFFS came into existence. The atmosphere of the club seemed to foster a good-old-days mentality, and encouraged the "old guys" to plan some fishing trips come spring. Bill seemed genuinely happy to be involved. As a matter of fact, in the early spring, with the snow still covering the path to the river, Bill confided in me that he was grateful the STIFFS had become a reality. He smiled and said thanks, adding that he was looking forward to doing a little more fishing this year. Being a STIFF appeared to lessen the effects of his arthritis, and made the thought of walking to the river a little less painful. I'm sure he only envisioned bright days that would make tying flies to his leader an effortless task. The fading evening light didn't factor into his plans.

As we talked by a warm fire one cold, winter night, we were the only members left. We were both reminded of our many shared conversations by the fire at the Crossing House. Then, we'd been the only members of our club—and a very exclusive one, at that. Neither one of us would have traded what we had for the biggest trout in the river. And for Bill, for the first time in years, the promise of the upcoming season seemed brighter than the last.

Chapter 14

March 18, 1928

I had always accepted and looked forward to winter, if reserv-
edly, the season change forcing me from my river to the warmth of
the fireplace, insisting that I put away my fly rod and relinquish my
single-minded pursuit of trout. I accepted its influence as I would
advice from a good friend. But this winter has made everyone an
enemy with its meanness, and made prisoners of all things alive.
Like the unwanted, ill-mannered houseguest, it has long overstayed
its welcome.

Sam's poignant comments on that winter of 1928 accurately
reflected my own feelings about the winter the STIFFS came into
existence. It just would not go away. It was during the loosening grip
of this brutal winter that I was motivated to write a certain essay.

It was shortly after my birthday and the ground was still white
in all but a handful of isolated, sun-drenched oases. The inspiration
came as I sat at the Crossing House, in Sam's old studio, gazing across
the snow plain to where I knew the river struggled to be itself again.
Snowmelt would be excessive this year. Ice helped hold the river to
winter longer than it had a right to. The season would be late. But if
there is one truism in life, it is that nothing stays the same. The snow
would vanish, the ice would eventually melt, the river would regain

its natural rhythm within the banks, and trout would once again rise to little flies. It would not happen as soon as I'd like, but it would happen.

In this mood of wishing and waiting, a perfect day on the river was what I most wished was mine. I was inspired to such melancholy because I had been reading one of Sam's journals, as I was inclined to do when I felt particularly pensive. I was pondering his musings on winter, and this entry, made in the time of an obviously more gentle spring.

June 11, 1926

I wonder about the importance of the need for perfection. I was moved to such thoughts as I watched a mayfly float past me on the river today. I was taken by how perfect its wings appeared in the sunlight . . . latticed, translucent, delicate machines, designed to carry life. But when the breeze blew hard, the perfect little wings were inadequate, and it seemed to me then that they should be admired for their beauty but not faulted for their deficiency. It seemed to me that few things, if any, are perfect. Although many things seem perfect for a time, nothing is always that way, nor indeed is anything ever more than perceived perfection. The mayfly's wings were perfect in the calm of a beautiful day, but they were inherently flawed when gusts of wind whipped the trees. To me they were always things of beauty, but even that is subjective. I suppose many people would find them neither functionally perfect nor things of beauty.

I now have a dilemma: While their imperfection seems logically undeniable, their beauty could be defended with vigor. I suppose that I could only use the term "perfectly beautiful" to describe what I see. It is not of much value to someone else. What is beautiful or perfect is a perception, and what I see as perfectly beautiful may go unnoticed by someone else. That's fine with me. It makes me appreciate my insight all the more. It might have been that someone did not see my

Elizabeth as beautiful. I cannot imagine that, for she was, in every sense, perfectly beautiful to me.

When I read that for the first time, I wondered what kind of person, what sort of mind, could connect philosophical pretense, insect wings, and the love of his life. Yet somehow I understood, and it made perfect sense to me.

What does all this have to do with fly fishing? Well, in my melancholy state of mind and in my wishing for the perfect day on the river (and I'm honestly not sure which came first that day, the wish or the reading of the journal), things wedded naturally in my mind. What would be an ideal day, or, as Sam so elegantly argued, my perception of a perfect day on the water? Like Sam, I put my musings on the subject of perfection in writing. However, unlike the secretive Mr. Tippett, I made my opinion available for public consumption by having it published as an essay. Little did I know that it would lead to trouble in paradise. My intent was simply to state what I perceived as perfect, not to create fodder for a feud.

I could have written that essay about a walk in the woods, or what a perfect home my little cabin had turned out to be, or how unparalleled those evenings were that Bill and I spent together, talking fishing and life by a Crossing House fire, or that perfect lady I once knew and how perfect our relationship was, or could have been—or even the perfection of a mayfly's wing. But I didn't.

Instead, I wrote about a perfect day on the river, and since that involved stating my personal philosophy, by its very nature it came into conflict with any other opposing philosophy or contrary doctrine. Again, in my defense, my intent was only to paint a picture, not to draw battle lines.

Maybe I should have written about a "beautiful" day on the river; in essence, I suppose I did. To quote Sam: "The beauty could be defended with vigor." But, instead I wrote about a "perfect" day on the river; as perceived perfection, it becomes a personal truth, and as such it becomes a philosophy and a love and a passion, to be defended with vigor.

Ultimately, I did just that.

Chapter 15

Perfection
By Benedict Salem

Spring will be late this year. The only path to the river is a maze of tracks in the snow, frontiered by the deer. The river is not fully alive, still ringed and scarred with ice. Spring will be late this year—but it will come. It will be spring.

And, when I finally step into the water, I will be home. It will be like slipping into my favorite, warm flannel shirt on a cool, spring morning. It will be perfect.

The stream will push gently against my legs and sweep away any worries and wash from my mind the residue of a forgettable winter. Cedar waxwings will be there to greet me, hawking the mayflies and caddis that manage to escape the feeding trout.

For eons, an altar of rock ledge has commanded the river to dig a deep hiding place for the trout. I know that a trout—a big, wild, stream-wise trout—lurks at a point in this ledge. Even if I had not fished this place before, I would know he was there. It is a perfect spot.

There are many things that I have come to know . . . parts that make me whole. Truths that make me what I am. Everybody has them . . . knows them . . . believes them.

I know that the most enjoyable way to be alone on the river is to have someone you love waiting for you when you return. I know with the confidence born of years on the water that if I make a perfect cast, I will be content with the results—hit or no hit; hookup or not; fish or no fish.

I know, for example, that a size 14 or 16 Deerhair Caddis—brown body, a bit on the dark side, palmered through with a brown or dark-ish dun or even grizzly hackle, trimmed flush to the body on top, the remaining barbules just slightly longer than the hook gap, the deer hair not too stiff, a color that complements the light, a subtle blend of black, tan, brown, and gray, the hair ends stacked even, and when laid on the hook, the fine tips extending past the bend in the hook in a graceful flow to form a faultless, tent-shaped wing, a couple of turns of a front hackle that matches the palmered feather, just to give the bug some movement, a little life—I know that this creates the perfect fly.

It should be fastened to a delicate 6X tippet (a 5X should the conditions so dictate) on a warm, slightly overcast, late-spring dawn, the sun working as an ally and waiting until later in the morning to burn the clouds away. Standing thigh-deep in my favorite stream, a rising trout within ideal casting distance, no trees to foul my back-cast, no devilish crosscurrents to corrupt the drift, caddis flies no less perfect than mine dancing on the river—I know that this little bug is as infallible a fly as can be created. I know, on that beautiful early June morning when a trout sips that fly as confidently as it would a true fly, my faith will be reaffirmed. It is perfection.

Chapter 16

This was the article just as it appeared in my monthly column, culled from the notes I'd scribbled on the back of a Crossing House bar napkin. The essay was conceived in March, and it was to be my contribution for the May issue, but didn't find its way into print until June. As it turned out, the paper was on the stands just a couple of days before the first Thursday in June.

On the days the STIFFS gathered, I usually arrived at the Crossing House early to take advantage of Bill's library. If Bill wasn't too busy running around, hopefully I'd be able to have a beer with him and maybe catch up on any local gossip of importance. That week was no different. I was enjoying a cold ale, reading a reprint of an old volume containing fly patterns from the turn of the century, when Mark appeared in the doorway. He knew I'd be there early for the meeting.

"Don't have time to talk," he said with a Cheshire cat's grin. "Just thought I would tell you about the fourteen-inch brown I got yesterday on a Bugger—just below the rapids. I was going to use one of those perfect Caddis flies you wrote about, but I didn't think I could get a good float with such a small fly in the rapids . . . you know, where the big fish hang out. I went with a Woolly Bugger because I didn't have a size four Caddis with me."

"That's one of your problems," I said. "No confidence to go with your lack of ability. If you knew how to make a halfway decent cast

87

with a little Caddis, you might be bragging about an eighteen-inch fish."

"Oops—do I detect hostility in the room? I'd better get back to the kitchen where I'm appreciated. See you at the meeting. Save me a window seat."

I crumpled up my napkin and threw it at Mark. He nearly ran over Bill, who was coming into the library, as he attempted to dodge my paper fastball.

"Seems Mark got a decent fish yesterday—fourteen, he says."

"Shit. I've been hearing about that damn fish since he got here this afternoon. Probably more like ten or eleven—if that."

"He would get a respectable fish just in time to take a shot at me about that Caddis article. But you know, given the opportunity, I'd rather cast to those bigger fish with a Caddis than with a Bugger."

"Preaching to the choir there, BS. But if the question becomes, would you be more likely to catch a bigger fish, a sixteen-inch trout, on a Caddis or a Woolly Bugger, well . . ."

"If that's the question, I don't know what the answer is. I've taken sixteen-inch trout, and bigger, on some pretty small dry flies. I was talking purely from a perfect place in that essay," I explained. "That article was about the most perfect way for me to catch a trout—a sixteen-inch trout, if you will—not necessarily the easiest way, or the most predictable way."

"You are aware, I'm sure, that the perfect fly is simply a Hendrickson during a Hendrickson hatch, a spentwing Trico during a Trico spinner fall—hell, a fruit fly if berries are falling onto the river," Bill commented. He was stating the obvious, but his point was well taken.

"That certainly is true," I said. "But again, that was not the point I was trying to make. I've caught a lot more fish, fishing a Caddis during a Hendrickson or a Trico hatch, than the other way around. You know, I sometimes fish the wrong fly during a particular hatch just to see what happens. I got that cockamamie idea from you. And let me say this: If I have on the wrong fly, please let it be a Caddis. I know it always works, and it can always catch fish, no matter what else is hatching at the time."

"No argument from me," Bill concurred.

"No argument from Bill? What the hell—did someone spot a flying pig? What could possibly be up for consideration that Bill doesn't feel a need to argue about?" Andy bellowed upon entering the library, beer in hand. It was fun when Andy joined us; his opinions and knowledge and his personality always added some extra life to any get-together.

"A Caddis can usually catch a rising fish, and if no hatch is present, a fish will probably be more likely to rise to a Caddis than to something else," I quickly summarized.

"Possibly," Andy commented. "I'm guessing your last column started this discussion."

I nodded.

"Good article, by the way; I really enjoyed it. It contained just enough bovine turd," Andy said, smirking. "I had to read it twice. However, if I was out there on that perfect day you proposed, and I wanted to take a fish—and I mean, the best fish—I would swing a Woolly Bugger or a Muddler by his nose."

"Here we go again," I quipped.

"You know how I feel about those rising, smaller fish," Andy continued. "The bigger guys are cruising around under them, either taking nymphs or eating those little folks."

"That, of course, is not always true," Bill said, sensitive to our shared philosophy of fly fishing.

"Oh, it's true more times than not," Andy countered. "The fact that a bigger fish will, on occasion, take a Caddis or whatever on the surface still doesn't mean he wouldn't prefer and actually more readily take a nymph, or one of his own bratty, little children."

"Help!" I shouted. "Listen—I was only commenting on a perfect day for me. *For me*," I repeated emphatically. "Hell, I'm already getting tired of explaining this, and it's only six o'clock," I joked, looking at my watch. "Pay attention. I was making an observation on a perfect day on the river—for me. I would, as I just told Bill, rather catch a given fish on the surface with a dry fly, and day in and day out, a Caddis has proven to be the best fly for that job. There are caddis on the water from April to October—they are always there. The imitation, if properly tied, is sturdy and floats like a little cork in most types of water. The fish know it and eat it, and I rest my case.

"I can't interpret a perfect day for anyone else; that's not possible. But I can tell you what's perfect for me. The very first time I came to the Crossing House—actually the second, but the first time I fished—Bill sent me to the river with a small brown Caddis. I think that's the moment I realized just how smart Bill is." I glanced over to see if Bill was paying attention. He just rolled his eyes.

"He sent me to a glorious spot on the river . . . a rock. . . . Remember, Bill?" I looked over again and I could see him smile. He nodded. "Well, that was a perfect day—a perfect trip. It only lasted a short time; it was getting late when I got to the river. A sixteen-inch brown, on a little brown Caddis—a big, fat, native brown on a little, brown Caddis. That's what happened. I remember the whip-poor-wills started calling as I revived the fish in the shallows. The sun exploded the sky into reds and purples. I had discovered a new place, made a new friend—it doesn't get a whole lot more perfect than that."

"Christ, you're starting to talk like you write," Andy joked. "You're a very successful fisherman," Andy said to me, "no doubt about it. I'll bet that no one catches more trout in this river than you. Not even Bill has more success than you—at least now. In the past I'm sure that wouldn't have been true, right, Bill?" Andy looked at his friend for confirmation.

"Maybe," Bill humbly responded. He took a swig of beer, mostly to keep from saying anything.

"Maybe? Christ, you were the king of this swamp. I'll bet even old man Tippett couldn't outfish Bill. Anyway," Andy again directed his comments toward me, "given that you are one of the most successful anglers here, who do you think consistently catches the most big fish in this river?"

"If I had to venture a guess, I'd probably say the old fart that runs the general store in town." Baiting Andy, I continued: "That old bastard spends half his time fishing in the dark . . . now that's fun. I've got enough trouble wading and tying on flies when I can see."

"Well, that old bastard gets some damn nice fish." Andy patted himself on the back.

"I get some damn nice fish, as well—just in case you weren't paying attention. And when I catch them," I added, "I can see to enjoy them."

Bill snickered at my comment. We both knew that fishing at night was probably the best way to take large trout, but neither of us did it anymore; our priorities on the river had changed.

"The last time I fished at night was quite a few years ago now," Bill said. "I slipped on the moss-covered rocks and took a shitter just above Big Hole—bent the handle on one of my best reels. I've left it that way as a reminder not to go traipsing around the river in the middle of the night anymore."

"I don't go at night anymore either, despite what you two clowns think," said Andy. "But you could argue that those dark hours before dawn can still produce some mighty fine fish. Not a whole lot of caddis hatches going on, though—at least ones you can see," Andy teased. "However, getting back to our discussion, if I was writing that story— if I could write, of course—I wouldn't be on the river in June, but rather a warm May morning. The water would be a touch discolored from a recent rain, maybe some drizzle in the air, a couple of hours before sunup. I'd have on . . . let me think . . . probably a big, ugly, brown marabou Muddler. Now, that's the definition of 'perfect.'"

Andy looked over at me and then glanced at Bill, checking for our reaction. We remained stoic, our predictably good-natured way of annoying him.

"Bill," Andy said, finally giving in, "how about you?"

"I have to say, if things were different, or if it was earlier in my life, I would have to agree with BS."

"See, I told you he was an intelligent man," I said.

"However," Bill continued, "things being as they are, and accepting that I'm having a bitch of a time tying on those confounded bastardly little flies, and that walking to those isolated pools is becoming damn near impossible for me now—"

"For Christ's sake, quit your pissin' and moanin'," Andy interrupted, trying to steer Bill away from reality for the moment; after all, we were talking about perfection. "You could still outfish us all anytime you wanted to, you old turd."

"Okay, okay," Bill said, responding to the prodding. "Anyway, given what I just said, my perfect day now would be in the warmth, I don't care what month or even the time of day. I'd want moving water, broken surface, and tied to my leader, a big, juicy-looking hopper or a stonefly—yeah, a yellow stonefly, big, unsinkable. Bounce it down a chute, around a boulder, along a ledge, a place where you know there's a big fish . . . and there's that anticipation, waiting for what you know will happen, and then . . . slam!

"The water explodes and the trout whacks the fly, and even though you believed it would happen, the suddenness still startles you. And he's on and in the rapids, and the water is on his side and the battle intensifies, and as great as the fight feels, it's no better than the hit."

"It's amazing how different—how imperfect—'perfect' can be," I said.

"Perfect is perfect is perfect," Andy followed.

"What about Sam?" Bill posed. "Andy, remember that part of the journal when Sam talked about his perfect day on the river—seeking pure fishing pleasure?"

"Oh, I remember it," Andy answered. "I think at that point, poor Sam might have been in the woods by himself a little too long."

This is what Sam wrote, near the end of his reign at the Crossing House.

May 22, 1931

During a recent day of fishing, when I released a tenacious brook trout, blood trailed from his gills. I knew he would not live long. I had inflicted a fatal wound to one of my fish. It has happened before, an unavoidable consequence of my pastime, and I sometimes wish I could make it less a circumstance of the pursuit. If I kept a fish to eat on occasion, then it really would not have mattered; I would have kept that one . . . but I don't. I have lost all desire to take fish for food or folly. I live for my time on the river, but I do not wish to harm the trout. I so look forward to the tussle, the battle of wits and the fight against the bamboo. When I saw that little trout bleed, I decided to settle on some days, not all, to focus simply on the battle of wits—almost always on sunny days, warm days, when just being on the river satisfies my soul.

I decided to tie the most beautiful flies, the most perfect flies I could. I used the best materials and spent extra time at the vise, attending to detail. I cut the bend from the hook shank, effectively removing any ability of the fly to impale a fish. I counted splashes to the fly and not trout brought to hand.

Soon, I found myself tying more perfect flies and concentrating on making flawless casts and spending more time in stalking the trout. I was more aware of the nature around me and what it took to trick a fish. Not one was harmed by hook. I definitely miss the battle in my hands, but I do not miss the blood that takes a young brook trout's life. I miss the graceful, rainbow arc of the bamboo, the beauty of the trout I can touch, but I have gained in the intensity and pureness of the act—a fair trade on many days.

I directed my comments to Andy: "I know it's another romantic notion, but that concept might have some merit. I mean, heck, just to live what we love to do on another level, almost as a religious experience—seeking the pure essence of the act. Wouldn't that be a rather noble aspiration?"

"It could simply be, of course, that old Sam's trolley had jumped the tracks," Andy said as he sat back in his chair and tipped his bottle to get the last few drops.

"Now, wait a minute, Andy," Bill quickly responded. "It's difficult to make a judgment if you can't identify with the concept. But, I can . . . sort of. I told both of you the stories many times, about when I first bought the Crossing House, how I advertised for fishing guests. Then those two assholes came back with big fish they had killed, displaying them like trophies to the folks around the inn. Both of those lying bastards told me, before I sent them to the river, that they wouldn't kill and keep fish.

"I remember feeling very strange about those events. I would have liked to have booted their asses right off the front porch, if only because they'd outright lied to me. But it was more than that. I had killed and kept fish all my life. Sarah and I would enjoy a fresh fish dinner nearly every week. But somehow I felt bad for those two particular fish—and not because I wasn't the one who had killed them. First of all, I would never take such large fish from the river. At the time, I didn't know that it was all right—a good thing, really—to feel bad about those dead fish. But when I found Sam's journals and read that entry . . . well, it just all made a lot of sense to me. Anyway, I think what I'm trying to say is, the older I get, the more valid Sam's idea seems to me. It may, in truth, be the ideal attitude for the ultimate angling experience."

"Jesus, Bill, you're spending way too much time with BS," Andy groaned. "You'll both be committed if you're not careful. I'll come and visit, though. Just because you're off your goddamned rockers doesn't mean I don't care about both of you."

"Thanks, Andy," I said, "and just because you haven't progressed beyond a Neanderthal mentality doesn't mean I don't care about you either."

"Just because I keep a fish once in a while, it doesn't make me a heathen," Andy defended. "Hell, I practice catch-and-release as much as anybody—except for you two do-gooders."

"Yes, you do," Bill agreed, "and just to show you how much I respect your efforts, let me buy you a beer and we'll toast to catch-and-release."

"If you're buying, I'll toast to anything you wish," Andy said, laughing. Bill got up and went around the corner to get the fresh beer.

"Seriously, for a minute," I said, turning to Andy, "since you've read his journals, you know as well as I do that Sam Tippett is solely responsible for the fishing we enjoy on this river. What do you think it was like for him while he was here?"

"That's a very interesting question," Andy answered. "When you think about the emotional investment that he must have had in this river, and its trout, I suppose his attitude is not really all that hard to understand."

"Maybe there's hope for you yet," Bill said, having heard most of Andy's comment. He handed each of us a beer. "To catch-and-release," he offered.

"To Sam Tippett," I added.

"I'm still not fishing without hooks," Andy said. "I can accept Sam casting for the fun of it, but I want a fish battling at the end of my line."

"I'm afraid we all do," Bill said, aware of one of the vivid realities that our shared passion incites. "Oftentimes it seems as much a need as a desire," he added.

"It could be that we just haven't reached a high-enough level of understanding," I said.

"I understand this: I want to fight the fish, and I want to be able to experience that feeling," Andy responded. "It's one of the main reasons I'm out there on the river."

"Maybe if you fished with dry flies more often, you'd be more in touch with the art of our sport," I teased. "Dragging the river with those ugly buggers you call flies is dulling your senses to the finer points of angling."

"Not if you want to catch big fish," Andy quickly countered. "I'll stay with my ugly buggers and you go with those dainty little bugs you fish with, and we'll see . . ."

"We'll see what?" Bill interrupted. "Who will have the most fun? My friend, I will remind you that we would have to wait 'til the day was done to see who caught the biggest fish."

"It's about time to get started," a voice said. It was Mike Hartland, announcing that it was meeting time for the STIFFS. Everyone was waiting in the studio.

"We'll finish this discussion later, possibly even tonight, after the meeting," Andy said with a smile. He brushed his snowy locks back with both hands. "I'm not through talking yet."

"Shit, you're never through talking," Bill chided. "Even when you're not saying anything."

"What the heck are you guys yammering about now?" Mike asked.

"Come on, I'll fill you in," Andy said as they started to walk toward the meeting room.

"Don't believe a word he tells you," I called after them. "You won't have any idea what we were talking about if you listen to Andy's version—you know he exaggerates."

"Might as well get in there; we're not going to change that old fart's mind," Bill said with a chuckle.

As he slowly got up from his chair, Bill put his hand on my shoulder and spoke softly, like the time he told me about the best place to fish when I first met him. "That was a real nice article you wrote. With all this talk about Caddis flies and perfection, well, I'm not sure you'll hear much else, but just to let you know: It sure was a lot more enjoyable being alone on the river knowing Sarah would be here when I got home."

Bill stopped and stared straight ahead, out the doorway, his eyes sad, but almost hopeful, as if Sarah might suddenly appear from around the corner, her arms piled high with laundry. He paused for a moment longer, then squeezed my shoulder—communicating silently, the way friends do—and we headed to the meeting.

Chapter 17

The STIFFS filtered into Bill's back room, and the routine milling around and casual banter, which took place before any "official business," got under way. The fishing season was in full swing now, so the pre-meeting chaos took longer, and consisted of a lot of hands spread apart, gesturing to indicate the approximate length of various trout that were caught or had gotten away since the last meeting. (I must point out that I use the term *approximate length* advisedly.) So, with everyone sufficiently supplied with liquid refreshment and the chatter growing ever louder and hands getting farther and farther apart, I attempted to call the meeting to order.

"Let's go, guys," I said loudly. It produced no change in the noise level in the room. "Hey, let's get going before the sun comes up," I shouted, and slowly the din subsided.

"Our unofficial treasurer," I said, gesturing toward Bill—he had agreed to become the keeper of the money, allowing us to use the Crossing House safe to stash our cash, but refused to accept a title for his efforts—"informs me that we have a fairly substantial amount in our fund. It's June, so I think a decision is long overdue on what project we should sponsor. Agreed?" Without a formal show of hands, everyone mumbled and nodded consent. "Let's see what we've got."

I proceeded to read from a notebook that contained the rivers we were concerned about. The choices ranged from large streams to some pretty small feeder brooks; if I recall correctly, maybe twenty or so possible projects made our list. All waters were within a couple of hours' drive. The perceived problems that landed them on the list varied widely, but they qualified because of firsthand knowledge. The details of the debate that followed are of little value to this story. Suffice it to say that everyone had a pet project, but in the end, two streams became the finalists: a little brook named Day, and predictably, our own beloved river.

Day Brook was a top priority because it fed our river not far above the Crossing House, but below my home. We were worried that it was becoming tainted by fertilizer, even though local farmers whose lands it traversed didn't seem to share our concern. They didn't place a priority on preventing the banks from eroding, and they also allowed too much timber to be taken from the land immediately surrounding the Day Brook watershed. These problems affected the water not only in the brook itself, but potentially the water downstream from where it entered the river. What could we do about it?

The other project encompassed several places on our home water, where the banks were becoming unstable because of poor streamside cover. Silting and erosion can become a major concern if left unchecked. It was our desire to stabilize these areas as naturally as possible. It was also suggested that the construction of deflectors in several chosen areas could vastly improve the habitat by forcing the water to the far shore, scouring out and reshaping shallow stretches that were not beneficial to both trout and angler.

These were not problems that would have killed our river. Left to nature, the stream and the trout would have survived. There was no question that addressing and actively seeking solutions to any negative impact affecting the quality of the water and the fishing in our river was an admirable goal. I believe all we ever intended to do was make our river a better place. It did occur to me, however, as we considered our choices, how apparently selfish our motives were. Despite the fact that they were well-placed concerns, other area streams needed much more help than our river did, but as the list was whittled down, I noticed that the farther away a river was from us, the quicker it was dismissed as a possible candidate for our help, and our money. In the end, it was no surprise that the two remaining options were in our own backyard. Although we clearly wanted to help, the fact that we were self-serving in our choices might appear a bit questionable.

The next couple of hours passed with little formal procedure or orderly debate. As a result, not much was accomplished. Those seeking the immediate and the obvious opted for projects on our river. The members with more of an eye toward the future came down on the side of Day Brook, arguing that if left unchecked, the long-term impact of a tainted waterway constantly feeding our river would eventually be more harmful, and thus should be addressed first. Even though I wasn't convinced that both could not be done simultaneously, I was willing to acquiesce and go along with the majority, returning to the second choice in the near future—a pragmatic approach I believed was best.

Acknowledging our predictable mob mentality and ambivalence toward commitment, resident politician Jack proposed that before the next meeting in two weeks' time, we would individually go out and assess the two waters in question. (Although no formal vote was taken, after two hours of arguing and drinking, it appeared we were in agreement.) This simply amounted to an excuse—not that any of us needed one—to go fishing a couple of times. Then, with the latest data in hand, we would make our final choice. Considering the source of the proposal, we were merely doing what every government organization seems to do when a decision has to be made: postpone the inevitable, form a committee to study what you already know, and gather information that will pretty much substantiate the same.

Our collective bar tab was getting larger than usual after what was for us a marathon session. Most were ready to move to the post-meeting bullshitting session that always followed, but I had to offer up one more bit of business before we adjourned. Mike Hartland spoke briefly about the possibility of the STIFFS getting involved in starting a fly-fishing club or an ecology and stream-awareness group at his school. I thought it was one of the best ideas I'd heard since we'd started the STIFFS, but no one wanted to discuss it at this point, after our two-hour debate over which project to pursue. We decided it would be the first item on the agenda at our next meeting—along with our "fact-finding" reports, of course.

As I closed our meeting, from the back of the room, Rick Meade jokingly suggested that we should adopt a club fly, sort of as a mascot. It brought a good amount of laughter from the group, including mine. Having read my essay, he said he knew what my vote would be, but stated he was partial to his own creation, the Rick's Wreck, suggesting it would be the ideal fly to represent the STIFFS. Andy jumped up and laughingly seconded the motion, but said he'd reserve his choice pending further discussion. We all ordered another round of drinks with smiles on our faces, and the rest, as they say, is history.

Chapter 18

Our meeting adjourned with the last thing on everyone's mind not the important project to help our river or Day Brook, or the possibilities for Mike's wonderful proposal, but the silly idea of a mascot fly—the perfect fly to represent the STIFFS. As we left our seats and fragmented into smaller, social groups, this seemingly inane concept was the first topic of conversation at each table. The studio was not a large room, and with the cozy, low ceilings, eavesdropping was not an art form but rather an unavoidable inconvenience. As a result, we were all aware that most of us were discussing the same odd notion. A raised voice was picked up by nearby ears and seemed an open invitation to comment.

I had partnered with Mark and Dan Sunderland when I'd asked them about the last time they had fished Day Brook; you see, truthfully, I was done with the discussion of a mascot fly before it ever got started. Other things seemed far more important to me at the time. However, before either had a chance to respond, our trio became a quartet when normally staid Wilson Davis joined us with his unsolicited opinion of a fly worthy of being adopted by the STIFFS.

"There's only one fly we should choose for a mascot," the slightly inebriated Wilson offered, pulling up a chair.

"I think the idea was a joke, Wilson," I said, hoping to put an end to it then and there.

"Oh, I know that," he said, continuing to plow ahead, "but it's kind of an interesting thought. If we were to elect the perfect fly to represent us, I think it should be the Hare's Ear."

And like the fool I oftentimes appear to be, I responded, "Why?"

"Because it's probably the best all-around fly ever created. Swim it along, dead-drift it—you can't name a better fly."

"A good choice," Mark said.

"A pretty good choice. However," Dan continued, being diplomatic as his good upbringing had taught him, "I would rather be represented by a graceful, fully adult, beautifully colored mayfly like an Adams, or even something iconic like a Royal Coachman . . . something traditional, classic. I don't mean to seem noncommittal, but I don't even care which fly it is, as long as it's floating high, wings up, sailboat-like in the current."

"I'm sure BS will agree with you in principle, but I think you may have the wrong species of fly. Shouldn't it be a Caddis, Mr. Salem?" Mark teased.

I buried my face in my hands. "When we were out last Monday morning," I said to Mark, "what were you catching all those trout on—Muddlers, Hare's Ears, Mayflies? And last fall when we went to the Coventry, I believe a Caddis is what you tied on to hook that big rainbow. And back in September, on the Sycamore, wasn't it a Deer-hair Caddis that took that nice brown?"

"Maybe I *will* vote for the Caddis," Mark said. "There's no denying success. Let me buy you a beer for helping me see the light," he added, patting my back in a mock gesture of appreciation. We spent a lot of time fishing together, and although he enjoyed playing the role of devil's advocate, especially when he had an audience, we were both aware of how important the Caddis fly was to his on-river accomplishments. Mark was not the most competent fly fisher in our group, and he relied on Bill and me for much of his angling success.

"Well, I still say my fly is better," Wilson said loudly, the alcohol making the scattered conversations grow in decibel levels.

"And what fly might that be?" Rick Meade responded from the next table, in an attempt to remove himself from his present situation. Rick found himself part of an odd trio with Mike and Dave. It seemed both he and Mike needed some work done on their vehicles, and our meetings were the most convenient place to corral Dave and set up an appointment for service. It seemed that Mr. Whitkowski was being uncharacteristically opinionated that night; not only were arrangements not made for auto service, but he and Mike also had to listen to Dave retell his favorite story of bass fishing on an old farm pond with night crawlers. It was a tale we had all heard versions of many times before, but because Dave always made it so amusing, we usually listened politely—and with some anticipation, I might add, because the fish could vary in size from six to ten pounds, its weight having a direct correlation to the amount of beer Dave had consumed … The more beer, the bigger the fish. That night, it was a ten-pounder.

Dave also seemed intent on making the point that any big fish would most likely be taken on live bait, so if you wanted to catch the biggest fish, then you should fish with an imitation of live bait, like a streamer, a Muddler, a crayfish, a Woolly Bugger, or even a worm imitation. Any of those would make the ideal choice for a club fly; choosing anything else would be a bad move, or, as Rick said, quoting Dave, "goddamn stupid."

As Wilson relaunched his treatise on the virtues of the Hare's Ear, Rick, having been silenced in his last trio, promptly cut Wilson off, because he too had something to say. Rick was a pretty competent fly caster, and, like the rest of us, relied on a technique that worked for him. He enjoyed fishing emergers during a hatch, and when there wasn't much visible activity, he would search the water with imitations of escaping insects. His preferred fly was a pattern of his own design—Rick's Wreck, the one he'd proposed as our club mascot fly at the end of our meeting—a combination of colors and feathers and ribbing taken from several proven recipes. It was a very effective fly. I had tied some, fished it on occasion, and often traded with him, a Caddis for a Rick's Wreck, when we fished together and one or the other of our favorites was producing better.

I listened in silence, nodding passively. As Rick neared the end of his dissertation, I slowly pushed myself away from the table. As I got up to leave, I heard Mark say, "What the hell is a Hare's Ear supposed to be, anyway?"

Rick and Wilson both had strong opinions on that, but before I got involved (because I also had a theory), I excused myself, saying, "I think I've heard all this before." As I stood up, I heard Andy's voice: "Hey, come here a minute. Let me buy you a beer."

My bottle was half full, and so was I. I graciously declined, but Andy insisted I join him, along with Bill and Jack. He then confessed that the mascot fly was his idea. He thought it would be an amusing continuation of our earlier discussion in the library. Andy had talked Rick into proposing it because he thought it would be more effective—and definitely more humorous.

It was an amusing idea, all right. It probably would have made for an interesting, philosophical discussion in the library with Bill. However, I told him to look around the room. Hands were flailing; voices were caroming around the walls like gunshots in the Grand Canyon.

"I find it an interesting thought," Jack said, throwing in his two cents.

"That it is," I said, "and now I suppose I'll have to listen to your opinion of it all."

"Shit," Bill responded, "he was already well into it when you got here. Unfortunately, Andy was half agreeing with him. You can imagine how difficult it was listening to two people talk out of their asses at the same time. At least now you can help me interject some intelligent opinion into this debate. Please, sit down."

As I mentioned earlier, Jack is a pompous, self-appointed expert on many subjects, including fly fishing, and although he may have been correct in some of his arguments, his presentation could often be interpreted as confrontational. His often-irksome religious views gave him a self-righteous arrogance and a sanctimonious moral air that I personally found to be both offensive and a pile of delusional, self-serving crap. He was also one of the few people I knew who, as a first choice, fished wet flies—old-fashioned, traditional, wet flies. Bill, Andy, and I—and, of course, Mark, when given the opportunity— would rile Jack with the opinion that anyone could fish a wet fly; just cast it out, let it swing through the current, strip it back, and at some point in its travels through the water, "pray" that a fish bites it. That is, of course, a simplification of what can be a sophisticated technique if carried to its fullest potential. Jack was not capable of that level of proficiency and he knew it, and I think that's why he took some of the ribbing so personally.

"You take a good wet-fly pattern," Jack started in his best lawyer-esque style. "If a trout has any inclination to feed, I would propose to you that he would take an insect that swims by his nose before anything else. Even the movement would entice him to hit before he would take a dead-drifted nymph. The movement is all an invitation to react, to strike the fly."

"I would guess that the fly you keep at the ready on your dry-ing patch is your choice of the perfect fly to get that job done?" I responded, being a bit of an instigator, seemingly unable to stop myself. "A Probe—isn't that what you call it?" I asked knowingly.

Jack always had a couple of wet flies on his vest, a particular pattern he had concocted, like Rick had his Wreck. In truth, all of us who tie flies have our own creations, attempts to personalize our philoso-phies and somehow be more in control of our own successes.

"Yeah, I call it a Probe," Jack snarled, very unlawyerlike. He had not yet become accustomed to the ribbing he received because of his boastful outbursts, and his fly's name. "I call it that, as you already know, because I use it when I start fishing to search the water."

"Oh yeah, now I remember," I said, sipping down my dwindling beer. "I thought for a moment that you called it a Probe because you use the hook point to probe the head cement out of the hook eyes on the flies you tie." It was probably uncalled-for, but somehow Jack seemed to deserve it.

Bill and Andy started laughing—that goofy, spontaneous, contagious laugh that comes from drinking too much and being a little too tired. Even Jack tried to force a chuckle, just to show he was not a complete horse's ass and did have at least the semblance of a sense of humor. But his eyes were not smiling. Before he could respond with an attorney's defense, which I was sure he was formulating as he waited to regain the floor, Dave elicited a collective gasp from the room when, in the midst of this collection of fly fishermen, he suggested rather loudly that maybe a Rapala would outfish most flies for big fish. Jack would have a bit more time to draft his closing argument.

We were intermingling, reacting to loud arguments from surrounding tables, siding with allies, rebutting those with whom we disagreed, and nearly banishing Dave from the room. We liked Dave, we needed Dave, and ultimately, we understood Dave. After all, he was the one who, after another especially long meeting, wondered out loud if a trout could live while swimming in a river of beer.

Although several people were orating at the same time, eventually, without anyone realizing it, the barriers that divided us into smaller groups had disappeared and we were becoming a single, unruly crowd.

Jack had had sufficient time to concoct his response to my dig, and when he had the floor to himself, he stood up to propose a bet that his Probe would outfish any dry fly. Bill looked over at me and rolled his eyes. "Everyone aboard the ark," he shouted. "The little Dutch boy in Jack's brain just let the water go."

Mark, never missing an opportunity, fired back. "Didn't you get the idea for both the design and the name of that Probe of yours when you tried to match the hatch by tying an imitation of a squashed insect that you'd probed out of your car grill after returning from the river one evening? It's a very good imitation, by the way."

Laughter erupted, and Jack did his best to remain unflappable, which his lawyer and councilman reputation demanded.

"Well?" he said, calmly at first. "Well?" he repeated a little louder.

"Well, what?" Mike Hartland asked, as the only completely sober person in the room.

"Well, are there any takers? I'll bet my fly will catch more trout than any dry fly," he confidently asserted.

Jack was the only one standing. All eyes were on him as he repeated his challenge. He had painted himself into the proverbial corner, and his stubbornness, pride, immense ego, and a whole lot of scotch prevented him from backing down—or slithering out a window.

"The only way that could possibly happen would be if you gave the fly to someone else to fish with," Mark said, adding more fuel to the already-smoldering situation.

"Hold on now," Andy quickly intervened, before Jack burst into flames. "That's an interesting proposition. Your fly against what?"

"I don't care; any dry fly you choose," Jack said matter-of-factly.

"Any dry fly?" Bill questioned.

"Are you talking the most trout, or the biggest?" Dan asked.

"Whatever you want," Jack responded without any thought.

"Can I throw my emerger into this battle?" Rick asked. "It can float in the surface film. Is that close enough to be considered a surface fly?"

"I've got a Hare's Ear that will out-catch any floater," Wilson said, joining the fray, intentionally (or unintentionally) offering Jack at least some perceived support for his challenge.

"Well, this is getting mighty interesting," Mike said, with a clear head and a challenging tone.

I knew it was coming, especially after all the turmoil he'd created. Jack looked over at me, his face ruddy with exasperation. "I'll bet your perfect Caddis won't outfish my Probe," he huffed, now with the quasi support of at least part of the room.

For the past few minutes, the usually opinionated Andy had remained rather subdued, but apparently calculating, as well. Before I could respond to Jack, Andy rose from his chair.

"Let's cut all the bullshit and empty rhetoric and settle this controversy on the water. Let's have a contest."

Chapter 19

I looked around the tables and became aware that without any conscious plan, we found ourselves in an interesting alignment. On one side of the room were the people who fished wet, all or most of the time. Seated with Jack on his side were Andy, Dave, Wilson, and Rick. Seated with me on the opposite side were the STIFFS who fished primarily (or certainly preferred to cast) dry flies: Mike, Mark, Dan, and Bill. When I think back, the fact that we naturally arranged ourselves in those groups still fascinates me, but there we were: wet versus dry, almost as if it had been preordained.

It would take volumes to tell, in its entirety, what took place in the next couple of hours. The discussion waffled between the profound and the absurd, reality and ego-massaging fantasy; claims were made, prodigious forecasts were offered. There were personal attacks on abilities, attitudes, character, and, probably most importantly, on angling philosophy. Talk was vociferous and dirt-cheap.

But the logistics of such a contest, at least as we perceived it, called for far more planning and procedure than anyone had first imagined. This was not going to be a case of simply walking to a stretch of water with a favorite fly and starting to cast. Rules would have to be constructed to ensure that our contest would be fair and equitable. When it was over, we wanted a clear winner—no whining or claims of unfair advantages.

Here are the things we considered as we proceeded to develop our rules:

How would the flies be selected?

Could the size or color of a fly be changed during the Contest?

Who would get to fish where, and with whom, and for how long?

What time of day—morning or evening?

How would a winner be determined: The biggest fish? The most fish?

This long night was clearly going to get much longer. It was not going to be easy, as all of these decisions would have to be made among a group of men who would have trouble agreeing on whether it was raining outside.

Even though everyone in our club fished both wet and dry, including me, oddly enough, we seemed to have little difficulty choosing our preferences. We had naturally divided ourselves, five on a side, with no forethought of a contest or a battle. It's even stranger if you consider that if we'd sorted by personality type, we would have teamed up differently, and by friendships and compatible fishing partners, differently still.

We eventually agreed that we would become five teams, consisting of two men each, one dry and one wet. The pairings would be determined by lottery.

Bill representing the dries and Andy the wets would take a map of our river and create five distinct and separate sections. We all had favorite places on the river; some knew the water better than others, and some were simply better fishermen. To neutralize any advantages, it was decided that each of the five pairs of anglers would get to fish each of the five sections, which would be determined by draw.

The river sections would be listed in our rules as A, B, C, D, and E. They would be fished in rotation, starting on Friday evening from 5:00 p.m. until dark. The contest would continue in four more sessions: Saturday morning from 6:30 a.m. until 11:00 a.m.; Saturday evening from 5:00 p.m. until dark; and then two more trips on Sunday, following the same time schedule as Saturday.

If your team started in section A on Friday, you would move to B on Saturday morning, to C on Saturday evening, and so forth. If you started in section D on Friday, you would move to E on Saturday morning, and then to A on Saturday evening, etc. Team number 1 would start in section A; team 2 in B, and so forth. This was as simple and fair a concept as we were able to arrive at in the middle of the night, and with only Mike Hartland's sober head to rationally contend with all the constant, petty bickering.

To give some indication as to just how significant this whole thing had become to us, in our alcohol-altered judgment we decided to hold the Contest on the upcoming weekend—starting the next day. The weather forecast for the days ahead was a mix of sun and clouds, warm days and cool nights, and no chance of showers. The weather for the following (or any other) weekend could be anything, and besides, in our misguided enthusiasm, this was far too important to be delayed for another entire week.

The men were going to have to lie and connive and manipulate to free themselves from real-life commitments in order to participate in this marathon, the only reason for which was an attempt to ascertain the perfect trout fly. Could anything this seemingly unimportant cause ten responsible men—with lives and families and jobs, businesses to run and meetings to attend, with less than twenty-four hours' notice— to put aside their responsibilities to attend such an event? In the world of fly fishing and challenges to philosophy and personal truths that motivate passions, you bet they could.

Now came the decision on flies; this was, after all, a contest to find the perfect trout fly. Each of us had favorites, but we sorted out any conflicts rather easily, and decided quickly which fly we would use. Nevertheless, to no one's surprise, problems rapidly arose. Mike, a little more practical and clearheaded in his approach, was concerned about size, and asked if he would be able to change sizes but continue to fish the same pattern. Rick asked about changing colors. Within the restrictions of a one-fly contest, these were not minor considerations.

Our conflicts were escalating, and in the pursuit of fairness, these were real questions that demanded real answers. We were trying to determine the perfect trout fly here . . . the if-you-could-fish-with-only-one-fly-for-the-rest-of-your-life fly. The single best fly, not the best variety of fly—that's what had started all this. In truth, this was not like most fishing contests, whose ultimate goal was just to catch the biggest, or the most. This was conceived to see which fly could do that job the best. So, in the end, it was decided that once your pattern was selected, you would be able to change the size of your fly, but not the color; color options offered far too many possibilities, especially with some of the wet patterns. This could certainly alter some decisions, because a good morning fly is not, much of the time, the best evening imitation, particularly during times when specific hatches were prevalent. Some concessions would have to be made by each participant.

I honestly believe that despite all the drinking and shouting, the decisions made that night concerning fly choices would have been pretty much the same even if we'd held our meeting at a Sunday-afternoon tea. These were choices born of years of angling experience—decades of successes and failures, likes and dislikes. These choices encompassed the beliefs in which one had unwavering confidence, reflections of each man's angling philosophy—his best memories, manifesting themselves and being represented in one single, simple choice.

Here is a quick run-through of the flies that would contend for the title of "The Perfect Fly." The STIFFS that comprised the wet team made the following choices:

Andy chose a brown marabou Muddler, confirming what he'd said earlier in the library. He said that while he didn't expect to catch the most fish, he did expect to take the biggest.

Dave went with a black Woolly Bugger, and after all the commotion he'd caused, spouting "big bait, big fish" theories, there was little doubt he would be tossing it in larger sizes. Subtle was not Dave's style.

Wilson, who had argued so vociferously for the Hare's Ear, naturally chose it.

Rick went with his Rick's Wreck, certainly no surprise there. Being limited by the rules to one color, after some thought, he opted for a version in olive. His fly was not known by many people outside the STIFFS, but it was a very effective pattern; I'd witnessed it catching trout both big, and often.

Jack chose an orange and brown Probe. I didn't know a lot about it except that it was Jack's concoction of a wet fly. In fairness, he did have some productive days on the river; whether or not he was fishing a Probe on those occasions is not known.

The quintet of dry-fly proponents, of which I was a member, armed itself this way:

Mike chose a Blue-Winged Olive. It may not have been his favorite fly, but he was more pragmatic than the rest of us, and it was a very good fly for this time of year. There were few times when an Olive, well presented, would not take a feeding fish. It was a well-conceived choice.

Dan went with tradition, just as he said he would. An Adams would be his weapon.

Mark chose a Caddis. He opted for one of my creations—a caddis imitation with two wings, a short underwing of deer hair with an elk-hair wing over the top. It created a larger, more-floatable fly (almost like a small stonefly), and showed a more-tempting silhouette to aggressive fish, especially in the riffled and faster-moving pocket water that was common in the Crossing House river. He decided on tan for a color.

Bill surprised everyone, including me, when he announced that he would fish a fly whose pattern was only to be found in one of Sam Tippett's journals. It was a fly without a formal name (although we would eventually give it one), and Bill would make available the recipe for everyone to see. He wanted to be sure everything was on the up and up, even though none of us would ever suspect Bill of any attempt at deception.

That left me. My choice was, for the most part, predetermined, but I would not have made any other decision, no matter what the circumstances. I would angle with a brown Deerhair Caddis.

It soon became obvious that when one strives to define and then implement what constitutes fair and equitable—well, reaching those lofty ambitions becomes blatantly impossible. Every suggestion offered, every position proffered, every recommendation tendered, only seemed to add another amendment to our expanding edicts of conduct. Ultimately, we came to the realization that a goal of the least unfair, or minimally unjust, was the only attainable standard. When the concessions and compromises began to overwhelm the intent of our endeavor, we simply, out of pure reason and common sense, decided to abandon the entanglements and opted instead to invoke the adage "Keep it simple, stupid." As is often the case, and not only with anglers, it took us far too long to become aware of the fact that when men and philosophy attempted to mix with perceptions, opinions, and alcohol, trouble usually ensues.

So, here is what we eventually decided: When a team arrived at their assigned river section, a coin flip would determine who had the privilege of being the first caster. That person then had twenty minutes to fish a run, or an "agreed-upon" reasonable stretch of water, not to exceed two perceived separate pools.

When the first angler had used his twenty minutes, the time being monitored by the partnered non-angler, the second angler then had twenty minutes to challenge the same water. When that time was done, that angler would then move to the next successive run, applying the same "agreed-upon reasonable stretch of water, not to exceed two perceived separate pools," and start his new twenty minutes of angling first in that water. The "next successive run" was the agreed-upon wording in the rules, to keep a person from going to great lengths to get to a distant, favorite piece of water, passing over all the water in between. Once the entire section of river was fished (and each section was a length that ensured this should happen with time remaining), whichever caster's turn was next could return to whatever run he wanted, and a twenty-minute opportunity was his. The next angler could then opt to fish his time there, or move to his choice of water.

It was believed that if these simple, honest rules were followed, and if a sense of fairness, sportsmanship, and respect prevailed, then the two anglers involved should be able to sensibly and amicably resolve any conflicts that might ensue. After all, we were friends involved in an honest contest.

There was still the need to crown a winner at the end. Everyone agreed that it was inherently unfair to potentially have one single, large fish as the winner. It would be just as unfair to have a bunch of six- and eight-inch trout reach a number sufficient to have a "most fish" total as the titleholder. So, after a rather short discussion, we arrived at the "total inches caught" as the best and most equitable way to determine the victor. Each fish was to be landed by the angler, but measured, recorded, and released by the non-angling teammate. These were the basic rules. There were additional amendments and other points of contention, and as I continue this tale I will relate some of them as they affected this story.

In our last bit of business, we decided that a trophy would have to be designed and constructed. We also voted two hundred dollars of the STIFFS bankroll, to pay fifty dollars for the largest trout caught, fifty dollars for the most trout caught, and one hundred dollars for the ultimate victor, the man who caught the most total inches of trout, and would thus be named the proud possessor of the "Perfect Trout Fly."

Thinking back on that evening, maybe the most amazing thing of all was that it was never suggested that we postpone these proceedings until we'd had more time to work things out. This contest was destined to start the following day. And so, with a show of hands, the rules were accepted and agreed upon. I'm not convinced that everyone had a full and clear grasp of what they had actually agreed to, but forward we plunged.

All that remained was to establish the teams. We numbered ourselves on the dry team: Bill, 1; myself, 2; Mark, 3; Mike, 4; and Dan, 5. The names of the wet squad were written down on evenly sized pieces of paper, folded in half, and placed in a nut bowl from the bar. To keep it elementary, Team 1 would start in section A, Team 2 in section B, and so on.

As dry-fly team member number 1, Bill was the first person to reach into the bowl that Andy held over his head. He retrieved a slip of paper and slowly opened it. A half-smile crossed his lips as he made eye contact with his partner. "Andy McDonald," he read.

"Well, this will be the easiest twenty dollars I've made in a long time," Andy said, referring to the twenty dollars we had decided that each man should ante up, to be won or lost in a personal head-to-head competition, as an incentive, a friendly challenge, a contest within a contest—totally oblivious to the opposite effect it could have. We had consumed a lot of alcohol, and all of this was being debated late into the night.

"Team One, Bill and me," Andy announced. Mike wrote it down for the record.

"You're next," Andy said as he moved the bowl with four remaining names in my direction. "Let's see who gets to fish with the Caddis man."

"Well, what do you know," I responded after opening my slip of paper. "Designed by fate, I'm sure. You get to live out your challenge for real, Jack."

"Benedict," I heard Jack call from across the room.

"Jack," I replied.

"Here's to a fair and spirited competition," he said, working his way over to me, his scotch glass held high for a toast.

Jack Windermere and me, fishing together for two and a half days. My initial thought was, How would I be able to do that without killing him? I spent the rest of the night trying very hard to put a positive spin on my luck (or lack of it) at drawing Jack as my partner. Maybe, I fantasized, I could shove that Probe of his somewhere that would give the name of his fly an entirely new meaning.

Mark was next. "Rockin' Rick Meade," he announced.

"Oh, great," Rick responded. "At least I have someone who can rustle up a snack on the river."

"The only thing that's going to get cooked out there is your goose," Mark answered.

Even though we had all put away a lot of alcohol, corn like that brought a loud groan from the room.

"Sorry," Mark apologized. "Even I'm embarrassed by that."

Mike was next. I could see him take a little breath as he reached into the bowl. He knew there were only two names left, and he would have preferred not to draw Dave's; Mike was far too subtle a caster for Dave's bullish ways.

"Wilson," he said with a smile. "Looks like it's the two of us."

"Well, Danny boy," Dave said loudly, "I'll be seeing you on the river. I'll bring the beer—although I'll try to stay sober enough to land a brown the size of your leg. Keep your wallet with you; I could use the twenty bucks to pick up an extra six-pack or two to celebrate my victory," Dave taunted. Dan just nodded; he knew he was in for a long weekend.

Bill and Andy agreed to get together over morning coffee with a copy of the aerial map of the river that Bill kept at the inn. They would mark out the five areas that would indicate our battleground. With the intimate knowledge they both possessed of our stream, this would be an easy task.

With everything said and done and dutifully recorded as "The Rules," everyone headed for the front door and at least a few hours' sleep before work and the start of the Contest later that evening, for it was now well past midnight. Everyone had committed to this, and some time on Friday would be devoted to clearing schedules for the weekend-long event.

Rick would have car trouble and be a little late for his Saturday-night gig.

Dave would close his garage, because it was his, and he could.

Wilson would have to take care of a personal matter and reschedule a Saturday-morning meeting at the bank.

Dan would feel a bit under the weather and not be able to work on Saturday.

Mark . . . well, Bill would see to it that his hours were covered, and that the staff took care of inn business for a couple of days.

For the rest of us, the adjustments were minor; we would all be there. This was going to be a civilized contest decided among civilized men.

This was going to be a war.

Chapter 20

I say everyone headed for the door, but that was not entirely true. Everyone headed to the door but me. Damp and overcast weather on Tuesday, Wednesday, and early on Thursday that week had made Bill's leg hurt. I knew he wouldn't admit it, but I was sure he would have preferred to postpone the Contest for a week or so. I also knew that he wouldn't complain, nor would he have missed this event for the world. He had to be part of it. Despite the pain in his leg and his failing eyesight, I could plainly sense that some of his old enthusiasm was returning—encouraging to see, as this had been the original impetus behind the creation of the STIFFS. I sometimes lost sight of that, especially after a night like the one that had just ended.

I volunteered to help Bill shuttle beer bottles and dirty glasses the short distance from the studio meeting room to the kitchen, where they would become a big part of someone's Friday-morning cleanup. We talked as we slowly cleared the mess. With hardly half the glasses and trash carted to the proper point of disposal, Bill returned from one of his trips with a couple of cold beers. During the last of our meeting I'd been beer-free, watching, listening, and contributing when I could without having to raise my voice over the clamor, and waiting for the welcome arrival of my second wind. It was here now.

"I'm leaving the rest of this crap 'til morning. What the hell; it's not going anywhere. Here, have a beer."

"Thanks," I said, reaching out for the bottle.

We headed to the library to be more comfortable and to get away from the debris. As we settled into the comfortable chairs, I lifted my drink toward Bill. "Here's to the dry team and victory."

"Hear, hear," Bill said as we clanked our bottles together.

"Do you think you can fish for three days alongside that windbag Windermere without slicing a hole in his waders and booting his ass into the river?" Bill asked. (I sensed he was only half joking.)

"I'm not sure, but if he does wind up in the drink, I'm positive I'll be able to honestly plead temporary insanity."

"If you execute a proper, decisive coup de grace, I'm sure you'll get off with a plea of justifiable homicide," Bill laughed. "What do you think of that fly he heaves around?"

"I really don't have an opinion that means anything," I responded. "It's just odd enough that it could catch fish."

"Oh, I have no doubt that it can catch fish, but I have a tendency to believe what Mark said to piss him off—that his fly would be far more effective if someone else fished it," Bill commented.

"Yeah, that was a great shot, wasn't it?"

"Maybe we shouldn't be so tough on poor old Jack," Bill said.

"You almost can't help it; the pompous ass always seems to deserve it," I said. "But please, spare me any more aggravation tonight— enough about Jack and his frickin' Probe. We have far more important things to consider."

We talked a little strategy, but could only speculate on any approach we might take, as decisions would have to be made on the spur of the moment, depending on the conditions at that particular time in whatever section of the river we were fishing, and in whatever position we happened to find ourselves in respect to our teammate and the Contest as a whole.

The hour was getting late, but we didn't seem to care. It had been quite a while since Bill and I had sat around until the wee hours in one of our powwows. Bill's work at the inn, his health, my deadlines, and even the gathering of the STIFFS every other week seemed to fill or replace much of that once-cherished time. Without a word to acknowledge it, I knew we both missed it. The fact that the Contest would start the next evening—actually, that evening, the hour having wandered well past Thursday into Friday some time ago—mattered little.

"I was a little surprised at your fly choice," I said to Bill.

"I noticed your reaction, and you weren't the only one. I figured having some of Sam's insight during this ..."—Bill paused, searching for a word, and finally settling on a war term—"this engagement could only be a positive thing."

We were both silent for a moment. I was thinking about what Bill had just said, about having Sam's insight as a guide. I sat back in my chair and placed the still-cool beer bottle against my temple. I closed my eyes, making a concession to the slight headache that was becoming a nuisance. In the quiet, something happened that I've never told anyone, not even Bill. I sensed a strange chill and the eerie presence of Sam Tippett. I opened my eyes with a start. I believe I'd simply slipped into one of those momentary naps—it's happened to all of us, mere seconds of unconscious drowse.

Bill was finishing the last of his beer.

"I wonder what Sam would think about his trout being the jury in determining the perfect trout fly?" I asked.

"I wonder what Sam would think about being part of a contest?" he responded.

I thought for a minute and then told Bill I didn't think he'd approve. "Reducing the passion and the beauty of fly fishing to a lowly barroom fish-catching contest ... I really don't think that would have enthralled Sam."

"But what about the essence of it all?" Bill countered. "What of the desire to find the most perfect fly? Don't you think Sam would have found that an intriguing proposition? Don't forget: He took fly fishing a whole lot further than the rest of us in search of perfection; he even removed the hook in his mission to find it."

"Well, when you put it that way ... ," I said. "But our intent was born of a drunken confrontation, and besides, when we are done with this, what about the variables of abilities and knowledge of the river and the fish? I would have to believe that one person, like Sam or you or even I, alone on the river, over a period of time, could best determine the most perfect fly. The variables would be fewer and more controlled. You know, that's really all I was saying when I wrote that the brown Deerhair Caddis was the most perfect fly. I think Sam would have appreciated that deduction on my part, whether or not he agreed with my fly choice, just as I would have accepted his choice of a perfect fly—or yours, I might add."

"Sam Tippett in a fishing contest ... that sure is an amusing thought, isn't it?" Bill smiled.

"Somehow, you and I in a fishing contest seems just as absurd," I said. "What a strange turn this evening took. Here we were, trying to make an important decision to help our river, and we got sidetracked by the preposterous concept of determining the most perfect trout fly—a mascot fly, yet. I hope we put this much effort and energy into whichever river project we choose."

"Sarah would have thought I'd gone completely off my rocker." Bill leaned back in his chair and laughed. "But she would have been up before dawn on Saturday morning to make sure I ate a good breakfast. She would have made me a snack to take to the river. Then she would have reminded me how childish all this was before giving me a kiss and telling me to watch my step and be careful. Then my angel would have wished me luck and told me to get the heck out of her way—she had more important things to do than look after an old fool like me."

Bill's eyes gazed into the past. He slowly tipped his head back to stare at the ceiling. It was a little sad to realize that such pleasant thoughts and comforting memories could hurt someone so deeply. "I guess we better get some rest. Andy will be here to map out the river before I get to bed."

"I think he'll probably be a little late," I said. "Mr. McDonald had a bit more beer than he's used to, I'm afraid. By the way, how are you fixed for flies?"

"Okay, I think. I was hoping to tie up a few in the afternoon."

"Take a nap instead. I've got to tie some for myself, and Mark asked me if I could possibly tie a few for him. I'll put together a handful for you, too. I'm actually one of the few people who know the pattern."

"Thanks. That would be a big help," Bill said. I could tell his mind was still on Sarah.

"I'll stop by late in the morning—just after lunch at the latest," I said, stepping out on the porch, still not quite ready to leave. I stood alone, leaning against one of the large white posts that defined the railing end at the top of the stairs. The night was dark and clear and still tinged with the coolness of late spring; the only light came from the low, warm glow inside the Crossing House.

I watched the stars for a minute or two and wondered if Bill, like me, had ever felt the spirit of Sam Tippett. I was sure he probably had.

Chapter 21

Despite catching only a few hours' sleep, I was awake early on Friday morning. Lying in bed, I felt a little like I did as a child on Christmas morning, or later in my youth, as I waited for sunrise on the first day of fishing season. Anticipation made resting in bed impossible.

I made extra coffee that morning, planning to spend hours at the tying vise. As I patiently tied, I thought about what Sam had written in his journal when he confessed to fishing with no hook on his fly, striving for perfection. I was consciously doing the same thing now. Actually, we were all going to define perfection—at least, as it existed in our little corner of the world. My sense of Sam's presence made me try to be as perfect as I could be—as perfect as he would have been.

Bill's Tippett's Crossings (as we came to name this pattern of Sam's) looked especially fine. I gave them an extra turn of my very best hackle to make them float better. They were the best-looking Tippett's Crossings I had ever tied. Hell, they were some of the best-looking flies I had ever tied, period. I even put a couple aside for myself. I didn't know why, but Bill's flies seemed more important to me than my own Caddis. I thought at the time it was because I desperately wanted Bill to come out on top in his one-on-one with Andy; later I came to believe something else.

The Caddis I tied for Mark and myself looked as if they might fly away when I freed them from the vise; they were only slightly less perfect than Bill's flies. Sam certainly made his presence felt that first morning of the Contest.

While I worked at my vise, my mind did much of its customary wandering. For me, tying flies has always been similar to being on the river—a pleasant, reflective time alone with my thoughts while involved in a task I love doing. A couple of thoughts dominated my time that morning. One was that the STIFFS were a group bound together by the common thread of fly fishing; different personalities, different philosophies, but somehow united. The glue was the love of angling for trout with a fly, and initially, at least for me, getting Bill back to the river. We were friends in spite of our differences. In the shadow of the Contest, however, the STIFFS fell victim to human nature—the disharmony that can arise between the desires of the individual and what is good for the group pulled up a chair and sat among us.

Anyway, it was now early June and we had the river, the quality time alone or with a chosen companion, the cherished solitude on the water that we all sought. We often didn't need or want the confines of a group. On a beautiful June day, the mind-set that initially instigated the STIFFS is often contrary to the innate beliefs of a fly fisherman— at least, to those seeking the solitude and serenity of the native pursuit. I believe most fly casters may secretly desire, consciously or not, to be Sam Tippett.

I also believe that contrary philosophies, opposing beliefs, and any personality conflicts made themselves evident that Thursday night in the studio. Under the guise of a quest to find the perfect trout fly, our true colors, our individual biases, got the best of us. We became, once again, ten individuals, not a group of passionate men willing to compromise our personal beliefs and desires to function as a group. Community became secondary to the individual, a sad state of affairs for people living in a society or striving to function as a respectful aggregation of fly casters. Nevertheless, we suddenly didn't care quite so much about the feelings of our neighbors. We showed the ultimate disrespect for our comrades, challenging each other's angling dogmas for no worthwhile purpose.

I said there were a couple of things that dominated my thoughts that morning. In addition to the evolution, or deterioration, of the STIFFS, the other was my inability to shake off the aura of Sam Tippett since my experience the night before. I guess what happened to me was that although I didn't then (and still do not now) believe in ghosts, I have come to believe in and accept the existence of spirit. I will confess here that this newly discovered awareness of the eternal presence of spirit made me honestly believe that Sam and Sarah were the only people who could have possibly kept this contest in focus— the only people who could have understood and accepted it for what it was. On Friday evening, as we prepared to get started, I don't think any members of the Samuel Tippet Fly Fishers had a clue.

Chapter 22

I was unable to keep my promise to Bill.

I had become so consumed with tying flies, morning had drifted into afternoon before I'd finished my third cup of coffee. By the time I had readied my leaders, sorted my fly boxes and added my newest creations, inspected my equipment, and packed my car, it was nearly two o'clock. I figured I still had plenty of time to deliver Bill's bugs and discuss a little strategy in the library before the others started arriving. Before I left I put Bill's flies in a box and wrapped it with ribbon like a Christmas present.

I reached the Crossing House parking lot at about three o'clock. I wanted to surprise Bill, so I quietly creaked open the front door and headed for the library, where I half expected him to be napping in his favorite chair. I peeked around the corner and found my friend totally absorbed in a book—one of Sam's journals, to be exact. Slowly I made myself visible in the doorway, the box extended before me as an offering. Bill didn't budge. I cleared my throat like a schoolboy trying to get his pal's attention during class. Bill's eyes jerked up, his head hardly moving.

"Is it my birthday?" he asked. "That could easily slip my mind."

"Christ, I thought your ticker had shit the bed. It would be just like you to screw up this contest by having a heart attack."

"What, and miss all the fun? I'm saving my bout with the big one until I spend all the money I'm going to win this weekend. After that, I suppose, there'll be precious little to live for. What's in the box, Santa?"

"Perfect little trout flies. I believe gray was your color of choice." I handed Bill the box and sank into the other chair. I suddenly realized, for the first time, that I hadn't eaten since my token breakfast early that morning. "Man, am I starved," I said without thinking. "I've been tying flies all day and it just dawned on me that all I've had is three cups of lousy coffee and something solid—although I can't recall exactly what it was."

"So, you're saying you could eat the north end of a southbound skunk. Tell you what—I'll trade you some skunk ass for this box of flies. Would you like some yak urine with that?"

Without waiting for my response, Bill started for the kitchen. "I'll wait 'til I get back so I can leisurely enjoy opening my present, which I know would be impossible with you whining next to me. I gave Mark the day off," he continued. "He said he wanted to get a new line and some leaders for tonight. I hope this new person he hired a few days ago knows how to make a sandwich. Probably can't make cereal . . . probably doesn't even fly-fish. Hell, I don't even know the poor soul's name. Maybe I should introduce myself."

I sat down and closed my eyes. I had hurried to finish the flies and get to Bill's before the others, and now that I'd stopped moving, I felt tense. I eased my head back into the cradle of the overstuffed chair. Without any intent, I reached for the journal Bill had been reading. It fell open to a page marked with a napkin. He'd been reading the section about attaining perfection on the stream—Sam's pursuit of the pure essence of fly fishing.

Bill soon returned with a turkey sandwich every bit as impressive as the roast beef sandwich he'd delivered to me during my first visit to the Crossing House, and he also had two bottles of Harp in his possession. He plunked himself down in his chair—and it was definitely his chair. Indentations in the cushions precisely fit his body, actually making it uncomfortable for anyone else that was, on rare occasions, allowed to sit in it. He gestured his beer toward me and offered a toast: "To kicking the wet team's ass."

We took healthy swigs to our success. Bill then took the box from the table and slowly untied the bow. "Shit," he uttered. "You weren't kidding. These look damn close to perfect."

"What do you mean, close?" I mumbled through a mouthful of lunch.

"These are better-looking than . . ." Bill took one of the flies out of the box and held it over his head to view it from the bottom; he wanted to see what the trout would see as it approached to take the fly. "You outdid yourself. These are as nice as any I've ever seen," he said, continuing to examine the fly, moving it slowly to study it from different angles. It was unusual to see him so absorbed, his mind seemingly miles away.

"Perfect," he announced as he placed the little bug back with the others. "Andy left only a couple of hours before you got here. Here's our itinerary." Bill took a piece of paper from his shirt pocket and unfolded it to expose a map of the river. I silently looked over the five sections, quickly visualizing the runs and pools and secret hiding places.

"I wonder if everyone has a secret honey hole or two in our river," I commented.

"Hard not to," Bill said. "If you spend time in a place and you pay attention, it would be odd not to pick up a secret or two."

I had intimate places and fish I knew personally in each of the five sections. Bill and I had few secrets when it came to our river, but I wondered if even he had a secret riffle that he'd kept to himself. I started to ask but changed my mind, not really wanting to know.

"It's funny . . . After all the years I've spent fishing this river," Bill said, "my favorite places are right behind the Crossing House: the

Ledge Pool, my rock, the riffle below the undercut by the root. It doesn't get much better, here or anywhere else, for that matter."

"You've got that right," I said.

"I insisted to Andy that we make it section A. I figured that I would get to fish it first, and since you were starting in section B, you would have last crack at it."

"Thanks, you sly old fox."

We talked while I ate, and I took a rain check on a second beer. Maybe I too was more serious about this contest thing than I'd realized. We had discussed our way through section C and started on the fourth area when Rick showed up in the doorway.

"Secret meeting?" he asked. "Is this where the dry team meets to discuss its plan of attack? Should I head for cover and await the arrival of my allied troops?"

"Well, the enemy has arrived. We'll have to continue our conversation in code for now," Bill joked, pulling himself forward in his chair. "We'd better head to the Frog before the entire enemy camp shows up." He paused momentarily before his strong hands forced his ailing body from the chair. Bill didn't care for extended groups in his library, and with the others soon to start drifting in, he was conscious about keeping a crowd out of his favorite room. It was only a little after four, and although we had fully expected some of the participants would be early, we were both a bit disappointed we didn't have more time with just the two of us; some things would have to wait until later that night, after the first round of the Contest was over.

Bill put the journal back in the barrister bookcase that held his prized books, and locked it. As Bill and I followed Rick out of the library we could hear Andy plowing through the front door.

"I hear tell there's a fishing contest about to get started, and I'm planning to kick some piscatorial butt," he announced.

"Well, that evens it up," Bill said.

"Did you bring your money?" Andy laughed, addressing Bill.

"Did you bring an extra shirt along with your pocketbook?"
Bill responded. "You'll need one before the night's over, you cocky
bastard."

"What, feeling the pressure already?" Andy chided. "You guys seem
a little edgy and tense." He turned to me. "Not concerned your perfect
Caddis will fail, are you? You're going to need steady hands to make
those perfect casts. You know how unforgiving these trout can be."

Andy was in his element—a good-natured soul with something
fun to do. He also seemed to be the only one who was able to maintain a lighthearted attitude about our impending confrontation; at
least, so far. Even Bill and I were not our usual selves. Maybe not
enough sleep or too many toxins still in our systems from the night
before. Whatever it was, as the remaining players trickled in, it
became apparent that the STIFFS had undergone a bit of a character
transplant.

Naturally, we congregated as teams. There was some joking, as
friends this familiar with each other routinely do, but the barbs
seemed rather pointed. Retorts seemed somehow mean-spirited. If
any bad blood had been created—and it must be remembered that
it had been only a few hours since the idea of this contest had been
conceived—it was obvious that not enough time had passed to allow a
healing bloodletting to occur.

The teams took time to look over the maps. Low, indiscern-
ible murmurs of strategy could be heard rumbling from each group,
now assembled at opposite ends of the tavern. Honey holes and
personal secrets, discovered by trial and error over years of fishing,
were revealed to other team members—an act that underscored how
important this contest had become. It also struck me that suddenly an
odd sort of mob mentality was developing: team against team. Wasn't
the original impetus of this whole thing to find the most perfect
trout fly, not the best way to fish the river, whether it was wet or dry?
It appeared that, to many, this was developing into something much

more significant than just the pursuit of the perfect trout fly. Competition can do that. A day on the river with a friend and fishing companion would cease to exist; at least, it wouldn't exist for the next two and a half days.

When is fishing not just fishing? When is a day on the river not just an enjoyable time on the water? At five o'clock on a beautiful June evening, when we paired up to head out, we were all still friends—we were still STIFFS—but we could have used the wisdom and insight of Sam Tippett or Sarah Cahill to keep us on our intended path.

Chapter 23

Although our rules stated that the evening sessions would start at five o'clock, and even though all the STIFFS had arrived well before that time, the two groups found themselves huddled at separate ends of the Frog, studying the copies of the maps each was given, talking strategy and trading any intimate information that each teammate might be willing to exchange. This contest had been initiated to crown a perfect fly, truly an individual endeavor. The dry against wet, the creation of teams, the reassuring support of a like mind, the offer of prizes for the biggest and most, and the bragging rights associated with all those things had quickly altered the focus of our event.

So, at five o'clock on that Friday evening, we were still at the Crossing House discussing tactics as if designing a battle plan for war. Fortunately, this was June, and the evenings were as long as they get. Eventually, pushing five-thirty, the teams paired up; handshakes were offered, *Good lucks* were exchanged, and we headed out.

When I was discussing things with Bill earlier, he did acknowledge that he and Andy had sort of tweaked the map by making section A right behind the Crossing House. Since we would be fishing both above and below that area, it made sections D and E upriver of the inn, and areas B and C below. No one questioned why the river was so designated; everyone just accepted what Bill and Andy had decided. Two vehicles would part ways: One would carry Mark and Rick to downstream section C, while the other would tote Mike and Wilson to the furthest spot upriver, area D. The rest of us would walk to our assigned spots, B or E, on either side of A.

Jack and I started down a path away from the water that would more quickly get to the top boundary of our B section. Bill and Andy indicated obvious landmarks to designate an area's beginning and end. A large midstream boulder was our starting point.

I should also mention here that another of the disputed rules eventually agreed upon was that the first caster had to start his angling at the first perceived run in the section—on the upstream end. This was to keep the winner of the initial coin flip from simply going to the best pool within that section first; it was the "next successive run" amendment that soon followed, and this was designed to prevent the second caster from running to what he perceived as the best pool. (I apologize if this recitation is at all burdensome, but creating fair and equitable rules really did prove to be a difficult task, and what I'm relating here is, believe it or not, our idea of simple.)

We talked very little as we hustled our way to the side path that led to the river. Several times I slowed my pace out of what I hoped would be perceived as polite behavior, to allow a huffing Jack to catch up, even though our jaunt to the river was not a long or difficult one.

I reached the water just above our bouldered starting point and scanned the surface for a few seconds before my panting partner emerged from the wooded path. I'll admit that it was a little difficult for me to ignore the sweat beading on Jack's forehead and the gulps of air he required, but I truly didn't want to ruffle feathers before we'd even made our first casts; we still had two days to go after this evening ended.

I slipped my hand beneath my waders and reached into my pocket for a coin. I continued to watch for rises as Jack removed his hat and mopped his brow with his sleeve.

"I'll flip and you call," I said, adding, "if that's all right with you."

"Sure," a winded Jack tersely replied.

I flipped the quarter, but made no attempt to catch it.

"Heads," Jack called before it hit the ground. The coin landed tails up in the matted grass at our feet. "Looks like you go first," he said.

My attention was still focused on the water. It was early for my best fishing time, and there were no signs of rising trout. I was also conscious of a nice run along a fallen tree that I've always had a lot of success casting to, just a couple of pools downriver. "Jack, I believe I'll defer my advantage and give you first crack at catching a fish."

Jack was caught totally off guard by my offer; not only did he immediately challenge whether the rules allowed me that option, but he also questioned my motives.

"Doesn't winning the coin toss allow me to choose among the available options?" I asked.

Jack, who had by now regained his breath, suddenly showed his lawyer stripes. "Doesn't the rule state that the winner of the coin flip goes first?"

"I don't believe it does," I argued. "Doesn't the rule imply that if a person wins the toss, not only does he have the right to go first, but that he could also opt to go second if he so chose?"

"Why?" Jack suspiciously countered. "Why would you not want to go first?"

"Simple; it's early in the evening and I've noticed a lack of surface activity," I quickly responded. I purposely did not mention the major reason—the Log Run, a few holes below us.

"Hmm—trying to gain an advantage already? Afraid your Caddis is not up to the task?" he feebly taunted.

"I'm not too worried about my fly choice," I replied, "and most certainly I'm trying to gain a sporting advantage. Isn't that in keeping with the spirit of a friendly contest? If, however, you cast first and catch a fish or two, then you will have gained an immediate edge— and who knows, it might be an edge I won't ever recover from."

Jack responded with an annoyed laugh as he unhooked his Probe from the hook keeper and moved toward the water.

"Good luck," I said in a liltingly sarcastic tone.

Jack's competence as an angler probably fell somewhere in the lower half of the pack of the STIFFS, but his perception of himself allowed him to strut through life with an air of confidence that belied his rather ordinary abilities.

I sat on the bank away from any errant backcast and watched as he stepped into the water.

"You haven't started keeping time yet, have you?" he called back.

"No, Jack; you're not on the clock yet—not until you make your first cast," I replied, amused that he was concerned about the edge he believed I was attempting to gain. "Don't worry; you'll get an honest twenty minutes."

Jack waited a minute or so once he was in position before casting to the boulder. On the fifth or sixth swing through, a small brown took his fly, and five minutes into the Contest, Jack had a seven-inch lead. I thought he might crow a little and was surprised when he didn't; however, it was obvious he was enjoying the position in which he found himself. Hoping that at some point in the next couple of days I might receive the same courtesy, after measuring, recording, and releasing his fish, I told Jack he had twelve minutes left in his time. "Just in case you want to try the next riffle below," I said. "I'll even wait until you make a cast there before I start tracking your minutes again."

Jack offered a cursory wave of acknowledgment with his free hand and slowly backed out of the water, moving the short distance to the next run. It was a trough that famously held a fair fish once in a while, and Jack did manage to take a brown of just under eight inches on his second cast. When I measured it, I told Jack we would call it eight even, trying not to appear too charitable.

"A pretty fair first go," I congratulated Jack when his time had elapsed.

"It's a start," he replied. "Now, if I understand correctly, you have twenty minutes in this water and then you start a new time in the next hole or two. Is that right?"

"That does appear to be what was agreed upon. I think I'll try the boulder."

I waded cautiously into position, taking a bit longer than normal, wanting the water to rest some before making an attempt. When I was standing right where I wanted to be, I spritzed a little floatant onto my fly and blew on it, wasting even more time. I dropped my Caddis just above the boulder and snaked some slack into the water before mending the line to keep my fly from dragging. The bug nicked the large rock and it was ambushed as it glided past. The trout was not much larger than Jack's first fish, and measured out at eight inches.

Oddly enough, I now had a dilemma. Another of our provisions, again in the name of fairness, was that if a person caught and landed three trout in his allotted time, counting both consecutive twenty-minute sessions, he had to relinquish his remaining time in that session. At the time, I'd perceived this amendment to be a thinly disguised attempt by some to keep the Contest within everyone's grasp. Certainly, some members were superior anglers, and thus held an unfair edge in both angling ability and river knowledge. But somehow it seemed just as unfair to the best fishermen not to be able to prove the effectiveness of their fly. After all, we weren't trying to prove who the best angler in our group was. How did the potential embarrassment to a fellow STIFF get to trump the point of the Contest—the attempt to establish the most perfect trout fly?

Oh yeah, this was supposed to be a way to resolve a sporting challenge among friends, I was reminded by the less-talented casters. This was supposed to be fun. I gave up any point of contention.

I now had one fish in one cast and still had most of my time left in the first two holes. I had given up my starting advantage so I could get to the Log Run first, and one more fish in either of these initial runs would seriously alter my plan—two more, and I would be forced to forfeit the first opportunity at the downstream hole altogether. Should I just tell Jack I wanted to give up my time in these two runs and move lower and start my new twenty minutes? Did our rules even allow such a move?

This seemed a perfect place to put to the test the theory that partnered anglers could amicably work out any disagreements. I knew that despite all of his annoying behavior, Jack was a fairly intelligent (and dare I say, calculating) man who could certainly see the advantages in the availability of a new strategic weapon in his future tactics. There was also the positive aspect of willingly giving up time in less-productive water, thus allowing a quicker trip through to the end of the section being fished, so that more time could be spent returning to places in which an angler would rather be casting. It was this point, and all the potential it offered, that had Jack agreeing to allow me, after giving up and not transferring time, to head downstream.

My issue settled, we hastened our pace to the next pool—the one I'd plotted to arrive at first. I had fished this spot earlier in the week and lost a fine fish there. As we approached the run I told Jack to loop around me and stay away from the water's edge.

"Afraid I'll spook your fish?" he asked sarcastically. "Don't want to lose that edge? Oh, wait a minute, I'm ahead; you've already lost your advantage."

"Come on, Jack," I said, "a little common courtesy shouldn't be too much to expect, even from you. And as far as that advantage you have—well, if I were you, I wouldn't make fun of the crocodile until I've crossed the river." We had been on the stream together for less than an hour, and we were already butting heads. It hadn't taken long for my partner to start annoying me, even though I was going out of my way to avoid conflict.

The Log Run had developed where the water ran deep, forced to flow against and under a tree that had fallen into the river, parallel to the shore. I watched for a minute or so, hoping to find a rising fish. The only activity was in the shallows off the lower end of the log. I wanted to be sure not to let my fly float down that far; I really didn't want a six-inch fish ruining my plan. I was familiar enough with the place to know where the best chance of a hookup could be found, rising fish or not.

I positioned myself to make a cast. The fly landed near where I wanted, but it bounced through the run unmolested. I quickly gathered the slack and picked up the fly before the eager little brookies patrolling the flats could grab it. I brought the fly to hand and blew on it as I contemplated my options without casting.

"Time's ticking," Jack called out.

I ignored his modest taunt. I reached into my vest, thinned for the Contest to hold only brown Deerhair Caddis in varying sizes, and took out a fly box. I clipped off the small size 16 and knotted a larger size 14 to my leader, tied on the plump, bushy side. "I'm putting on a larger Caddis," I announced to Jack.

My cast with the new fly was better than my first attempt with the smaller bug, and halfway along the log a decent fish splashed to take it. I knew I would have time left, so I tried to move the fish quickly out of the run to disturb it as little as possible, urging her into the shallow water below. The net slid under an eleven-inch brown. I couldn't help but relish the disgusted look on my partner's face.

After several fruitless casts I turned to Jack and asked, "How much time do I have left?"

"Three minutes and ten seconds," he responded.

"What an asshole," I mumbled to myself. The preciseness of Jack's answer irritated me. So, at that moment, knowing the rules and it being early in the competition, I hastily removed the larger fly and put the smaller Caddis back on. Without moving, I sailed my fly to the lower flats and hooked a little seven-inch brook trout. I figured, What the hell—a third fish, small or not, was better than a couple more fishless casts, and besides, it might further annoy, and put some pressure on, Jack.

Jack spent an unproductive twenty minutes heaving his fly along the log. He did manage to hook and lose a small brookie in the shallows. He was already showing signs of frustration as he splashed his way out of the water when his time ended. And so, away we went, down to the next series of riffles. Jack had lost his early advantage, and I sensed that this fact was eating at him, even though we had only just begun our challenge.

The remainder of the evening was rather uneventful. Jack's weighted fly and some sloppy casts probably had fish scattering for cover. Twice I exercised giving up time, as I had to get to the Log Run, and abandoned any hope of catching fish, having to follow Jack into the same water. I caught a ten-inch brown and a nice brook trout of nine inches, and missed two other fish on the way to the final pool in our section. Jack was able to land a ten-inch brown and missed one other.

It was getting late when we fished our last pool. We headed back upstream, each taking time to fish a preferred spot. In the spirit of sportsmanship I gave him first choice of a pool to return to, telling him I was ahead and that it seemed the fair thing to do. (My real reason was that I wanted to cast as close to dark as possible.)

Jack went to the first boulder and did manage one small, eight-inch fish. I chose to end my time at the Log Run, and in the last bit of light before darkness fell, I hooked the biggest fish of the evening. The trout fought hard before winning the battle by dragging me into the submerged tangle of branches under the log.

There was obvious relief in Jack's voice as we made small talk on our short walk back to the Crossing House. Although he had landed only one less fish, he trailed the equivalent of a twelve-inch trout. Oddly, he had to be happy with that; if I'd netted that last fish, Jack would have been well over two feet deep in the hole.

Chapter 24

Quite a few cars occupied the parking lot by the time we reached the Crossing House. It was a beautiful Friday night in June, so along with the guests at the inn, many locals were also there for dinner.

The Winged Frog would have far too many paying customers for our rowdy reappearance, so Jack and I went straight to the studio, where we knew anyone who had returned from the river would be congregated. We were greeted by Andy, Dan, Dave, and Rick. Mark and Bill were momentarily absent, checking on things—Mark, on the condition of the kitchen, and Bill, making sure his staff had everything under control. So, when we entered the room all the STIFFS were accounted for except Mike and Wilson, who had traveled the farthest to get to their water.

"Beer's on me—unless you caught a bigger fish than me," Andy roared as soon as we came through the door.

"Oh boy, this could be a long evening. How big?"

"How's sixteen-plus?" Andy crowed. "I thought closer to seventeen, but that pain-in-the-ass Bill would only settle on sixteen and a half. I take it that this will be top fish tonight."

"I'll have a Harp," I responded. "How many fish?"

"Three."

"The other two?"

"Ten and eleven," he replied.

"Hmm . . . sixteen and twenty-one is thirty-seven. Correct me if I'm wrong, but forty-five is more than thirty-seven, isn't it? I'm still going to let you buy me a beer."

"What did you do, catch nine five-inchers?" Andy teased.

"So what? Forty-five is more than thirty-seven. Hey, you were as responsible for the rules as I was. I'm just playing the game."

"How do you stand it, Jack?" Andy asked my partner.

"With much difficulty," Jack answered.

"It's always a little more difficult for the one playing catch-up, but we're all right, aren't we, partner?" I lightly mocked.

"Just great," he replied, heading out the side door to the tavern to get a drink.

"Problems?" Andy laughed.

"We're doing just fine," I answered, shaking my head.

"Forty-five inches?" Rick asked. "How many fish?"

"Five," I answered. "Nothing of much size, as the numbers might indicate, except for the one I lost right at dark. I doubt it was as big as Andy's, but it might have been close."

"Where'd you hook it?" Andy asked with interest.

"I'm not as dumb as I look, McDonald—you'll be fishing in that section tomorrow. I'll discuss that with Bill, and Jack can fill you in with his version. I'm sure it will be different than mine would be. How about you and Mark?" I asked Rick.

"Well, I have good news and better news—which do you want to hear first?"

"I don't think I'm going to like this. Go ahead . . . whichever."

"Mark got two fish, an eight-inch brookie and a ten-inch brown, and I was being generous in allowing that brown all those inches." He paused.

"Yeah, that's the good news—I know," I said, breaking Rick's dramatic silence.

"Why, yes it is. I, on the other hand, netted six fish. I could have had more if I didn't, at one point, have to stop after three before my time was up."

"And?" I asked.

"Oh yes—and I believe sixty inches or so."

I nodded. "Maybe you should be buying the beer." I turned to Dan. "And you, sir? How was your evening date with Dave?"

"A little slow," Dan said, rolling his eyes. "I got three fish, nothing big—about twenty-seven inches, I believe."

"Dave," Andy called out, "how'd you do?"

"Just one . . . fourteen . . . missed a couple," he reported between swigs of beer.

"Actually, he might have had two," Dan interjected, "if you could count the one I'm pretty sure he knocked unconscious with that bola he calls a weighted Woolly Bugger."

"You're just pissed because I got the only decent fish," Dave fired back.

"Just two more days . . . just two more days," Dan droned a mantra.

"How did Bill do?" I asked, anxious to know.

"Bill missed a few hookups early on—maybe three or four," Andy answered. "I'm not sure what the hell he was doing wrong. Said he just didn't want to get too far ahead so early in the Contest. Said he was just being a concerned friend and trying not to discourage or embarrass me. But once I got a couple of fish, especially that big one, he started paying more attention and he stuck the next couple—one about thirteen, off that ledge he likes so much, and then another smaller one, about ten or eleven . . . I forget. He just needed a little pressure, a bit of motivation, I guess, to get him going. He seemed to really enjoy himself out there, though—just a little slow on the uptake at the start."

Wilson and Mike wandered in, drinks in hand, having detoured through the Frog on their way to the studio.

"You two are the last to check in," Andy said as soon as they entered the room.

"All you want is numbers?" Wilson asked.

"For the moment," Andy responded, paper and pencil in hand.

"I got three—twenty-nine inches," Mike replied. "Is that right?" he questioned Wilson.

"Yeah, and I landed two—two small ones—but I missed at least two larger fish," Wilson said, defending his meager total. "The ones I landed were eight and ten."

"Well, this should come as no surprise," Andy announced. "The wet team caught more fish by one and totaled more inches by"—Andy paused while he finished adding—"nineteen inches. So, all you dry guys need is one twenty-inch fish and you'll grab the lead," Andy playfully taunted.

Andy's sociable and outgoing personality, and the fact that everybody liked him, seemed to naturally anoint him as ringmaster of this little circus. And now, after the first session on the river, he found himself serving as monitor of a couple incidents that needed some clarification, in the name of remaining fair and equitable, of course.

Mike and Wilson actually seemed a good pairing, both mature, reasonable adults. But they had run into a problem, and, strangely enough, it was the same one Jack and I had experienced, concerning giving up time to move to the next run. It was also odd that Jack and I seemed to have had a much easier time addressing the concern, at least as it pertained to us. We had reduced the problem to a personal issue, but it became evident after some examination and thought that it had far deeper implications.

Mike believed that the time designation was meant to mark the required period to be spent in a pool before moving along. Wilson, like Jack and me, believed that if it was your time, you could give it up and move, thereby leaving more time for both anglers to return to preferred waters. However, Mike apparently was able to maintain a grasp on why we were doing what we were doing, and brought up a valid argument—one that had escaped me, as well as the others, once we'd all become immersed in the Contest. As I've mentioned already on several occasions, what we'd lost sight of was the fact that we were supposed to be trying to find the perfect fly. It would be much fairer to determine the effectiveness of one fly compared to another if both flies were fished in the same water for the same amount of time, despite variables such as the wide-ranging abilities of the anglers, or the advantage of a fly being first to search the water.

After listening to Mike and Wilson explain their respective positions, Andy called me aside and asked if I thought we should open this up for discussion. "So much for partners working out disputes amicably among themselves," I said.

Andy nodded. "Maybe we should take a couple of minutes and quietly talk this over and see if anything else of consequence crops up. I guess none of this should come as a surprise; after all, we are a bunch of men, competing together. The real problem here is that this is just the first session."

"A 'couple of minutes,' and 'quietly talk this over'; those are two phrases that don't usually get uttered in the same sentence with reference to this group," I reminded Andy.

"Yeah," Andy sighed, "but still, we should address this and any other obvious things before partners start exchanging gunfire out on the river."

"If you grab everyone's attention," I said, "I'll cover your back as best I can."

We pulled a few tables together and congregated to hear everyone's conflicts. I'll not bore you with the details, but because the resolutions agreed upon this first night would have a direct bearing on the future of the Contest, I need to briefly relate the results of our discussion.

Two revealing points influenced our impromptu debate about time. Ultimately, despite what Jack and I had amicably settled on, I had to side with Mike's conclusion that we should be required to spend our allotted time in the same water in an honest attempt to discover the best fly. However, the arguments that most prejudiced the final decision were more a commentary on the participants' perceptions of each other, as well as reflections of themselves, than statements about our contest.

The first point centered on a person spending the last few minutes of his time fishing in obviously troutless water, thus forcing the next person to spend at least part of his new time angling the same unproductive water.

A frustrated Dan Sunderland offered up the second point, and it was impossible for me to disagree with his complaint, because I suspected Jack was guilty of such behavior. It concerned the possibility of an angler fouling the water he was fishing when his time had elapsed, intentionally or unintentionally ruining a run. Becoming conveniently snagged and the resulting commotion to get unsnagged, or even consciously delivering bad casts, could virtually destroy the "fishability" of a piece of water for far longer than the next twenty minutes. This was a strong argument for exercising the option of forfeiting time and moving along as quickly as possible. So, within the rules that constrained his movement on the river, it was decided that each man could do as he wished with his time. Use it or lose it, so to speak.

As I listened to the arguments, I remember thinking just how far we had apparently fallen—how devious we had inadvertently become—to even be contemplating that a STIFF would consider such possibilities and tactics as ammunition to be used against a fellow member. Once again, in the name of fair and equitable, we had become unwitting victims of our inherent competitive fire, and found it necessary to protect ourselves against our own unfair and insidious behavior.

We then proceeded to drink and bullshit the time away as was our routine for these STIFFS get-togethers. There was the reality that we would all be back here in a few hours, some of us before dawn, ready to do it all again; two sessions, morning and evening, with a few hours off in the afternoon to deal with less-important matters. It was nearly eleven p.m. by the time the teams had finished huddling at opposite ends of the studio, talking a little strategy for the a.m. session. We were still all smiles as each man departed, albeit not grinning quite as broadly as when we'd arrived earlier in the evening to start this contest.

Chapter 25

I was nursing a beer in the library while I waited for Bill to finish up with the last of his Friday-night chores, which consisted mainly of saying good-night to the late help. I refused the offer of another beer, so Bill just dropped himself into his chair.

"This fishing business can sure tucker a man out," he said with a noticeable sigh.

"You don't see me up looking for a dance partner," I responded. "I know it's not really the fishing, though—it's what we've turned the fishing into that's the problem. Remember the old days? Oh, wait a minute . . . that was yesterday, before this thing got started. Remember how much fun fishing used to be?"

"That was just yesterday?"

"Indeed it was. What the hell did we start? Have you ever seen this group behave this way?"

"Not all at the same time," Bill said, chuckling.

"Could you ever have imagined the erudite Mike Hartland and the reserved Wilson Davis in a contentious argument over the judicious use of time? Or poor well-bred, well-mannered Dan Sunderland forced to follow Dave Whitkowski around the river, in the wake of Dave's bullish ways? Or even more bizarre, me and Jack, alone on the river . . . together . . . for two and a half days? I'll repeat: What the hell have we started here?"

Bill didn't answer. An odd little smile crossed his face as he slowly shook his head. "I guess it's a little easier for me, although I did notice that even Andy seemed to take our fishing a bit more seriously this evening. However, after I missed a couple of fish because my skills have apparently suffered from lack of use, I assured him that his reputation as an angler supreme should remain secure. It was not until after he took that nice brown out of the Beaver Hole that things seemed close to normal. I even busted him by not letting him claim that extra half-inch, just so he couldn't say he'd gotten a seventeen-incher—just the way I would on any other day." Bill took a thoughtful pause. "Yeah, it was kind of strange out there tonight, now that I think about it. Maybe I should just keep missing fish—that would keep things the way they've always been."

"Andy said you were a little slow on the uptake."

"Maybe a little. Just a bit rusty, I guess. Like I told Andy, probably just some stiffness in the old casting arm from lack of activity." And then, as if to put that thought to rest, he continued. "That Sam Tippett fly sure is an effective pattern. You really did it justice with the last ones you tied for me."

"Thanks," I said, "but I do believe we should deal with the fact that it's getting late and I'm planning to be back here early, before the others. Knowing that tomorrow you'll be in the section of the river I was in tonight, I need to tell you about the two fish I lost, one Monday and one tonight at the Log Run, just below the big boulder—you know the one?"

Bill nodded. We talked a little strategy for the morning—mainly how he should get to the Log Run first, as I had earlier. Although he had remained silent during the discussion in the studio, Bill made it a point to say how impressed he was with Mike's defense of the belief that each man should cast to the same water for the same amount of time. Despite the fact that this option had been rejected in favor of more-advantageous personal opportunities, we both agreed it was the proper position to adopt in keeping with the initial spirit of the Contest.

Bill said he was set for flies—for tomorrow, at least. I told him I planned to spend some time tying on Saturday afternoon, and that I'd put together a few more for him. Mark had already told me he could use a few more Caddis. "Mark's going to need more than a few good flies to challenge Rick, I'm afraid," I couldn't resist commenting.

Even after my exasperating day with Jack Windermere, I was not very tired. I closed the big front door of the Crossing House behind me and stepped out into another warm, star-filled evening. I wished I could have settled into one of the inviting rockers that lined the porch of the inn and had a little heart-to-heart with old Sam Tippett—but that wasn't one of my choices that evening.

Chapter 26

By the time I reached the Crossing House there was only enough light to etherealize the morning mist that blanketed the river valley. It was a perfect morning for fishing—weather-wise, at least. The second I opened the door I could smell the coffee Bill had brewing in the studio for the STIFFS.

"Muffin?" I heard Bill call out quietly, because of the early hour. "Blueberry?"

"Is there any other kind?" I said.

I poured a coffee and for a few solitary minutes pondered the possibilities for the day before Bill arrived with a warm, fresh-from-the-oven blueberry muffin. These were not your ordinary, run-of-the-mill muffins; they were famous in three states.

Bill and I sipped coffee and ate muffins while we talked about the day ahead. There wasn't really anything new to say. We'd talked last night, and knew what needed to be done. So, instead, during what was the calm before the storm, we two anglers and friends chose to talk of other things.

Bill's truck was scheduled for a tune-up with Dave the following Wednesday. I offered myself as chauffeur for the ride back and the return to get his truck.

Bill was relieved to say that he was confident he'd conquered the problem of beetles that were a destructive nuisance to his dearly loved roses and flowers and shrubs—life that had been planted and nourished by Sarah. They'd been her pride and joy, and now they were Bill's.

We talked about the desire of some to reassess the local proper-ties in an effort to raise taxes to cover budget shortfalls—a far greater concern for Bill than me.

"What the hell happened to the valid and reasonable concept of pay to play?" Bill asked. "Instead of closing a library, why not throw a couple of quarters or a buck or two into a pot when you use it, help pay some of the expenses of a service you're using? I believe that everyone should pay something to maintain our libraries—they're a valuable resource—but those that use them most by choice get the most out of them, so maybe they should pay a little more for that privilege, and I believe they should do so willingly. Everyone should pay for the school system, but hell, if I'm an old lady on a fixed income and already paid when my child was in school, or if I have only one child in the school, is it fair to pay the same amount as someone with ten kids in the schools?"

"It is indeed difficult to assess what's fair," I concurred. "What's fair sure seems to have a lot to do with how much it benefits you." It was so easy for me to make the connection that I almost ignored it, but I couldn't seem to help myself, so I added, "Look how difficult it was for us to create rules that we all considered fair for our little Contest—and we're all doing the same thing."

Bill shook his head and laughed. "And what about the . . . oh, to hell with it. Sometimes it seems we're all just pissing in the wind, and all this crap we get concerned about eventually will amount to . . . just a huge pile of crap, which is exactly what it was to begin with. Nobody's listening. Nobody really gives a flying rat's ass about what someone else is pissing and moaning about, unless, of course, it affects him personally.

"If there were no taxes and no social welfare, I honestly believe we might all just naturally care more about our neighbors—we'd have to.

We don't have to do that now—care for or about anybody else's problems. We believe that somebody else, namely, the government, will take care of it. Unfortunately, more often than not, the job gets done poorly; it's incompetently handled, especially if the government has a hand in trying to do it."

"I'll discuss the problem of tax distribution and the proper implementation of the rules and laws of society with our noted attorney and esteemed councilman, Mr. Windermere, this morning," I sarcastically remarked, getting up for a second cup of coffee.

Our conversation came to an end when, as no surprise, Andy was the first of the others to show up. Andy was required to be up before dawn every day to open his general store—early was his natural world.

"What the heck did you do, stay here overnight?" Andy joked, a little surprised to find me there so early.

"If you can eat it in two minutes, I'll get you a muffin," Bill said, already kitchen-bound.

"No problem there—I can eat two in that time." Andy immediately turned to me and continued. "You sneaky son of a bitch—Jack told me later that the fish you lost last night was a really good one."

"I told you that."

"Yeah, I know, but I thought you were probably just busting me because I got a seventeen-incher."

"Sixteen and a half," I was quick to remind him.

"That's what Bill would have you believe . . . Anyway, have you got a secret hole or two, or maybe a fish you know, stashed away in a riffle somewhere, that you'll reveal to Jack today—maybe one that Bill and I can get to this evening?" Andy laughed.

"Oh, probably a couple, but—no, wait, I'm sure you already know every honey hole and obscure spot that harbors a Crossing House lunker; this river holds no secrets from you, does it?" I smiled, hoping to plant an unconscious seed of doubt in his mind.

His jesting was not all that far off base. Strangely enough, I had promised myself not to fish, in Jack's presence, a couple of potentially productive, nondescript runs, camouflaged by their ordinary complexion. They were not in this morning's area, but rather in this evening's upriver section D, the area farthest from the Crossing House but closest to my home. It was my intention to talk to Bill about that very situation after the day of angling was done, and before he fished that stretch on Sunday morning.

With just the three of us the spirit of our competition seemed, once again, the pleasant diversion that it was intended to be. Andy taunted his partner and best friend about all the fish he'd missed yesterday, and wished him more of the same inept execution for this day. He teased me that the best I could hope for my "perfect fly" was an honorable mention, as part of a team of losers. Naturally, Bill and I chastised Andy for his insensitive and unrefined approach to angling, which missed all the subtleties and finer points that are the true soul of fly fishing.

With the rapid arrival of the other STIFFS, the atmosphere in the studio once again took on the feel of a war room as the teams congregated in two groups at opposite ends of the room. The plans for the day were briefly discussed and the anglers paired up to do battle.

"Everyone should be off the river, packed up, and back here by noon," Andy, our de facto leader, announced. And off we went, each to our own assigned battle front.

Chapter 27

Not counting our routine greeting in the studio, my day with Jack really started with the confined car ride to our designated, section C starting point. I thought I could just keep my mouth shut and rely on Jack's usually predictable grandiloquent manner to kill the time it would take to get there. It was actually a short trip, but prolonged silences, wedged between our brief, pointless exchanges, made the little jaunt much longer than I expected.

I had some paper and a pencil in my nearly empty, Contest-tailored vest with which I hoped to add to—and, at the very least, clarify—the sketchy notes I also carried with me. These notes would eventually become one of my future articles. It had crossed my mind the night before, as I tried to fall asleep, that a follow-up to the "perfect fly" essay that had started this contest might be an interesting avenue to pursue. It might even be humorous, as I hoped it would eventually be, after some time had passed. Right now, however, I found little humor in it all as Jack and I pulled up our waders.

The coin flip, this time off Jack's thumb, ended with the same result as yesterday's, but this time, as the winner, with no thought or discussion, I waded as quietly as I could into position to cast to the riffle that betrayed the several prime trout lies in the rock garden over which it flowed. Although the sun was now above the horizon, the light was still dim, and a silvery glow was suspended over the river in the mist. I looked through my fly choices, standing as motionless as possible. I knotted on one of the largest Caddis; it seemed only logical to try to entice a trout to believe that his effort to get through the current to the broken surface was worthwhile.

I methodically began to cover the run, starting with short casts close to me, extending each subsequent cast farther across the riffle. It was over the second of the larger submerged boulders that a decent fish splashed at my fly, startling me in the serene surroundings. The fish raced around the run, and I put as much pressure on him as I dared. Against the current, it was difficult to turn him, but I did manage to halt his frenzied flight for a minute and he dove to the bottom. When he decided to resume the battle I urged him downstream, out of the run, and gained enough control in the shallow flat before the next pool to corral him.

It was now Jack's task to record the trout, and as much as he finagled the tape to make it not so, the fish measured just shy of fifteen inches. I settled for fourteen and a half. I could see Jack do a slow burn as he made an anemic attempt to compliment me on the first fish of the day.

It had taken me longer to land that fish than I'd thought. I took a peek at my watch and saw that my twenty minutes was fast disappearing. So, instead of moving down to the next pool, and despite the commotion my battle to land that last fish had caused, I dried my fly the best I could as I moved purposefully back to the top of the boulder garden. After only a couple of casts, my fly was only half floating, having become waterlogged and a little beaten up in the fight. I needed to change flies.

"Three minutes," Jack announced, standing from the log on which he was seated and moving toward the water for his turn.

"Yeah . . . three minutes," I said, again glancing at my watch to confirm the warning.

Now, without a reasonable amount of time to change my fly, and irked by Jack's snippy attitude, I quickly squeezed the bug tied to my leader in my shirt to blot any water and blew on it. I squeezed it again. I fluffed the deer hair, blew on it once more, and put it in the air, making several hard, false casts in an attempt to dry it and improve its floatability. I measured the cast and powered the Caddis to the top of the run, above the outermost underwater boulder. The hastily conceived effort resulted in a pretty poor cast. I shuffled line into the water, but the current caught up and consumed the slack. The fly floated only a couple of feet, and already half submerged, it was swept under by the drag. I gathered up the bowing line, but before I could lift the fly from the water, a brown grabbed the fleeing Caddis as it swam by the large rock. The trout bolted back across the run, further fouling the water for Jack's turn. I was now past my allotted time, but that wasn't my only problem.

"That fish didn't take a dry fly," Jack admonished as he stepped into the water next to me.

"What the hell are you talking about?"

"That fish wasn't caught on a dry fly—on the surface with a dry fly," he repeated, attempting to clarify his protest.

"How big an ass are you going to make of yourself?" I asked, unrealistically hoping for an answer of some sort.

"Can I now put floatant on one of my Probes and float it through the run before I sink it?" he asked indignantly, the arrogance of a courtroom lawyer showing through his frustration.

While I continued to fight the fish, I responded, "I'll answer that question when you answer mine."

"What question?"

Paraphrasing to emphasize my growing impatience, I repeated, "How big an asshole are you intending to make of yourself?"

"My complaint is a legitimate one."

I slipped the trout into the net, but Jack made no attempt to record the fish. "Do you want to measure this fish, or not?"

"I don't believe it should count," Jack continued his protest.

"Eleven inches," I announced, laying the tape along the brown. I released the fish, knowing full well that our rules clearly stated that after an angler netted his fish, the non-angling partner was required to unhook, measure, authenticate, and record the fish.

"The rules of our contest were to make things fair," Jack said. "Dry fly versus wet fly—which implies that the dry fly should be floating; otherwise it's a wet fly. Wouldn't you agree?"

"Not entirely," I immediately responded. "The fly was floating. It floated down the run, the current unintentionally swept it under, beyond my control, and then a fish decided to eat it. I don't know— how unfair is that? If I was a lawyer and this was my courtroom, I would state that I did catch the trout on a dry fly."

"Well, this is our courtroom at the moment, and I ask you: When is a dry fly not a dry fly?" Jack arrogantly questioned.

"I can assure you that according to any book you choose to reference, I was fishing with a dry fly. Where it winds up in the river doesn't change that fact. And, I will remind you as a fellow angler and a fellow STIFF, despite whatever else may be pissing you off about having to spend your time with me, there is not now, nor has there ever been, any intention to deceive or cheat to win this challenge. I'm asking you, and not rhetorically: Do you really think I would have to resort to dishonest means to beat your ass out here on the river?"

Jack didn't answer.

"I don't need that last fish," I said. "I don't want that last fish. As a matter of fact, I wouldn't count it now even if you insisted. My time is up. One fish, fourteen and a half inches. Your turn," I grumbled, trying to remain under control.

Jack had opened a can of worms, so to speak. We spent the rest of the morning watching each other like a sixth-grade teacher keeps an eye on a suspected cheater during a math test. Every action was scrutinized as if we were trying to catch the other in the act of stealing secrets that threatened national security.

Jack caught only two fish—a rather nice, ten-inch brookie, and a brown, a littler smaller. He missed one other. I landed three more: another eleven-inch brown to replace the one not counted, and two smaller fish, an eight-inch brook trout and a ten-inch brown. I missed two others. My neck ached down into my stiff right shoulder, all the result of being far too tense. In my mind that was the excuse I leaned on for missing two fish.

It was about 11:45 a.m. when we got back to the inn. I was aware that I had just experienced the least enjoyable day of angling since . . . well, since the days that had led me back to the Crossing House. There were already two teams in the studio having coffee; actually, one and a half were having coffee. Dave was having a beer. It was Mike and Wilson who were also there. They had been forced to return over an hour early when Wilson had slipped on a rock, slamming his rod on a boulder as he fell, snapping off the top two inches of graphite. It was too late into the session to come back for another rod, so they had "agreed" to terminate their remaining time.

"The only exposed damn rock within a hundred yards," Wilson pointed out in disgust, shaking his head. "That Orvis was my favorite rod, too."

"We still had a couple of nice runs to go yet—my favorite pool in that beat was just around the next bend. I offered to let Wilson use my rod while we finished the section, but he didn't want to do it that way. He said he needed his sink-tip line for it to be fair, and changing reels every turn seemed . . . I don't know, a little too much like work for him, I guess," Mike sarcastically commented.

Mike told me later, before he went home for lunch, that he had the feeling Wilson's desire to not continue using one rod was heavily influenced by the fact that Wilson had landed two fish to his one, and that those fish allowed Wilson to erase his deficit from yesterday. Mike insisted that the virtual tie in which they now found themselves, and the reality that he still had his best water ahead, crushed any motivation Wilson might have had to continue. Mike did fall short of insinuating that Wilson had broken his rod tip on purpose to conveniently end the morning session.

It was hard for me to conceive that Mike—trusting, good-natured, beloved schoolteacher Mike—would believe that Wilson could be so devious. Yet, under the increasingly competitive nature of this contest, and with a broken rod, it was not outside my realm of understanding to consider that Wilson might try to turn his misfortune into an advantage. What was fair under these circumstances?

It was almost 12:30 by the time Mark and Rick came into the studio. Andy had drifted in alone about five minutes earlier, again losing Bill to inn duties along the way. It would be a short stay, each member simply reporting their morning results to Andy for the record before heading off for lunch and any business that might need attention before they returned for the evening session.

"We should all be back on the river by five o'clock, so plan accordingly," Andy reminded everyone as they filed out of the studio.

Mark stayed behind to ask me for a little angling advice. It seemed that Rick and his Wreck were making a shambles of their head-to-head.

"If there are no rising fish to cast to," I told my friend, "you need to get your fly as close to the ledge or boulder or tree branch or whatever structure you are casting to. These damn trout often won't move even two inches to take a fly. Tight against the structure is usually the place to be. It's also a good idea to change sizes often if nothing is happening—big to small, smaller to larger. Throw a few of those sparkle Caddis, the ones with the crystal flash in the wing. So, Rick is really kicking your ass?" I said, chuckling.

"Yeah, Rick is really kicking my ass," he mocked disgustedly.

"At the risk of overstating the obvious, the truth is that more fish are taken below the surface than on the surface, so a good wet fly fished by a competent fisherman is formidable competition for a dry-fly angler to overcome. Rick is a very competent angler, and that Wreck is a very formidably fly. I wouldn't be too disheartened because you're trailing him in this contest."

"But it sucks being second in a race of two. That would make me last, wouldn't it? My ass is sore from being whipped. Think about this: What if Jack was embarrassing you out there on the river?" Mark offered, defending his concerns.

"Well, first of all, Jack is not Rick," I said, putting my arm around Mark's shoulder in a friendly, sort of patronizing gesture, "and you are not me."

"Eat shit," Mark said.

"Close to structure—change flies," I said. "I'm going to tie some flies for Bill and myself this afternoon; I'll put together a few extra-special ones for you."

"Thanks, I appreciate that. Eat shit anyway. Speaking of eating shit, would you like a turd sandwich before you go home?" Mark asked as he was leaving to check on the lunchtime kitchen.

"As mouthwatering as that sounds, I think I'll pass," I said, licking my lips. "See you in few hours."

On my way out I ran into Bill, checking in a couple of guests. I told him I was on my way to tie up a few flies, including some new ones to add to his evening arsenal, and that we'd talk later that night, after the fishing.

"I'll let you buy me a beer," I said, to his answering smile.

The biggest trout of the morning was my fourteen-and-a-half-inch brown. The biggest fish of the Contest was still Andy's sixteen-and-a-half-incher from the previous night. The most fish, at ten, and the most inches, totaling 102, belonged to Rick. Despite the individual accomplishments of the wet team's Andy and Rick, after the first two of our five sessions, the totals favored the dry team:

Dry: 30 fish—292½ inches

Wet: 26 fish—268½ inches

I don't know if anyone at that time was aware of the particulars, but if the Contest had ended on Saturday morning, Rick's Wreck would have been the perfect trout fly.

Chapter 28

I spent longer at the vise Saturday afternoon than I realized, and didn't get to the inn until after four o'clock. Most of the STIFFS were already there when I arrived. By the time I gave Bill and Mark the flies I'd tied for them, everyone was leaving for the water.

I wasn't looking forward to being in a confined space with Jack again, but I could only hope that the ride would be the least pleasant part of the evening. I was eagerly anticipating the angling because we were headed to the uppermost section of our designated water, section D, and that was the water closest to my home, upstream of the Crossing House. I knew that stretch better than all the others, and I was confident I could put far more distance between Jack and myself, angling this leg of the Contest—maybe even enough to crush any hope my partner might have harbored of winning our personal competition.

We reached the large, sentry sycamore that marked the upper-end starting point. Here the surrounding land became a gradual, graded slope, and the river, a series of riffled runs. I would have much preferred to fish here on a morning beat, for mornings were my favorite time to cast a fly. I consistently caught more and bigger fish in what I felt were the pristine, untouched hours of the day.

It was early for me, just as it had been the evening before, so when we were about to get started, I offered Jack first chance at the water without a coin toss. He refused, stating that the rules didn't allow for that. At this point I realized I had made a bad decision. If Jack won the flip, he'd make me go first, knowing that I wanted him to start. He'd exercise this option as the winner, just as I'd done the night before.

I sent the coin spinning into the air.

"Heads," Jack called. "Heads it is," he confirmed.

"I know," I said. "I'll go first."

Jack nodded with a smug little smile. I smiled back and headed to the sycamore. I knew several trout that lived there on a personal basis, and I was hoping to persuade them to come out and play.

My second cast took an eight-inch brookie. My fifth landed a ten-inch brown. I still had a little time left, so I hustled the short distance down to the tailout where, at current water levels, a large rock just bumped through the surface. I quickly changed to a larger Caddis and floated it within inches of the exposed stone top. A fat, foot-long brown came along and ate it, fighting me past my allotted time, but our rules allowed that "Any fish hooked before an angler's twenty-minute session ends will be counted, even if it is landed past the designated time." Jack was as irritated as he was exasperated by his inability to do nothing more than watch and record the fact that he was falling ever deeper into this confrontational abyss.

I shook the dripping water from the net bag as I walked to shore to sit down. I turned to Jack, who was already in the water, having been required to measure my fish.

"It's all yours," I said. "Three fish—thirty inches."

Jack didn't respond verbally, but his face became ruddy, and telltale beads of sweat dewed his brow. He didn't bother going back to the top of the run, but simply remained where he was and started casting. Things didn't improve for him as he huffed and puffed, erratically heaving his Probe at the poor frightened fish. He flailed away during his first forty minutes, fishless. Not even a hit.

"The good Lord has a way of balancing the scales and rewarding the deserving," Jack commented as serenely as he was able. I got the impression, however, that the impromptu sermon was as much about Jack trying to convince himself of its merit as it was to taunt me. It was, indeed, Jack's little prayer.

Have I mentioned that Jack was an active member of the Catholic Church, and one of "God's humble servants," as he'd often remind those who would listen? After listening to him pontificate at length during one of our particularly late STIFFS gatherings, I added to his growing disenchantment with me by asking if he actually knew the meaning of the word *humble*.

Anyway, Jack did confess at the outset of our Contest that he had to tell "a bit of a falsehood" (what would be classified as a lie by the rest of us) in order to miss church, which fell during our Sunday-morning session. I had no idea what story Jack told to justify his untruth, but I'm sure he rationalized that God would forgive him, although obviously he doubted that his friends and associates who were closest to God would. Clearly, they wouldn't agree that a simple fishing contest was sufficient reason to shun his religious duty. I did find it interesting that Jack somehow found his participation in this event so important. I viewed Jack's often provokingly confrontational religious elitism as simply one more of the false haloes he wore with haughty superiority.

I made no cast to the water that Jack had just beaten into froth. I purposely walked past one of those inconspicuous trout holes that I called the Glide—a deep trough of what appeared to be mundane river that meandered under bushes nearly touching the water along the far shore. Jack wouldn't recognize it for what it was, and I had no intention of revealing its value. I would, however, tell Bill about this place for his Sunday-morning session.

I stepped into the river at the next obvious pool. I missed the take as a trout rose to my fly on the first cast because I was looking back at the water upstream in the run I'd chosen to keep secret. "Damn. Pay attention," I quietly scolded myself.

Three casts later I had an eleven-inch fish in the net, and when I moved down to the next run, I caught another eleven-incher and missed one. And so it went for the rest of the evening. I didn't have to reveal any of my secrets about the river—especially in my section. My total for the night was eight fish landed, the last one a fat thirteen-inch, chocolate-chip-spotted brown, right at dark. My catch totaled eighty-three inches.

Jack landed two fish for nineteen and a half inches.

At another time, in another place, under different circumstances, I might have felt sorry for Jack. I didn't enjoy the lack of compassion I had displayed these last two days. I didn't feel like it was really me. Yet, I seemed compelled, almost driven, to emphasize my displeasure with him for challenging me about my perception of the perfect fly, thus initiating this damn, pleasure-sapping competition in the first place. Jack and this contest had spirited away all that I had come to appreciate and enjoy about angling. I didn't like Jack very much at the moment, and it showed as we headed back to the Crossing House in virtual silence.

Despite the effect this all-consuming search for perfection was having on those involved, this was Saturday night, and nearly everyone had places to go and things to do—Saturday-night things that included other people who couldn't have cared less about our quest. As a result, the evening totals were somewhat hastily verified and recorded. There was little good-natured jousting. Much of the conversation was strained, and the excuses to leave, although no doubt true, were tersely related. Each man apologized for his abrupt departure, ending with the assurance that he would be back early the next morning.

Bill gave Mark a rare Saturday night off. He planned on making good use of it with the new weekday waitress from the Frog, someone he'd had a major say in hiring.

"How convenient," I was quick to remind him as he raced out of the studio to get ready for his date.

The studio was soon left to just Bill, Andy, and me. Andy had in-laws up visiting from Connecticut, and only stayed for a very quick beer.

"I'm leaving these totals from tonight with you," Andy remarked, handing me several sheets of paper. "You also have yesterday's catches in there. Since you and Bill have nothing better to do tonight—no lives to speak of, really—why don't you add all this up? Looks like you had a pretty good evening out there," Andy said, adding, "Jack inspiring you to great things?"

"Inspiration is not one of the emotions Jack brings out in me," I responded.

"See if you can give some advice to your friend Bill; he sure seems to be missing a lot of fish. He's making this contest way too easy for me. A little more competition would be a good thing—you know, make it more exciting." Then Andy tossed his head in an affably pretentious gesture of confidence. "See you losers in the morning."

Bill left me with a fresh, cold beer while he went to do a quick check of things around the inn. I took a couple of big swallows and began totaling the results of the Contest thus far.

Chapter 29

When I was finally finished with the Contest numbers, I took what was left of my beer and went to the library. Bill would know to look for me there. I was drained, and when he took longer than expected, I closed my eyes, put my head back, and lost myself in the relative silence of my surroundings. The voices that wafted in sounded a million miles away. The world, once again, seemed a peaceful, undisturbed place without Jack Windermere in it.

"Oh, excuse me." A gentle voice startled me. "I was just wandering around. I didn't know anyone was in here."

"Nobody . . . just me," I responded.

"What a quaint library," she said. "I've been here before, a couple of times for dinner, but I never ventured around the place. I'm here tonight for . . ." She paused. "I guess I'm here for a celebration of sorts. I never appreciated what a truly lovely inn this is. Oh dear, I'm sorry—I'm sure I'm disturbing you."

"You most certainly are not," I said. "I was going over some figures here, waiting for Bill, the owner of the Crossing House. He seems to be sidetracked at the moment. I only had my eyes closed in this Zen-like repose because I was praying for a stranger to wander in so I'd have someone to talk to. Who says there's no god? Would you care to sit, or do you need to get back to your party?"

"It's not really a party," she said, politely acknowledging my attempt at levity with a smile and a playful tilt of her head. "A few of us girls are here celebrating"—again she paused—"if that's the right word. We're here celebrating a divorce. Not mine," she quickly added. "I celebrated mine a few years ago. Oh, that's terrible, I don't even know you. I apologize."

"For what? Not inviting me to your divorce party?"

"You might have had a great time," she said, taking the few steps to Bill's chair. "I know I did." She sat down on the edge of the chair. (As I mentioned earlier, Bill's chair was molded to his body, and relatively uncomfortable for anyone else to sit in.) She put her drink on the small table between the two chairs and adjusted her dress.

"I don't believe I've seen you around here," I said. "In fact, I know I haven't. I certainly would have remembered. Do you live in town?"

"One town over; actually, one town up," she answered. "I'm a teacher there. And you?"

"No . . . I'm not a teacher there," I said, hoping my further attempt at humor would be recognized as such. Thankfully, she shook her head, trying not to be too amused at my response.

"But I was a teacher once—not here, but in Massachusetts, years ago. That was before I dropped out of society and became a recluse in the wilds of Maine."

"And now?" she pursued.

"I'm still a recluse. I fish a little, write a little. Actually, that's not entirely accurate. I fish a lot and write a little. However, I manage to get my monthly assignments in to my editors, and my Great American Novel is nearly complete—as soon as I'm finished with the self-edit. If I'm not mistaken, I believe this is my fifty-second revision."

"My, my, fifty-two—that's a lot of rewrites. Once you get all the commas in the right place, I bet it will be one great story," she said.

I was trying to compose a clever response when Bill came into the library, a scotch in one hand and a beer in the other.

"Bill," I said, disappointed to see him at that very moment. "This is . . ." I looked over at the lady occupying his chair. "I'm sorry to say, I have no idea."

"Lucy," she responded.

"Lucy," I repeated. "It's a pleasure to meet you. I'm Benedict Salem. For some odd reason my friends call me BS. Oh, and this is Bill, the owner and sage of this manor."

"I was just commenting on what a beautiful place this is," Lucy said, smiling at Bill.

"Thank you," Bill said. "I hope you're having an enjoyable evening."

"Very much so. My friends and I were saying how comfortable we all feel here. The Castle Lawn dining area is quite unique, and your tavern is wonderful. As a matter of fact, I believe we'll all be coming here more often in the future."

"That's music to my ears," Bill said, with an appreciative bow in Lucy's direction.

Lucy stood. "So nice to have met both of you. I'll leave you gentlemen to your business and return to my . . ." She glanced at me and smiled. "To my celebration party. Perhaps our paths will cross again."

"I certainly hope they do." I surprised myself with this unimaginative response to her inviting comment. Lucy walked elegantly to the door leading out of the library. She turned and gave a little wave without saying a word.

"Please wipe that stupid grin off your face," Bill teased.

I raised my eyebrows and gave a little schoolboy shrug of my shoulders.

"Lucy, huh?" Bill said.

"Yeah, she just wandered in. She said she was here with a few of her gal pals, celebrating her friend's divorce."

"I saw them in the Castle. Hard not to notice such an attractive bevy sitting up there when I went through to check on things in the dining room," Bill commented.

"I think I'll send them a round of drinks," I said, "with a note—as soon as I think of something clever to say."

"In the mood Jack's put you in, that could take the rest of the night," Bill needled. "In fact, I thought you might prefer something a little stronger than beer. You can have both of these if you want." Bill still held the beer and scotch.

"Beer is just fine for now," I responded. "I was relishing a few moments of escape into a Jackless world when that delightful lady showed up like a vision, as if to remind me of the way things should be. Maybe this serendipitous encounter is just what the doctor ordered to cure a case of Windermere-itis. Hey, you know what? I feel better already. Quick, get me a paper and pencil. I feel a clever thought—an ode to beauty, perhaps—struggling to free itself from my addled brain. Let's see, what rhymes with Lucy . . . juicy?"

"Careful," Bill chuckled, "you may not want to start there. You don't even know the lady."

"You're right; bad idea. Something more subtle. Let's see . . . Lucy . . . moosey . . ."

"Yeah, that's it. I know I've always found women are swept off their feet by being compared to large, antlered, cud-chewers."

We shared a good laugh. The brief encounter with Lucy had actually done a great deal to relieve the Contest-induced stress I was feeling. Lucy seemed, at least for the moment, a more significant influence than Jack. What a welcome revelation that was.

I did compose a note—in rhyme, and signed "BS"—that would arrive at the ladies' table before they left. There was one more conse-quential effect that Lucy had on the evening . . . but I will reveal that later on.

I said to Bill, "It's becoming clear to me why I find Jack so objec-tionable: He's an idiot. His disagreeableness increases the more time I spend with him. At least in the STIFFS meetings I can walk away or involve myself in other conversations, but this being stuck with him, one on one, all day long—I don't know if I can last another day. He's so . . . frickin' grating. He's unbearable!

"I've actually entertained the notion of killing him. Maybe tomorrow, while he's terrorizing the fish, I can devise a plan to execute the perfect murder. I could anonymously write an article about it for the benefit of those forced to fish with folks they find to be bad company. No one should be required, under any circumstance, to fish with someone they find intolerable."

"Easy." Bill put up his hand like a stop sign. "Jeez . . . has it been that tough out there? He's not getting too close for comfort, is he?"

"He's so damn far behind me now, I could decide to not even show up tomorrow and he still couldn't catch me. Hey . . . that's a great idea. I could just stay home tomorrow. That would really frost his ass—the entire day on the river to himself and still not able to catch me."

"Not so fast. Did you forget who you're dealing with?" Bill asked.

"Not for one damn moment—believe me."

"He would no doubt come up with something, some lawyer's perspective; as a no-show, you'd have to forfeit the Contest to him. He would win, no matter how far behind he was," Bill said.

"How very true. Thanks a lot for dashing my hopes. But then at least I wouldn't have to endure the misery of spending another day with him."

"Yeah, but just think how much greater your victory will be, how much sweeter the taste of triumph, when you trounce him even more tomorrow, further adding to his humiliation."

"Believe me, I'll try to hold on to that thought with all the power I can muster," I said.

"How badly are you beating him?" Bill asked.

"By nine fish and nearly a hundred inches," I quickly answered, having just dealt with the numbers.

Bill roared. "Shit, maybe you should stay home. Jack's liable to shoot you out there at some point tomorrow just to save the embarrassment he'll have to face at the next STIFFS meeting."

"I'll keep a close watch on him, check him for weapons before we get started," I said. "Before I reveal these interesting Contest totals, what do you really think about this little competition we've created? I use the collective *we* here, even though most of the blame truly rests with Jack . . . and I guess Andy's not completely innocent, either; he's the one who suggested and actually encouraged this farce."

Bill took a long, thoughtful pause. "What do I think of it? Well, nothing brings out the best and the worst in folks than a little competition. But don't you think it's the person's attitude about winning that dictates much of the atmosphere during a contest?" Bill proposed. "When you and I compete on the water for a dollar, or a beer, it doesn't detract from our enjoyment while fishing; on some level, it may even enhance it."

"We also like and respect each other," I commented.

"There you go," Bill said. "That's it. We respect each other, so we keep things in perspective. We know our friendship, our mutual respect, is far more valuable to us than winning a competition. We also respect our activity and the importance it plays in our lives. To allow that respect to be tarnished by placing victory above our regard for each other would be sacrilegious to us, demeaning our appreciation for angling. It would ruin it for us."

"Have you been rehearsing that little sermon, waiting for the proper question?" I asked. "That's exactly how I feel about this damn contest. When I'm on the river with Jack, any semblance of enjoyment and even fair play seems to vanish. I have no respect for him or his attitude, and being with him in places that I love, doing what I enjoy most in the world—well, he simply takes all the fun out of fishing. That clown is out there quoting scripture like he has a direct line to God—as if God gives a shit if he wins a fishing contest. Unless he has one divinely endorsed, unimaginable day tomorrow, it looks like God has more important . . . fish to fry, if you'll pardon the pun."

"Now, now . . . take it easy," Bill quietly admonished.

"You know, the tone of a contest is shaped not only by what was challenged, but by how it was challenged," I continued, ignoring Bill's gentle reprimand. "Calling into question what someone believes to be true for the sole purpose of pissing him off just seems . . ." No adequate words came to mind. "I couldn't care less what Jack believes about the ability of that Probe of his—or about his choice of automobiles, his political beliefs, or his religious beliefs, for that matter.

"I don't care what Jack believes as long as he keeps it to himself and doesn't flaunt a perceived superiority because of those beliefs. This is exactly the point I was trying to make: Look at the interactions between the others here—what this contest is doing to them. This isn't the way I normally act around people. This isn't me . . . it's—"

"Oh, it's you, all right," Bill jumped in while I searched for words. "It's you being influenced—maybe infected is a better word—by Jack Windermere. Like I said, competition, contests, challenges, call it what you will, certainly bring out the best and the worst in people. This is just bringing out the part of you that you don't like very much. What? Didn't think you had it in you?"

"I hate to admit it, but you're right. Maybe if I get a good night's sleep and try really, really hard, I will be less hostile and more pleasant and amenable toward my angling partner tomorrow," I said. "Maybe I'll even show him a couple of secret trout runs—that is, if God doesn't help him out first. Don't hold me to that. I'll see how obnoxious Windermere the windbag appears to me in the new morning light."

"Wow, Jack has really gotten under your skin," Bill said. "In all the years I've known you, I've never seen you this miffed."

"I'm telling you, it's this cursed contest. Look at Wilson and Mike," I offered as evidence for my tirade. "Here you have two levelheaded,

intelligent men who I daresay respect each other, who are finding
each other more than a little . . . irritating, if you will. Now, these guys
have been interacting socially for years in more than the world of the
STIFFS. They have functioned compatibly at events for their children,
both school and sports. Wilson once told me that Mike was his kid's
favorite teacher, and I know Wilson was instrumental in securing the
financing for Mike's new home. I also know for a fact that they have,
on many occasions, enjoyed fishing together, as well as having a drink
together. I can tell you that both have talked to me privately about the
character and integrity of the other man.

"Now, look what this contest may have done to their relationship.
When I saw them together this evening, they sure didn't seem like
they were enjoying each other's company very much. They're both
still pissed off about their disagreements over time allotment and
broken-rod conspiracies and who knows what else. Will they be able
to see each other in the respectful light of friendship again, or has this
contest permanently altered their view of each other?"

"I noticed they were a bit at odds," Bill said. "What's their situation in the Contest?"

"Almost dead even; Mike has one more fish and is only five inches
to the better," I responded after a quick check of the numbers. "But
it's everyone," I continued. "Before this contest started, Dan could
tolerate Dave—joke with him, even get deeply involved in talking
about fast cars. But in this competition, no common interest seems to
hold things together; their different philosophies and lifestyles, and
certainly their diverse approaches to angling, are all perfectly tolerable when they're in Dave's garage or Dan's bank or in the studio for
a meeting. But that odd couple, united in this competition—Christ,
it looks like Dan is about to lose his mind. Dave knows he can be an
obnoxious bastard if he chooses to be, and I'm sure he's trying hard to
drive Dan right into the bughouse."

"Boy, you hit the nail on the head describing those two as an odd couple," Bill commented. "Dan has got to be ahead in that pairing, isn't he?"

"Yeah, by quite a bit." I flipped the pages to find their results. "Dan by six fish, nine to three, and by forty inches. But how's this for a stat? Dave has the largest average per fish of anybody in the Contest, so far."

"Besides me and Andy, that only leaves Mark and Rick to discuss," Bill said. "Mark must be getting his ass kicked."

"That's a kind description of what Rick is doing to Mark," I said. "Rick has twice as many fish, with fourteen, and over twice as many inches, with one hundred and forty-three," I said after verifying the numbers. "And look at these guys: two friends—they hang out and drink and fish together. However, this contest has emphasized the disparity between their on-river abilities. Rick is far more accomplished overall. Fishing together within the context of a competition creates conflict, especially for the inferior competitor.

"Mark told me before he left tonight that if things got much worse out there, he was going to challenge Rick to a cook-off, in an attempt to get things into a more-competitive arena for himself. There's not a more laid-back soul than Rick—he still wears that hippie spirit proudly—and yet I noticed that even his jesting seems tinged with, I don't know . . ."

I stopped talking, as I am inclined to do, not sure what I was trying to say, not wanting to say something I really didn't mean. Finally, I continued: "Having fished with Rick many times, I do think it's important to him to display that fly of his in the best light. There is no way, if he can help it, that his Rick's Wreck will be outfished. With his performer's ego in play, he wants that fly to be perceived as the best, the same way he wants his music to be best. It's just a little unfortunate that Mark is in the unenviable position of having to endure the 'wrath' of the Wreck while Rick proves the bug's worth."

"There's no chance you're overanalyzing this whole thing, is there?" Bill asked.

"Sure there is," I said. "Probably a very good chance. But I know what I see, and you see it, too. It's really undeniable. Whether I'm correct in my assessment of what's happening, I don't know, but I do know that things seem to have taken a drastic turn for the STIFFS."

"I can't wait to hear what you think about me and Andy."

"I don't have a single astute thought about it," I said, "not that you'd give a squirrel's nut about what I thought. However, since you brought it up, what's all this complaining Andy's doing about you missing fish—fudging all the hookups? You know, he thinks you're doing it on purpose to keep the Contest close. He says you only start to hook and land fish after he catches a few and gets a lead on you, and the totals so far actually back up his speculation. You both have eight fish, and he's ahead of you by only seven inches," I said, watching Bill's face for any telltale reaction. "It appears to be pissing him off because he resents any placating behavior on your part, especially when it comes to fishing, where he feels he's anyone's equal. Any comments?"

"Just lucky, I guess," Bill said, "catching a few fish when I need them." Bill smiled slyly.

"Yeah, what luck," I said, still staring at Bill, looking for something that would expose any other reason for such good fortune.

"My guess is that Andy is getting a little paranoid in his old age, while I've simply mellowed—sort of like a fine wine or a top-shelf whiskey," Bill said, holding his glass of scotch up to the light to examine its color. "And of course, those perfect Tippett's Crossings you tied certainly help."

"I think you're full of shit," I responded, bending forward as if interested in looking at Bill's glass of scotch through the light. "Seriously, Andy seems quite annoyed at your missing all those fish."

"Well, he'll just have to deal with it—for at least another day," Bill responded.

"What the hell does that mean?" I questioned, believing now that there must be something to Andy's suspicions.

"Just that there's only one day left in this contest."

"Do you have any idea how many fish you've missed?" I questioned, still probing for insight.

"I have no idea—maybe a half-dozen, eight?" Bill answered without thinking.

"Bill, my friend, you're so full of shit your eyes are brown. You're yanking Andy's chain, aren't you, you old bastard?"

"I haven't a clue what you're talking about," Bill said. "I'm a little rusty out there. You know I haven't been fishing anywhere near as much as I used to."

Knowing I wasn't going to be told anything Bill thought I didn't need to know just then, I gave up.

"Okay," I said, "I'm done. But if you happen to need an extra fish tomorrow, let me jog your memory about that spot upriver where you're apt to find a good one." And with that I reminded Bill of the Glide, the run I'd walked Jack past—a trough that indistinguishably falls from the visibly shallow river bottom, the deeper water slipping under the bushes.

We were both tired, and there was still one more early start facing us in the morning, our last day. Before I left I read Bill the totals so far:

The dry team had 49 trout, for a total of 488 inches. The wet team had landed 40 fish, totaling 424 inches. The biggest fish belonged to Andy, his sixteen-and-a-half-inch, first-night brown. I had landed the most fish, at seventeen, and since the true winner was to be determined by the total inches, I was the current leader.

On my way off the porch I stopped and glanced back at the motionless row of rockers. Sam Tippett was still nowhere in sight. I would have loved to sit down and talk with him for a few minutes about the brown Deerhair Caddis—what was, on this Saturday night, still the most perfect trout fly.

I may have also mentioned Lucy.

Chapter 30

Both Andy and I were again early enough to have a muffin and coffee with Bill before the others arrived. Andy was his usual jovial self, provoking Bill by assuring his friend that there was absolutely no chance of him winning their head-to-head challenge. He was, however, humorless when he expressed his honest concern that the dry-fly guys might just win the overall competition. In his mind, the true focus of the Contest—determining the perfect fly (by most inches caught)—was still up for grabs . . . for some. He also reluctantly acknowledged my rather substantial total.

"But anything can happen out there, as you are well aware. I've had many a day that would easily erase your lead," he said. "Maybe I should have a little private talk with Jack . . . about things," he added with a devious squint.

"If you can't beat 'em with skill, sabotage the son of a bitch. Is that your new, panicked modus operandi? Seriously, Andy, is this the sort of legacy you want to leave your grandkids? I won, but I had to connive and cheat to do it?"

"There will be no cheating . . . maybe just a bit of psychological warfare—as I'm convinced Bill is waging against me. I'm not completely sure what his motivation is, but I can assure you, it won't work. He's got to land a fish over seventeen inches to top my biggest fish— my biggest so far—and he's also trailing in total inches. I don't believe for a minute that that Sam Tippett concoction has the ability to catch and beat the proven, and dare I say, perfect, marabou Muddler."

"Well, I must humbly point out that your far-from-perfect Muddler is trailing far behind the perfect Caddis in this contest," I said. "And when my dear friend Jack gets here, I will endeavor to put that sculpin of yours so far behind that you'll be embarrassed to be associated with it."

"You two should be fishing together," Bill commented, picking up the muffin plates as the others started to arrive. "That would put this whole shebang in perspective."

"I would love that," Andy said, devilishly curling the ends of his mustache. "If you and I were out there together—"

But before he could continue his thought, Bill jumped in. "Yeah, yeah, and if a frog had wings he wouldn't whack his ass every time he jumped. However, you're stuck with me, old man, so let's get our gear together. We're on beat D, and that means a ride. You drive."

When Bill, with Andy in tow, left for their morning beat, everyone else followed close behind, as if he was the Pied Piper of the Crossing House. All except for me, because Jack hadn't yet shown up, even though our proposed a.m. starting time was fast approaching.

I had already poured myself another cup of coffee and taken it to the porch when Jack, dust flying, skidded to a stop in the corner of the parking lot. He grabbed his gear from the trunk of his Mercedes and trotted across the lot. I remained seated, not the least disappointed at his tardiness, having convinced myself while I waited that the later he was, the less time I would have to spend with him. He scrambled up the inn steps to where I sat.

"Sorry," he said, sounding almost contrite.

I was ready to respond with a few, calculated, smart-ass comments, having taken the opportunity to rehearse several while I'd been waiting there, sipping my coffee. But Jack seemed almost pathetic, his chubby, red face already beaded with sweat.

"I got hung up—had some stuff to take care of," he sputtered. "I apologize."

"Yeah, well . . ." My affronting barbs filtered through my mind, but I uttered none of them. "We're upriver in beat E. You going to be able to walk up there?"

"Of course," Jack responded, taking shallow breaths to help disguise his agitated state.

"I'm going to slip into my waders here rather than carry them. You?" I asked, not knowing whether Jack would rather take a little time now to put them on or make his walk upriver less strenuous by traveling in his sneakers.

"I'll put them on when I get there," he said. "You take your time."

"Can't take too much more time," I said, "or our morning session will be over." Jack just nodded, aware of the situation he had created.

When we arrived at the top of our section, it was well past our supposed first-cast time. Jack was painfully slow getting into his waders after a dawdling trip to get to our starting point.

"Why don't you just start," Jack proposed, an offer he'd insisted was outside the rules when I'd suggested he go first yesterday. I was about to call him on that, but instead I agreed. I thought it might benefit both of us to have him sit and relax and regain some of the old Jack—not that it would be better than this new Jack, but maybe just less of a concern.

I caught a fat, foot-long brown at the tail of the first pool. Jack seemed to have regained some of his color and peevishness when he was forced to come and record the catch. He gritted his teeth but remained silent as he measured the trout. I was somewhat relieved to see the pain-in-the-ass return, as it was far more satisfying, and far more justifiable, beating up on him if he could fight back.

Jack caught a small, nine-inch brown and an even smaller brook trout of slightly over seven and a half inches. Despite his mild protest in the name of honesty and respect for our rules, saying he didn't want to be shown any favor, I recorded the fish at eight inches.

"You've staked yourself to a small lead this morning," I commented as we shuffled downstream.

"It's a start," he responded, trying hard to display the serenity of the saints he so admired. "I know I'm a long way behind, but the road to respectability may just begin with a couple of small fish—and a little help from above."

I let Jack walk slightly ahead of me as he talked, and, as if I had someone next to me to respond to my irreverent reaction to his gibberish, behind Jack's back I rolled my eyes and shook my head. "That just may be true," I said.

But Jack's trip down the road to respectability was a short one. In my next turn I caught another twelve-inch brown just three casts after I'd taken a ten-incher along a downed tree, and just for good measure, I landed a beautiful nine-inch brookie that exposed his lie by ambushing fleeing caddis from the cover of some submerged midstream boulders. Three fish ended my time early. Each trout was measured and noted by my increasingly irritated partner.

With the ever-widening gap between us in the Contest numbers, not only did Jack's frustration mount, but his apparent stress-related issues seemed to resurface. He lagged behind on each move to the next run, and there was also an increasing amount of muffled mumbling—beseeching prayers, I assumed, and maybe a bit of concern over where to find the answers.

Our abbreviated morning session ended with Jack continuing to seek solutions to his deteriorating position, and no doubt cursing himself for ever issuing his inane challenge in the first place. The need to shelter his ego was becoming even greater than he could have imagined. Despite my momentary feeling of sympathy for Jack when he'd arrived that morning, huffing and puffing, once on the river, with our "partnership" resumed, I seemed to lose all compassion. I continued to show no mercy for my humbled partner as I landed more trout. As Bill had insightfully revealed to me, I was acting like someone I didn't know, or particularly like, but entangled with Jack, I seemed unable to help myself.

Mercifully for Jack, the slaughter on beat E eventually came to an end, and he dragged his out-of-shape ass back to the inn. His meager totals of three fish for twenty-nine inches had dropped him an additional five fish and nearly forty inches further behind. A few small, but appreciated, brook trout of seven inches added more to my total, but had a big impact on lowering the average size of my morning's catch: eight trout for just over seventy inches. I truly wanted to feel some pity for my partner, but I couldn't.

The players clamored around the studio for an hour or so. Those ahead in their personal confrontations were noticeably in better spirits. To a man, each had tragic tales to tell about fish lost; predictably, nearly all the trout not brought to net were bigger than any landed. But, as was evident by the totals, fish over thirteen or fourteen inches are not so easy to come by. It's not that we don't have eighteen- or even twenty-inch browns in our river, but it must be remembered that we are angling for what are truly native trout, original Sam Tippett progeny, and eighteen-inch fish didn't get that way by being stupid or careless. Some, I'm sure, even became much smarter and far wiser after being caught a time or two as youngsters, in their formative years.

I sat with Andy and helped to compile the numbers from our next-to-last session. As we added the figures, it became evident that with only one session remaining, the dry-fly team, barring a complete collapse, was realistically beyond reach of being caught, so far amassing a total of twenty more fish and over 160 more inches—162 to be exact.

However, as witnessed by the STIFFS' behavior, tensions were rising between the pairs comprising each team. It remained so on Sunday morning. I will refrain from listing a bunch of numbers here, but I will mention a few things of interest between individuals who were partnered—just a little insight, at least as I perceived it, before the final trip to the river.

Andy still had an issue with Bill missing fish, complaining to me that he honestly believed that his good friend was, in his words, "purposely provoking my congenial ass."

Mark happened to have a very good morning on Sunday, landing six fish. Unfortunately, his catch was not as good as Rick's eight fish, and he fell another twenty-seven inches further behind.

Mike managed to put a little distance between himself and Wilson. They were still sufficiently irked with each other to complain openly about questionable behavior concerning stream etiquette and misuse of time.

Dave seemed the least affected by the hubbub and grumbling, apparently able to just go fishing amid the turmoil and flying accusations. His partner, however, couldn't wait to get this over with. Dan had an insurmountable lead of ten fish and eighty inches, and was so annoyed by Dave's plundering ways that he seriously asked me if he could just not show up for the last session—what I had joked with Bill about doing with Jack. I was honestly sympathetic when I told him I didn't think that it was a good idea; it was not in keeping with the spirit of the Contest.

This contentious tournament had started as a quest for the most perfect trout fly. Now, as I scanned the numbers, one thing jumped off the page: There were only two people who had a legitimate chance at winning this contest, and that was Rick Meade and me. Rick had landed 22 fish for 225 inches. My totals, no doubt motivated by my unappealing desire to embarrass Jack, were 25 trout and 243 inches. With one session left to contend, as had appeared to be the case on Saturday night, the brown Deerhair Caddis was the fly to beat.

I was oddly taken with the sense that suddenly, Jack didn't matter. My initial lack of enthusiasm for this contest was sparked by the fact that I now had the opportunity to verify a contention that was important to me. Although this wasn't exactly how I would have considered doing it, having been pushed to this point, maybe I should just complete the challenge.

I was reminded of the quote by former Boston Celtics coach, Red Auerbach, who once said (and I may be paraphrasing here), "As long as you're going to keep score, you might as well try to win."

I stayed and had a late lunch with Bill. I confirmed what he had always assumed would be the case—that there was no way the wet team was going to beat the dry team. After he had assured me that he wasn't going to allow Andy to catch more inches of trout than him, he also pointed out (unnecessarily) that he really hadn't tried very hard to stay in the running.

When he asked me who I thought would win the Contest, I told him only Rick or I had any real chance. He nodded his approval, saying, "That's good. We all fish both ways; it's only right that it comes down to one dry and one wet vying for the cup. That's the way it should be."

Chapter 31

I spent the majority of the afternoon contemplating my situation in the Contest. I'd been opposed to it ever getting started. I am averse to the entire notion of contests when they involve the artificial need to validate something I already know, or at least believe to be true. I have always fervently defended my passions and my philosophies, but it was a totally foreign concept to have to justify their worth by way of a competition.

If Jack had challenged me to a friendly competition for a couple of beers, his Probe against my Caddis, I have no doubt that it would have resulted in something quite different from what this contest had become. It might have even had the potential to be enjoyable. Instead, he had created a monster by issuing his challenge not in private, but in a room full of liquored-up anglers, like waving a red flag in front of a bull. So now, here we were—all of the STIFFS acting like a bunch of unethical, immoral, childish oafs—and, unbelievably to me, I was one of them. What the hell had happened? Was it too late to do anything about it? I had been challenged and now was in a position to prove myself right, with all of my fellow STIFFS as witnesses. Was the cause important enough to need to win? Ultimately, why did I even care? Why, indeed.

Even though I was hoping to be the first one back to the Crossing House, both Andy and Rick beat me there. They were in the studio talking with Bill when I showed up.

"Keep it down," Andy joked, "here comes the king you must depose."

In the spirit of the moment, I raised my arms and waved like royalty hailing a cheering throng.

"Please, please . . . be seated, my vassals," I said with a sweeping gesture of my hand. "And might there be a minion available to fetch me a cold tankard of ale while William the Wise and I contemplate the most effective means of implementing the plans for the evening?"

Just then, Wendy, the afternoon waitress who tended to the often large, often lingering Sunday-brunch crowd, walked past the studio. Knowing everybody in the room, she stopped to say a cheery hello.

"Might the lovely wench Wendy have the time to fetch us all some refreshment from the tavern?" I asked, smiling.

"Lord knows I've tried to ignore what people say behind your back, because I like you," she responded, "but I'm starting to believe that BS really does stand for what many of them say it does. What can I get you gentlemen—and you too, Sir Benedict?"

"I thank thee, oh beautiful lass," I said, bowing in her direction.

She playfully tapped me on the top of my head with her tray, took our orders, and sashayed slowly out the door, purposely swaying her very attractive behind.

"You've got a great section to fish tonight," Rick said to me. "Maybe the best section. It will be tough to catch you, but I'm sure as hell going to try."

Andy joined the conversation. "We wet guys can smell victory, especially if the finicky trout this evening are locked in on sulphur or cahill or some other non-caddis delicacy."

"I'm afraid what you smell is not victory," I said, "but rather the piles of shit you're shoveling in my direction. For victory smells far different than what you're inhaling. Victory smells sweet. It really is too bad your Muddler isn't in the running."

"Don't count it out yet," Andy blustered, knowing he had no chance of winning the Contest. "My main focus now is to tighten my grip on the biggest-fish money, and to be sure Bill owes me twenty by the end of the night."

"I'll bet you a beer that Bill's Tippett's Crossing will defeat your Muddler—total inches, as the rules state."

"You're on," Andy quickly responded, coming over to shake my hand to seal the deal.

For a brief while it seemed like the good old days (of four days ago)—friendly, sporting, noncombative jousting among friends, the way it used to be—the way it should be. We continued our good-humored give-and-take while we sipped our drinks.

The others soon started to arrive. Mike was first; Jack followed, showing up earlier than usual, maybe to relax before another stressful session, or possibly thinking it would make up for his tardy morning arrival. Dave was next, a brew from the Frog in hand. Then Wilson and Mark walked in together, having reached the inn at the same time. Last to appear was Dan; I chuckled to myself when he skulked in, sure he was counting the minutes until this nightmare was over.

Everyone knew that only two of us were in the running to be named the ultimate winner, and in the name of sportsmanship offered Rick and me a "good luck" handshake or an encouraging pat on the back. However, there was no doubt that each man had become consumed by the competition with his partner—in truth, to the exclusion of the original intent. The game within the Contest had taken precedence. The best trout fly be damned; all that mattered was to win your one-on-one, or cover any convoluted side bets made, at this point the only part of this thing you had any control over.

Ultimately, no one's mind was going to be changed; each man would always believe that his fly was the perfect one. This contest would do nothing but supply one man with bragging rights. It was of more immediate concern to protect yourself from humiliation.

Rick and I talked briefly alone in the studio, after it emptied out. We were good friends, and although Rick was one of the people who had initially expressed no enthusiasm for this contest, I now sensed an intensity in him, or at the very least, a competitive will. In our frequent tavern encounters, he had mentioned how others often misinterpreted his lack of initiative to compete in the cutthroat world of music as him not caring enough. He defended himself against the view that his perceived complacency meant failure, or, in other words, a lack of success, which he adamantly assured me couldn't be further from the truth.

I wondered if maybe Rick needed to prove that he could get to the top, for the pinnacle here (albeit insignificant to anyone outside our realm) was certainly within his grasp. Exactly how owning the bragging rights to the best trout fly might compare to reaping the rewards of a hit record, I'm not quite sure, but somehow, I understood his desire to succeed. I could find no fault with Rick's ambition to prevail in his attempt to validate perfection. It would, indeed, feel nice to be victorious.

Rick and I exchanged a sincere handshake on the Crossing House porch. One of us would return here in a few hours as the possessor of "the most perfect trout fly in the world." One of us would return here a winner.

Jack, seeing Rick and I part ways, started on a leisurely trek down the path to the river. There was no need to ask him to wait up; I would catch him long before he reached the water. The river behind the inn—the ledges and runs, and even the trout that had initiated my enduring connection to my new life here in Maine—waited to determine my place in STIFFS history.

I honestly had not come to terms with exactly how important winning this really was to me. As I caught up with Jack, I was determined not to let him interfere with my evening's activities. Believe it or not, I didn't want Jack or Rick or this contest to influence what I did tonight. I wanted to prove to myself that I was capable of calmly rising above the fray and still completely able to enjoy an evening on the river, despite the turmoil and any self-imposed pressure.

Jack, on the other hand, had only one option left to save himself from complete and utter humiliation before his fellow STIFFS— and himself. There was no chance of defending his initial challenge by winning the Contest, or by catching more trout than me in our personal battle. He could save face, however, by winning at least one session of the Contest, or, should he get lucky, by catching a bigger fish than me. I had brought a fourteen-and-a-half-inch brown to net, and it was within the realm of possibility for him to catch a larger fish—provided, of course, that I didn't catch a bigger one—and we were in the section of river where it was most possible for any of those things to happen.

"Tails," he called, the opposite of what he'd called every other time.

"Tails it is," I informed him.

Without so much as a change of expression or a smart-ass remark, Jack slowly walked to the river to position himself for a cast. I moved out of the way and sat on a log, comfortably back from the water. Jack waded into the shallow current that riffled over the gravel- and rock-strewn bottom. He bent down and picked up a few double-fist-size rocks and appeared to examine them.

"Jack, this is no time to pan for gold," I shouted to him.

"Yeah, yeah," he said, not turning around. "I was just checking temperature." He set the small boulder back in place. "And the conditions," he added. He took a small rag from his shirt pocket, wiped his hands, and pulled line from his reel to make a cast.

I watched with momentary interest as he uncharacteristically changed flies a couple of times after only a few unproductive casts. It appeared he may have picked up some useful information from watching me, I reasoned; quick fly changes—presenting even subtle differences in hue or size—is a ploy I routinely use when working uncooperative fish. Often that's all it takes to entice a finicky trout to bite.

My favorite series of ledge pools were coming up, not far downstream, and I started plotting as to how I could be the first to cast to them. I was deep into my thoughts when a splash commanded my attention. Jack was hooked up.

"Looks like my luck may have changed," Jack said, dragging his fish to hand in the shallows.

"Sure looks like it," I responded, thinking nothing of the fact that the man who was such a stickler for protocol already had his fine twelve-and-a-half-inch brown landed and unhooked, in violation of our rules, waiting for me to measure it.

"You still have time—six or seven minutes," I said without checking. I knew Jack would have a handle on his own time. "I'll get out of your way."

I planned on paying little attention to Jack's numbers this evening; I was only concerned with my own success and how it might compare to Rick's. By the time I reached my log seat my partner was battling another fish. I remained where I was and watched in surprised silence while he, as efficiently as possible, brought the fish to net and knelt to unhook it.

"BS," he called to me, lifting the netted trout out of the water to show me.

"I'm coming," I mumbled, not loud enough for him to hear me.

I measured the brown at one inch smaller than his first fish. "A twenty-four-inch first twenty minutes—pretty impressive," I quipped.

Jack took a sighing breath, as if exhausted from his efforts. "The best I've had so far," he said. "There's a bigger fish than yours to be caught tonight, but now you're up."

He had run several minutes past the allotted time, but I just chalked it up to the effort of measuring and reviving the fish. I certainly didn't want to start the session off by being as petty as he had been most of the time.

I thought my way through the next series of runs to the ledges that I wanted to cast to first. With that as the goal, I told Jack I was abandoning the run in which he'd just caught a couple of nice fish, with the veiled complaint that he no doubt had cleaned it out of all the decent fish. So, down the river to the next run we headed.

We were in the section of the river that held the biggest trout. It was also the area that I knew nearly as well as the water by my home. I believed a few decent fish would be enough to keep my lead over Rick; however, if it didn't work out that way, I had myself pretty well convinced that was just fine.

Jack shuffled behind, even while moving the relatively short distance to the next run. He was uncharacteristically silent and noticeably reserved, seeming to ignore the golden opportunity he had to crow a bit. Eventually, when he'd caught his breath, he appeared unable to restrain himself any further, and was compelled to fire a verbal harpoon at me as I scanned the water.

"Plan your strategy well; I've just begun my assault," he said.

I turned my attention from the river to Jack. He looked to me a drained and beaten man, the ability to change things for the better, out of his control. So, he continued to do what he was most comfortable doing: talking a better gig than he could play, to borrow a wonderfully descriptive phrase from my musician friend Rick. Jack, no matter what else was happening, seemed unable to interact without some measure of bluster and confrontation. His motto, especially if things were not going his way, was surly: "If you can't impress them with intellect, baffle them with bullshit."

"Actually, in my strategy for the evening, you're not even part of the equation," I snapped. Damn, Jack was making me behave like I'd promised myself I wouldn't. We were only at the second riffle, I hadn't even made a cast yet, and Jack had already started to annoy me enough to make me annoyed with myself. How in the hell was he able to do that so easily? Why did I let it happen?

"Maybe you should reconsider your strategy," Jack said with a snicker. He could see he was getting under my skin, and I knew he'd be determined to pursue that perceived advantage. I was just as adamant about not allowing it to happen.

"Time's a-wastin', Jack." I stepped into the water. "I've got fish to catch."

For the next twenty minutes I would lose sight of the Contest, and my competition with Rick for the trophy. I became solely intent on erasing the lead Jack had been able to acquire with his lucky catch of a couple decent fish. I needed to exercise my superior ability as a fly fisher for the purely selfish reason of further humiliating Jack, taking away any thought he might have had of putting a dent in the lead I held over him, or the hope of winning our final session, all the while consciously aware that I was violating the promise I'd made to myself not to let this very thing happen.

"You're on the clock," he called out to further bait me. I amused myself with the image of putting his eye out with a properly aimed backcast.

I then focused on a subtle rise toward the far shore, along the shadow edge of an overhanging branch. When the fish rose a second time I stripped line from my reel, false-cast to gauge the distance, and dropped the fly to float through the fading surface rings. The splash at the bug indicated a good-size taker, but when I lifted the rod tip, there was nothing but slack; he had missed or refused at the last second. In either case he hadn't felt the sting of the hook, and that meant there was still a chance of getting him to hit again.

"Oops," Jack said, chuckling loud enough for me to hear. I refused to turn around.

After years of dealing with the idiosyncrasies of Crossing House trout, I knew that this fish wouldn't come back for the same fly. So, careful to not disturb the run, I slowly retrieved my fly and replaced it with a smaller Caddis with a lighter-colored wing. I waited a couple of minutes before my next cast. Several good floats through the same spot brought no success. Jack thought the outcome was just fine. This was the perfect place to cast a completely different pattern, but this was a one fly-pattern contest, so that wasn't an option.

I didn't want to spend much more time on this fish, but since it did appear to be bigger than average, and had been actively feeding up until it missed my fly, I decided to try one more thing. I clipped off the smaller fly and tied on one of my sparkle Caddis with a slightly longer wing. As my time ticked away, much to Jack's silent approval, I waited a couple more minutes before making a final attempt at the fish.

The first cast was short. The second skirted the surface shadow and rode the current, drag-free, to duck under the bowing branch. A healthy splash, and my rod was straining under the pull of a heavy brown. I was hard-pressed not to turn around to see Jack's face; my ego wouldn't let me.

The fish rolled to the surface twice with low, porpoise-like jumps, each time stripping line as it powered away. It was imperative that I land this fish, and as a result, I was far more cautious and deliberate than I'd normally be. After several minutes of careful, calculated battle, I slipped the net under the tired trout.

Jack slowly wandered over to log the fish. It taped out at just over fifteen inches, but I settled for a new, personal-contest best of fifteen even. As the rules dictated, and Jack had conveniently chosen to ignore with his two earlier fish, I waited for him to unhook my trout. He stooped to perform his required duties and squinted a puzzled look at the fly.

"What's this?" he asked, reaching down to remove the hook from the trout's jaw.

"A Caddis fly. What the hell do you think it is?"

"Yeah, I know, but what's this shiny stuff?"

The low sun glinted off a couple of strands of crystal flash that I often mix among the deer hair on some of my Caddis wings. Jack picked at the soaked deer hair. "This?" he repeated, holding the fly so the few shiny fibers were exposed.

"Flashabou," I snarled, certain where this was headed.

"That's not part of the standard Deerhair Caddis pattern, is it?" Jack questioned in a prosecutorial tone, looking over the fly and waiting for me to respond.

"Jack," I said, trying to remain as composed as I was able, "it's part of my standard Deerhair Caddis pattern. If you think for one second that you're going to rattle me with some bullshit accusation, some half-assed, half-witted complaint that I'm using, or need to use, an illegal or unapproved fly to beat your ass . . ." I could feel myself near the point of eruption, so I stopped talking—mid-sentence, mid-thought—in order to regain control, and simply waited for Jack to continue with the point he was tiptoeing around making. If he was going to accuse me of something, the indictment had to come from his lips.

"Well, I'm just wondering . . . Do all your Caddis patterns have some sort of crystal flash in the wings?" he continued.

"Nope."

"Then are you fishing with more than one pattern—against the established rules?" he pursued.

"Nope."

"Then how do you explain that your flies have different wings?" he asked smugly. "Wouldn't that make them different fly patterns, from different recipes?"

"No," I responded, having recovered most of my composure. "You see, a brown Deerhair Caddis is a brown Deerhair Caddis. Some of the bodies of my flies are palmered through with a hackle, some are not. Some of my flies have a front hackle, some do not. Some of my flies have light deer hair, almost like elk; some of the wings are from almost-black deer hair. Some of my flies have a strand or two of flashabou camouflaged within the wing, some do not. If you feel the need, I will let you go through my fly boxes here and now, and let you choose the flies you would like me to fish with—if you think you need such an edge to be competitive," I challenged. "Don't some of your Probes have palmered hackles, while some do not? Aren't some ribbed with gold tinsel, some with silver, some not ribbed at all?"

Jack's jaw flexed back and forth as he clenched his teeth in frustration. "Maybe we should ask for a clarification of exactly what constitutes a legal pattern in this contest?" he said, a feeble threat meant to intimidate, since he could now only weakly defend his own position.

"Absolutely," I calmly answered. "If you feel it will help you out here, absolutely. However, consider this: Are you a frickin' idiot? Have you completely lost what's left of your frickin' mind? Do you have any idea what an asshole you'd look like, asking the STIFFS to consider your complaint? How much more humiliation you'd face if it was perceived that you needed the STIFFS to bail you out of this contest? Do you?"

Jack's face was as red as a tomato. His eyes were wide with the fire of a revival-tent preacher. He flicked my fly into the water, bent down, and released the trout out of the confines of the net. I heard him mumble a passage from the Bible—something about revenge being showered down upon the unjust—and off he splashed to sit and watch, as my time was not yet up.

I now knew I could erase Jack's early lead in this session with a single trout, which would be a piece of cake in this water. After the ruckus created by Jack's unceremonious exit from the river, I decided to move to the very tailout of the riffle for a few casts. I was still ideally set up for the upcoming ledges. Things were aligning themselves perfectly.

I walked cautiously to an ideal casting position only a matter of eight feet below me. I regretted lowering myself to my partner's instigating level; nonetheless, I told him that I should be able to fish a little longer because he had wasted minutes of my valuable angling time by initiating that baseless confrontation concerning my fly pattern. And, much to my pleasure, as if things couldn't deteriorate any further for Jack, with only a minute left in my beat he was forced to record an impressive ten-inch brook trout, completely erasing his early advantage and even nudging me one inch ahead for the evening.

We were only a couple of runs from the ledges I so coveted. Big fish dwelt there, and with the aid of Bill's insight, over the years I had learned much about their character and their tendencies. My confidence was sky-high. I had no doubt that I could completely crush any optimistic expectations that Jack Windermere might have harbored for the day, as well as solidify my advantage over Rick. The water that connected to the ledges was now Jack's to fish, leaving the hallowed river through the ledges themselves for me to cast to first.

"Go easy through there, Jack—there are a lot of big fish around. Try not to scare them downriver, out of our beat."

Jack seemed almost desensitized to what was happening around him, and unable (or unwilling) to muster an adequate response. Was it possible that my partner was so intent on winning this leg of the Contest—or so consumed with landing a bigger fish than me—that he had become single-mindedly absorbed in what he needed to do to make either, or both, of those things happen? In any case, he completely ignored me and baby-stepped his way into the river.

As was my routine, I moved away to sit out of range of an errant backcast. Oddly, just as before, Jack knelt in the shallows, as if he was praying, and then took time to examine a few rocks. I could see him put his head back and take a couple of deep breaths—asking for divine intervention, surely. I was about to yell out some irreverent remark about praying to the fishing gods (deities we anglers know exist), but I said nothing.

Jack made a couple of casts to the flow that dug deep along the jagged edge of the far shore; technically, it was the worn-away remains of what, hundreds of years before, must have marked the true beginning of the ledges, but now it looked like hammered sandstone, pockmarked and eroded down to nearly river level, undeserving of the ledge designation. Without a hit, as he had earlier, he stripped his Probe to hand and hastily changed flies.

A few more fruitless casts and Jack took several steps downriver so he could reach the tailout of the run more easily. Once stopped he again switched flies, glancing back over his shoulder to see if I was watching him work the water. When he seemed ready to cast he tried to improve his position by a few more feet. With his eyes focused on the water, he stubbed his toe on a rock and took a commoving, splashing step to keep from falling.

"If you can't catch the fish in front of you, please try not to foul up the river for the rest of us. That would be me, Jack," I censured, relentless in my attack.

Jack simply motioned over his shoulder with his free hand, a contrite wave without any contrary commentary. Once again, he knelt in the shallows, picked up and carefully examined a few rocks, and placed them back in the exact spot from which he'd removed them. He was displaying a fresh, steadfast approach toward his angling, a self-absorbed intensity that was apparently allowing him to rise above the rather puerile behavior that he and I had recently exhibited. Maybe things had changed. Maybe this was a newfound serenity in his attitude toward me and the Contest. I wasn't quite ready to worship at the church of Saint Jack, however . . . not just yet, anyway.

Jack deliberately changed flies one more time. He lofted an awkward, looping cast to plop above the deep water in front of a large boulder that in times of high water had forced the swirling sands to end this run in a pair of shallow, submerged dunes—a place we called the Trench. I could see the flash from my shady, knollside perch. The boil on the river top confirmed that Jack was fast to a big fish.

"Thank God," Jack exclaimed as the trout bulled upstream, spinning his reel handle in a blur. I watched for a second or two in amazement, not knowing what to make of the scene unfolding in front of me. This could easily be the biggest fish of the Contest, and it was improbably tethered to Jack Windermere's line.

"Damn, Jack," was all I could come up with as I hustled over to the river.

In a steady pull the trout cruised back toward the lower end of the run.

"Try to keep him in the pool," I offered, almost encouragingly. "If he races out of here you'll have to chase him, and my guess is, you don't want any part of that."

Jack simply grunted, his eyes transfixed on the line slicing the water, seemingly in disbelief. He did a good job slowing the fish the best he could with only the pressure of the rod and the relatively light leader as a makeshift brake. But the trout was determined to flee the pool, and when he reached the large, run-defining boulder, he powered effortlessly past it and through the slit of deeper water between the decks of bottom sand, and into what would have been the second of Jack's two pools. Jack scrambled to keep up, awkwardly stumbling over slippery rocks, once falling to his knees. Instinctively, he kept the rod high and pushed himself upright with his free hand as the brown yanked line from his reel in a droning purr.

No matter how intense, no matter how one perceived the importance of the event as it was happening, this was the kind of scene that would be retold with much humor. But now, as the situation intensified, I realized that I actually had a personal stake in this brawl, because the fight was now being waged merely one short, energetic dash from the ledges—and I didn't find that particularly funny at the moment.

I waded into the water on the upstream side of my partner, just in case he had to start a sprint downriver after his fish. Jack was panting like a teenage groom, and his constricted breaths were taken between exaggerated blinks in an effort to wash the sweat from his eyes. The fish was, for the moment, content to hunker down in the deepest part of the current, giving both himself and his tormentor a chance to regroup. Jack appeared overwhelmed with the stress of the situation, struggling to bring to net his redemption in this contest.

Even though my sympathies were with the fish, I found myself inexplicably rooting for Jack. My concern about losing the advantage of being first to the ledges seemed lost to the realization that I might rather see this fish landed. Maybe, despite losing any potential edge or the ability to selfishly brag over a tavern beer, I would prefer to be inspired by personal contact with a truly impressive relative of one of Sam Tippett's trout.

"Well, Jack," I said as the standoff continued, "I may have to reassess my opinion of that Probe of yours."

"The only thing I'm thinking right now is that I would give my right testicle to land this fish," he huffed, very irreligiously.

"I'm not sure God would find that a fair trade," I said. "But, since I'm all the help you can count on at the moment, I can honestly promise you that I'll do whatever I can to see to it that we land this fish—and you can keep your nuts. You are aware, however, that in order for that fish to count in the Contest, you have to net it yourself?"

All the STIFFS had unanimously agreed upon this rule: "The angler is to be solely responsible for the landing or netting of his own fish, without the aid of his partner." That's the way the rule was written, and until Jack had curiously unhooked his own fish earlier that evening, in blatant violation of the regulation that required the non-angling teammate to "unhook, measure, and record the landed catch," Jack had been a pain-in-the-ass stickler for the rules.

"Yeah, I know," was Jack's concerned response.

"Can you turn him?" I selfishly asked, hoping to keep the trout out of the ledges. "Maybe a little side pressure without giving him any slack," I suggested.

Jack said nothing, but immediately began to do as I'd suggested. Neither of us had gotten a good look at this fish yet, and with the current on his side in the present standoff, we really didn't have a handle on exactly how big he was. Even though the Crossing House river doesn't compare to the Montana streams Bill and I often talked about, browns of over twenty inches are not unknown here, and this appeared to be one of those trout.

The fish reacted to Jack's urging, and although it initially, doggedly headed the short distance downriver toward the ledges, it shied away from the gauntlet of the brief, thin-water flat it would be forced to run to get there. The brown turned and carved through the current, heading back upstream, again reluctant to exit the perceived safety of the deep water to reenter the shallower trough, back to the pool in which it had been fooled. The fish was getting as anxious and weary as Jack, and it appeared that this battle would be decided where we stood. The trout took a tour of the pool and then offered a momentary truce by retreating once again to the refuge of the rocky bottom in an attempt to regain some fighting strength.

"Jack, I believe that if you can keep him from resting you'll have him under control; you'll have him where you want him," I said, sincerely trying to be of assistance. "However, under control is the key phrase here."

Jack was unconsciously biting the inside of his bottom lip to the point of drawing blood. He nodded to indicate that he'd heard what I said. He must have agreed with me, for once again he lowered the rod nearly parallel to the water and slowly exerted side pressure until he'd prompted the trout to reengage in the confrontation. The fish made two bids to twist free from the hook, crashing the surface with wild, thrashing bursts of power and energy. But the restraint remained fastened, and for the first time, Jack had the upper hand. The spirited and gallant trout had reached the limit of his ability to resist. Jack took several steps back, retrieving line and shortening his leash on the fish, ushering him into the shallows nearer shore. Now we had our first opportunity to get a good look at him. Even through the distorted window of the water, the fish appeared to be over twenty inches.

"Shit, Jack, what a magnificent fish," I said, watching my saucer-eyed partner virtually holding his breath as he clumsily shuffled backward. "Get him where you want him, where you're comfortable, and when you feel you've got him under control, I'll hand you the net," I said, watching the exhausted fish calmly finning in water barely deep enough to cover his back.

"Maybe I should just try to drag him to shore," Jack suggested in a panicked voice.

"You've got a shitload of rocks to work him through before you get to the bank," I offered, "but you've got to do what you're most comfortable and confident doing."

Jack stood like a statue, his rod held in a high arc over his head, the trout, gills pulsing, calm in the quiet water. Without saying it out loud, we were both aware of how explosive a fish, especially a fish of this size, could be when a human presence encroaches too closely. This trout was more than capable of breaking free during any attempt to land him, and the longer it took to make an effort to do so, the stronger he became at rest.

"Maybe you should net him," Jack oddly suggested.

"But then you couldn't count him in the Contest, according to the rules," I reminded him.

Jack, in stunned silence, stared at the giant fish. "Yeah . . . I know," he responded.

In that moment, Jack seemed incapable of deciding whether it was more important to land the fish and experience the thrill of success, or risk losing his trophy for the opportunity to claim an almost-assured additional prize.

"Jack," I said sternly, urging him to make a decision without asking him to do so.

"Yeah . . . ah . . . I'll, ah, try to net him where he is . . . not try to move him," he stammered.

"I'll stay behind you, at your right hand. I'll hand you the net, ready to go, when you ask," I told him, quietly slipping into position to make the exchange.

Jack, keeping the line taut, shortened it enough to be able to reach the fish, which remained rather docile. Jack reached slightly behind and blindly took the net from me. He lifted the rod and stooped to slide it under the fish. The water erupted and the big brown plowed between the rocks for the heavier water. Jack dropped the net and splashed a couple of floundering steps forward to catch up with the fleeing fish. I expected to see the rod spring straight up and the line swing loosely from below the top eye, but the graphite arced into an ever-grander curve and the reel clicked a short, uninterrupted whirr. Miraculously, somehow, the fish was still hooked.

I rescued the net. The trout's run was reactive and brief.

"Jack, that fish is beat," I encouraged. "He's done. You should be able to bring him back to the shallows here without too much resistance."

Jack looked pale and faint. This entire incident had become so stressful that he seemed unable to enjoy a single second of the encounter—this angler's dream. I truly started to feel empathy for my teammate. Then, in a moment of inexplicable compassion, I said, "Get him in here one more time and I'll net him, and we won't tell a soul."

In one of the rare instances since the hookup, Jack took his eyes off the water and looked at me. "Why?" he asked suspiciously, skeptical of my motives even during this once-in-a-lifetime opportunity.

"Don't know," I answered. Then without thinking, I quickly added, "Well . . . ? Just say 'No, thanks,' and I'll hand you the net one more time."

This truly was not a time for discussion. The offer was on the table, and Jack had to take it or leave it—immediately. This really was a win-win situation for him, unless he believed that acceptance would somehow come with the unbearable burden of a certain indebtedness to me for the rest of his life. This was a potential fate he may have perceived as even worse than losing the fish of a lifetime. My overture was made with no strings attached, but, considering our history, Jack might have found that hard to believe.

As he worked the trout back to the shallows, Jack had yet to accept or decline my offer. I sensed that he was mulling over his options and the potential consequences of any arrangement he might be entering into with me. However, once he got another good look at what was still only a potential trophy, he blurted, "Okay." Apparently the thought of losing that magnificent fish was too much for him. "Yeah . . . okay," he repeated, willing to forge a deal with the devil.

On his second reluctant return from the depths, the exhausted brown seemed resigned to his fate. With a minimum of urging, Jack applied enough pressure to lift the trout's head slightly, and I cautiously swiped the impressive fish into the net. Jack had his prize.

Chapter 32

This was a time for big smiles and high fives and riotous whoops of triumph, but Jack and I shared none of that brotherly camaraderie. I became nearly overwhelmed by a true sense of disappointment—that such a magnificent fish was wasted on two men who were unable to enjoy and appreciate this rare moment together.

"You do have your camera with you, don't you?" Jack asked, knowing I never went to the river without carrying it in my wader pocket.

"I've got it," I said, admiring the fish, holding him in the water, trying to stress him as little as possible. After all, he didn't know his life wasn't in danger. "Let's measure him—I'm guessing one, maybe even two over twenty."

"No—take the picture first. If he's spent he's less likely to thrash around. I think that would be better, don't you?" Jack responded, dropping his rod into the water and reaching for the net.

"Relax, Jack—I've got this under control," I said, still with a good grip on the net handle. "He's not going anywhere. Let me unhook him and—"

"No. Maybe we should leave him hooked to take the picture, in case he reacts and flops loose . . . That's happened to me before. I didn't get the picture or the fish," he nervously sputtered.

"For Christ's sake, relax," I repeated, fending off Jack's attempt to grab the net. I admired the big, hook-jawed male for a few seconds and then reached into my vest pocket for the measuring tape.

"Let me help," Jack said, kneeling at the net and aggressively reaching to unhook the fish.

"That's my job. You know, rules and all," I said, being sarcastic, since I'd already promised not to reveal the fact that I'd netted the fish in violation of those rules.

"It's my fish—let me have the honor," Jack stubbornly insisted.

As we engaged in a senseless tussle for the net, the fish became as irritated with us as we were with each other and made a wild, thrashing attempt to flee his restraints. Jack let go of his part of the net and with one hand reached for the fish, with the other making a wild stab for his rod, knowing that if worse came to worst, the trout would still be hooked. He was successful with neither of his endeavors and wound up sitting in the river, water running into the back of his waders as he propped himself up with his elbows on the bottom of the shallow stream. The trout, despite his valiant effort, was still swaddled in the net mesh, the leader wrapped around his snout.

"Jesus, Jack, what the hell is the matter with you? I'm trying to help you out here, and you're doing everything in your power to see that this fish gets away."

And then, Jack just seemed to give up. He put his head down and made no attempt to continue his aberrant behavior, or to right himself. He leaned further back on his elbows, allowing even more water to stream into his waders.

"What the hell is the matter with you? What are you doing?"

Jack just slowly shook his head, a vague, empty stare in his eyes. "Nothing. I'm doing nothing."

I started to feel a little concerned for him. He even seemed to lose interest in his fish, still waiting to be recorded as most assuredly the biggest fish of our contest, and then released. Jack sat up straight and with his hands together, cupped cool river water onto his face. "I'm doing nothing," he passively repeated. Jack, like the fish, seemed imprisoned in the moment, totally unable to do anything but gasp for air, and wait and hope for some compassionate help.

I turned my focus to the fish. Even after his attempted escape, he seemed in far better condition than my partner. I reached for the leader and gently unwound it from around the trout's jaws, careful not to bind it into his skin or let it slip to his gills. I slid my hand down the leader to unhook the fish.

"Jack," I blurted in disbelief, "what the hell is this?"

I looked over at Jack sitting motionless in the water, his eyes closed. He didn't even open them to see what I was asking; he already knew. I removed the hook from Jack's fish—not a hand-tied, Jack Windermere Probe, but a bare hook—a size 14, thin-wire, scud hook, the kind I use to tie my caddis worm and caddis nymph imitations.

"I'm going to ask this once more, and I don't give a shit what your condition is, I want an answer." I glared at my thoroughly demoralized partner and qualified my question by indignantly repeating, "What the hell is going on here, Jack?"

Jack knew that there was no adequate explanation, and in the heat of the moment I didn't expect to hear one that could justify what had taken place. Jack's silence was an admission of guilt for his unpardonable deed. Realizing that no defensible response was forthcoming, I didn't repeat my question. I spent the next eerily silent minute or two reviving the big brown. Then, without measuring, recording, or photographing him, I supported the trout in the water and ushered him to the edge of the deeper water. When he gave a powerful twist to escape, I gently pushed the fish free and watched Jack's magnificent trophy disappear.

I turned toward my teammate. He hadn't moved. I picked up my rod and walked past him in splashy strides. The Contest was completely forgotten in light of these newly created circumstances. Any further, conscious desire I might have harbored to humiliate Jack was also abandoned. He had already humiliated himself to a far greater degree than I ever could have. I sat under a tree and simmered in silent resentment, waiting for Jack to recover and respond.

After several interminable minutes, Jack righted himself, salvaged his rod from the river, and, with his waders so full that the water splashed over the top, sloshed his way to shore. He stayed away from me while he unhooked the suspenders and pulled off his waders, creating a puddle inches deep where he stood. He removed his shirt and socks, wrung them out, and hung them on a convenient branch. He made a token attempt to squeeze the water from the bottom of his pants, quickly giving that up as a lost cause. Everything was done in slow motion. He took labored, deep breaths between each deliberately performed task. I would have traded my favorite rod to know what was going through his mind at that moment. Eventually, he trudged over to where I sat, trailing a brooklet as the water continued to dribble from his pant legs. He stood in front of me, making no attempt to sit.

"I don't know what to say," he began contritely, refusing to make eye contact.

"You'd better say something," I said, compassionless.

"Honest to God, I didn't plan for any of this to happen. When this damn contest started I was actually excited, even eager, for an opportunity to prove what I believed to be true. I know you and I aren't friends. We may not even like each other all that much. I know what you and some of the STIFFS think about me—what's said behind my back. I'm not oblivious. I know I can be overbearing, that I come across as arrogant and a cocky know-it-all. Your perception of me is nothing new; I've dealt with it most of my life. I'm also aware that my personality often promotes these responses, but that's just the way I am. That's me.

"I know my attitude—the fact that I usually believe myself to be right—offends a lot of people. This contest was for me, at the outset, a chance to show people, the STIFFS, that I was one of them, worthy of their respect—an equal. It was a chance to prove that I had something positive, something of importance to offer here, that I'm as capable an angler as anyone—as capable as Bill or Andy or you.

"My presumed arrogance may be viewed as negative, and an indefensible fault, but it's part of my competitive nature. It fuels my drive to succeed and to perform up to my expectations, which I keep intentionally lofty. It has driven me to accomplishments that I'm very proud of, in politics and business and in the courtroom. But a motivation to succeed is often nearly the same as a fear of failure, and the latter has forced me, even encouraged me, to do things that I'm not proud of—things I'll admit to you here and now that I wouldn't want my wife and kids to know about. This is certainly one of them. My family is too innocent to understand, and I love them too much to violate their trust and faith in me by asking them to defend my inexcusable actions."

As he talked, it appeared that Jack's breathing couldn't keep up with his rambling speech. He had to stop and catch his breath and wipe sweat from his face, often stumbling over words and pausing to put his thoughts together, but on he trudged.

"It may appear just the opposite, but I'm not trying to make excuses or justify what I did. I'm just trying to explain why I did it. This morning, feeling defeated and beaten, I noticed a lot of stick-caddis casings on many of the rocks. Trout sure love those caddis, don't they?" he sidetracked with a spacey little smile, as if his caddis reference would garner some sympathy from me.

"So, I thought if I could just put one of those caddis worms on my hook—not every time it was my turn, mind you, but just once or twice, in the best pools . . ." His voice trailed off as he regained his breath. "If I could just catch one decent fish, bigger than Andy's, bigger than any you caught, just one fish to save myself all the bullshit and embarrassment that I was destined to face in just a few hours, all because of the stupid challenge I made, and partially under the influence, I might add . . ."

Jack continued to struggle, stringing different thoughts together. "And, to make things even worse, you drew my name. What luck. What damn, shitty luck for me. I know you're a better fisherman than me. I know you're more skilled, more knowledgeable, more competent. Maybe because I do know that, I became intent, preoccupied, almost, on proving that I too was competent and deserving of respect."

As I listened to Jack, honestly trying to understand, I was having a difficult time comprehending how a man who was so successful in so many other facets of his life could turn his participation in this contest into something so significant that he needed to cheat to remain competitive. Even more surprising, he found it worth the risk—and consequences—of getting caught. What a regrettable interpretation of what we'd started out to accomplish.

In my eyes Jack had fallen into a state of self-delusion where his own selfish goal had become more important than the initial objective. Even though there was no doubt that all of the STIFFS (and I abjectly include myself) were guilty of the same objectionable behavior, somehow, at this very moment, Jack's intent seemed far more devious and dishonorable. Jack's efforts hadn't even been focused on trying to preserve and protect a passion or a cause he truly believed in; he was simply trying to save his ass.

Despite his conciliatory admission of guilt, I got the distinct impression that Jack thought he was just clever (or arrogant) enough to get away with his actions. Getting caught with your hand in the cookie jar—or with a caddis worm on your hook—can make a man mighty contrite. There seemed to be more to Jack's aberrant behavior, however, and he didn't impress me with his job of explaining it. Jack was so deeply entrenched in my disfavor at the moment that I had no interest in knowing what made him tick.

"If you are so conscious of your"—I paused, searching for the right words—"your shortcomings, your . . . failings," I finally said, both weak descriptions of what I was trying to describe, "shouldn't you, by your very awareness of those faults, be able to prevent yourself from falling victim to them?"

"I didn't do what I did to win something. I'm guilty of my attempt at deception only to save myself from humiliation," Jack admitted.

"That doesn't answer my question," I continued to press. "This is not a political debate we're having. Answer the question, Jack: Shouldn't you know enough not to cheat, especially during our friendly little competition—and, not to be forgotten, a competition you were responsible for initiating?"

"Yes," he answered matter-of-factly, with a slow, deliberate head nod.

"Jack, we were fishing. When all this was settled, we would merely have named a fishing fly to use as fodder to good-naturedly harass and needle and otherwise liven up our friendships and STIFFS' meetings. Nobody was going to die. The worst that could happen was that you might lose a few bucks."

"Aren't you listening to me? I would lose much more than that," Jack defended. "Again, I didn't do what I did to win. I was at the point in this thing where it was far more important to me to save myself from further humiliation. I took a chance at doing that. I made a mistake."

Throughout his prolonged explanation, Jack still made every attempt to avoid eye contact. He was having a difficult time with this; I just wasn't sure if repentance was his motivation.

"You did, indeed, make a mistake," I said. "I just wonder if you honestly believe your biggest mistake here was getting caught," I challenged. "And now what? You're a lawyer; what would you do if I had cheated?" I asked, waiting for a response from a man who apparently believed that his sanctimony allowed him to be both a moral church parishioner and an immoral citizen.

"Yeah, I'm a lawyer, but now you're trying to be a judge," he responded.

"I think I'm even more pissed at you for creating the situation that made me one."

"So, what do you plan to do?" he questioned with some concern.

"Plan?" I said, thoroughly annoyed at the question. "You idiot, there is no plan. I haven't thought about what I'm going to do about this for two seconds."

I continued to watch Jack. He fidgeted with the belt loop on his pants and continually pulled at the shoulders of his wet T-shirt. He was pale and noticeably concerned that he had unintentionally empowered me with a whip hand, and ultimate control over his immediate destiny and his future fate within the STIFFS—a circumstance that I neither wanted nor appreciated.

"However little I want to deal with this, it must be dealt with—now," I said. "This contest is nearly over, and thanks to your incomprehensible actions, we have ceased to participate in it—at least until I get to the ledges—so, any suggestions, counselor? What the hell do you propose we do?"

"That was quite a fish, wasn't it?" Jack said, ignoring my question. He took several deep breaths. "I know you've caught a lot of big fish," he continued in a soft, almost reverent voice, "but that was the most magnificent trout I've ever seen, let alone had the good fortune to actually catch. Look," he said, "my hands are still shaking, and my heart is racing."

The smile on his face grew broader and his eyes stared into space as if he was reliving the adventure. "When I have time to think about it, the exhilaration of catching that fish might be well worth getting caught doing a devilish deed . . . That sure was one hell of a fish, wasn't it?"

And then Jack dragged himself the couple of steps to where I sat. He plopped himself down next to me, covered his eyes with his left hand, and with his right he clutched his chest. He took a gasping breath, and in the final hours of the Contest that he had instigated, Jack Windermere died.

Chapter 33

The newspapers printed a smiling photo and a glowing syn-
opsis of a life well lived, a review of impressive accomplishments
and high-water achievements in schooling and business and law. It
recounted dedication to community affairs and charity events. It told
of a respected local councilman who many had thought was primed
for an imminent run at a far loftier office here in Maine. There were
many who believed he'd had both the drive and the support to do so.
It detailed tireless devotion to work for the church, citing a long list of
successful fund-raising efforts to promote the word of God. He was
praised as a loving husband and caring father.

Of course, there was no mention of the things he'd wanted to keep
from his wife and children, and there was no mention of angling.

Jack's unexpected death immediately shoved our little contest into
the light of reality. As each man returned to the Crossing House from
their last session, one by one, their petty squabbles were overwhelmed
by shock and disbelief at the news of Jack's death. No one tallied
numbers that night, except to realize that the STIFFS now totaled
only nine.

Everyone expressed their heartfelt desire to help the family in any
way possible. The hour was late when the studio eventually emptied.
In one of those offers for which a person becomes eternally grateful,
as a friend to both Jack and me, Bill willingly offered to go, in my
place, as one of the messengers who brought the unimaginable news

to Jack's wife Cathy and their children. He later told me that it was probably the second most difficult thing he'd ever had to do. It might have been my first.

A few of the individuals in our angling fraternity, namely Bill, Andy, and Wilson, were much closer to Jack and his family than the rest of us. Dying has a way of nourishing sympathy for the dead and transforming, even eliminating, the intolerable and irreconcilable. The touch of death often allows absolution of what could never have been forgiven in life, before tragedy made deals and compromises acceptable. So, with a refined sense of mercy, I spent most of Tuesday evening at the wake. I also felt obliged to tell Jack's wife, as succinctly and compassionately as I was able, what happened on the river. I honestly made Jack my friend for a few tear-filled minutes.

Wednesday was dedicated to a High Mass, deserving of such a disciple. The church was nearly overflowing with Jack's family and friends and acquaintances, many with tears in their eyes. We, the STIFFS, naturally talked and mingled together at both the wake and the funeral. Bill personally told each of us that he was calling a special meeting of the STIFFS for eight p.m. on Thursday night as a farewell party for Jack—drinks on the house.

Oddly, Bill and I did not have the opportunity to get together on Wednesday night, because the local businessmen's association decided to keep their Wednesday meeting at the Crossing House, seeing it as an opportunity to honor Jack. Thursday would be lost because Bill had to travel out of town to deal with a snafu concerning a continual problem with one of his supply sources.

I needed to finish an article to beat an end-of-the-week deadline; I had let it slide in order to participate in the Contest, and, ultimately, to deal with the unfortunate aftermath. I found that I had little interest in writing, or even thinking, for that matter. It was not simply the melancholy and pensive mood of self-examination that the sudden, unexpected death of someone can initiate, although only three days out from Jack's death, those emotions were still raw.

What was most distressing to me was that I'd been the only one present when Jack died, and therefore, the only one who could tell the truth about what had actually happened. Considering the contentious nature of our relationship, this was both a daunting and unwanted responsibility for me to live with. I wished desperately that I'd had the chance to talk with Bill about the entire episode that had taken place on Sunday night. But that Thursday evening, as the STIFFS arrived at the studio, the only serious discussions I'd had about the circumstances surrounding Jack's death were with my own conscience.

I had been required to respond to different versions of "What happened out there?" from each of the members of our club, at the wake and the funeral. My answers had been purposely short and vague, acceptable responses because the men knew that more-detailed information would be forthcoming in the near future, under less-trying conditions. Now, the future had arrived.

"To Jack, for this excuse to drink," Andy said, setting the tone. He wasn't being insensitive, merely making a sincere effort to keep the spirit a celebratory one. "To a man we thought enough of to get this ragtag bunch of anglers together, to honor with a farewell drink and going-away party—an honor that the rest of us can only hope to achieve."

"Hear, hear—to Jack," everyone chanted in unison. Around the room, neighbors clanked glasses and bottles together. Then, one by one, toasts were offered. Some seemed forced, some sounded contrite. Some were serious, others humorous or anecdotal. Others were spontaneous and sincere and heartfelt. Some were all those things. The remarks ran the gamut of emotions, just as our reactions to Jack had on any other STIFFS' Thursday night.

The first eight toasts took each of us through a couple of drinks. All the toasts seemed to be presented with the sense that mine would be the last, for I was the one everyone was waiting to hear from—and not just with words of ceremonial tribute. I was the featured performer, so to speak, after all the opening acts had eventually played their way offstage.

I had prepared my toast ahead of time; the rest of what I had to say would be ad-libbed, by choice. I didn't know if Jack was in a place to hear what I said, and if he was, if he'd even give a damn. The only thing I knew for sure was that anything I said now was for the guys in the room—and for me.

"To Jack, and to things to be remembered for. It didn't seem possible to me that I could be impressed or surprised by anything that might take place while we literally battled our way down the river. But, in three days on the water with you, you certainly proved me wrong. So here's to you, Jack, and to keeping water out of your waders, no matter where you are."

The glasses and bottles clinked together once again, but after the requisite drink, silence. No smart-ass comments, no clamorous "Hear, hear" that had attended the other salutes. All eyes were on me. I still wasn't sure how I felt about Jack and what had happened between us. Nonetheless, I was now being required to face my heartfelt belief that if you didn't like someone when they were alive, you shouldn't necessarily like them when they were dead. I still wasn't sure what I was going to say, or even which version I was about to relate—so I just started talking.

"It's no secret to any of you that the connection that Jack and I shared was . . . well, often strained. We were the proverbial oil and water. We were the dry-fly versus wet-fly debate. We truly became the Caddis–Probe conflict personified," I tentatively opened, stating the obvious in clichéd images. "Our relationship was not, however, black and white. Things rarely are.

"My opinion of this contest of ours was pretty clear from the outset. Jack, on the other hand, seemed inspired to prove something once the challenge had been issued. We—and I include myself in that group—all began, to varying degrees, to encourage the idea of this competition, just for fun, for some novel diversion. But can we say that it turned out to be what we'd envisioned—what we'd hoped it would be?

"I know that for me, and I feel I can honestly say, for Jack as well, those days were not always the most pleasant hours I'd ever spent on the river. As a matter of fact, they were at times rather contentious and unpleasant, with petty arguments over inexplicable actions and ungrounded accusations and constant, unintelligible behavior—or, more accurately, unintelligent behavior—but, that was Jack and me.

"I know this is Jack's night, and I apologize for making myself so much a part of it, but unfortunately, there truly is no one else to tell what happened in Jack's last hours, so please bear with me as I ramble through this unprepared eulogy. There really is a point to be made.

"It must be remembered that it was Jack's challenge that set this whole thing in motion. Maybe because of that, and I hope I'm not assuming too much here, but Jack appeared to me to be more deeply invested in this contest than I was. As I have already mentioned, he seemed . . . well, driven . . . to represent himself and his fellow team members successfully.

"As things worked out, I was fortunate to run into some cooperative fish the first couple of days, and, according to our rules, enough to have a pretty comfortable lead on Jack. But, there was still the matter of the biggest fish, and as we anglers are very well aware, that hookup has the potential to occur at any place and at any moment—even on the very last cast of the day. The biggest fish can be far more significant to some," I said, giving Andy a little wave, "than to others. But there's no ignoring the pleasure and pride that comes with the bragging rights connected to a big fish. It truly is one of the most satisfying rewards of angling.

"And now, much to what will be Andy's chagrin and disappointment, I am telling you that Jack caught the biggest fish, by far, in this contest."

I saw eight faces—eight bemused, astonished, disbelieving faces—staring back at me.

"Jack landed one of the largest trout I've ever had the pleasure to witness being caught in our Crossing House river." The room, in stunned silence, waited for an explanation, not sure what to think.

At that very second, for what it's worth, I didn't really know what to say next. I was committed to saying something, to give an account of Jack's fish. I could have chosen to simply ignore the trout; after all, no one had seen it except for Jack and me. In reality, it was caught outside the bounds of our contest, meaning it didn't count. But it was such a magnificent animal that I couldn't dismiss it as though it was merely another fish, for truly it was not. It was a fish that deserved recognition.

"Let me say that again," I continued. "Jack landed one of the largest fish, quite possibly even *the* largest fish, I have ever seen in our river. It was, in a word, magnificent; a large, hooked-jaw male. However, there is one small problem: I can only estimate its length, because although it was landed and unhooked, it was only fleetingly measured against the rod for a quick reference before it found its freedom. It was never properly recorded. I am comfortable telling you that it was over twenty inches long—well over, by maybe two inches or more—and I will swear to that on Jack's life, for I was the one who handled it and unhooked it, and from whom it eventually broke free."

The room buzzed. I was conscious of my desire not to reveal any more about the situation than I wanted known. So far, Jack's trout was still a prizewinner. I knew no one would ask me the number-one question when a big fish is the topic of discussion: "What did you get him on?" We were, after all, fishing a one-fly contest, which took away the need to ask such a thing of honest participants.

"Over twenty?" Andy was the first to respond. "Where? You were in section A, right?"

"Yeah, Jack hooked him above the ledges—you know, that place we call the Trench, with the large boulder at the tailout. The fish wound up down below into the next pool, and it all ended there. It ended for Jack there as well, under the big sycamore, as we sat discussing his catch."

"Whaddya know? Would you believe that shit? Jack with the biggest fish," Mark commented.

"By a mile," I said. "There's no doubt in my mind that that fish deserves to be honored. And while we are presenting testimonials here, we should give thanks to Sam Tippett for what he left in our care, and for what he alone is truly responsible for: a trout worthy of a trophy."

"Jack Windermere and Sam Tippett, honored in the same ceremony—who'da thunk it?" Bill smiled, shaking his head at the absurdity of it all.

"Not me," I laughed, and raised my drink. "But here goes: To Sam and Jack—thanks for the memories."

We drank to my toast. There was a low murmur around the room as the STIFFS processed what I had just told them.

"I know that because of what happened on Sunday night, we have kind of ignored our contest. But after spending all that private time with Jack, I know how . . ." I paused, stumbling a little, looking for appropriate words. "I know how important success in this contest was to him, and how significant an achievement it would have been—how significant an achievement it was"—I corrected myself—"for him to have caught the biggest fish. And, as we talked late Sunday, he knew he'd done just that. In the spirit of the moment, he told me he'd never had such an exhilarating experience. Trust me; I was sharing a moment with a Jack I had never seen before—a Jack I hadn't believed existed. I can tell all of you here that Jack's last words were 'That sure was one hell of a fish, wasn't it?'"

My story was almost unbelievable, or at least, incomprehensible. We all knew Jack. We all knew how intense he could be, how inscrutable he was at times. Oddly, all of those often annoying and insufferable qualities we'd had to deal with when he was alive now worked in Jack's favor after his death. His attitudes and his persona made what I had to say acceptable to the STIFFS without much further detail. My Jack Windermere tale went unchallenged.

"What about the Contest?" Andy asked. "There wasn't really much left to decide before our last session on Sunday."

I had the stage, but I just shrugged my shoulders. I had completely lost sight of the Contest. The dry-fly guys had the undesignated team category pretty well wrapped up before we'd headed out on Sunday evening. The "Biggest Fish" prize had been stolen from Andy's grasp by the acceptance of my account of Jack's trout. With my abbreviated Sunday session, landing only two fish, I was fairly sure Rick had wound up with more fish than me. That left only one person left to crown, the true winner, the reason for the Contest in the first place: the caster of the most perfect trout fly. The only anglers left standing on Sunday evening to contend for that honor had been Rick and me.

"I'll take down everyone's totals for Sunday later on tonight," Andy offered. "But maybe the proper thing to do here, right now, since we're here to salute Jack, is to just declare the winner of this contest. Rick, BS, your totals for Sunday, please."

"If I may make a suggestion," I said before Andy went any further. "I propose that we name our prize the Jack Windermere World's Most Perfect Trout Fly Trophy."

I saw Bill raise his eyebrows and cast a skeptical glance in my direction. With a cynical half-smile on his face, he stood up. "I second that motion," he said loudly.

"All in favor?" I questioned.

The room responded as one voice: "Yea."

"The motion is carried," I said, formalizing the suggestion. I immediately continued, "I only caught two—a very nice fifteen-inch brown, and an equally nice ten-inch brookie—and it seems you'll have to accept my word on that," I added with a touch of humor.

"Umm," Rick reluctantly started, having done the math in his head, "it's not really fair the way this ended for BS. I suggest that he and I share the victory—if that's acceptable with everyone."

"Maybe not with me. Did you pass me?" I questioned Rick.

"Well . . . yes," he responded haltingly, ". . . but it wasn't really fair. You were dealing with far more important matters than catching fish and trying to win a meaningless contest."

"Then I don't agree to sharing the prize. I think Rick's Wreck should be declared the undisputed winner of the STIFFS' first Jack Windermere Trophy, and that, I might add, is hardly a meaningless prize. As much as I appreciate your very charitable offer, you can be comfortable in knowing you won fair and square—no asterisk needed."

"Well, I . . ." Rick stammered.

"Well, nothing," I interrupted, not giving him a chance to finish his thought. "Without waiting for our formal meeting, I think it's appropriate that we STIFFS, here and now, declare you, Rick Meade, and your Rick's Wreck, winner of the first Jack Windermere Trophy."

There was applause and cheering, signifying complete agreement among the group. Many other issues still needed resolution, such as who was victorious in the personal battles within each team, and, of course, side bets had to be settled. These, and any other things involving our Contest, were conveniently and harmoniously shelved until our next scheduled meeting. At that point we could guiltlessly carry on and conduct ourselves in the irreverent and courteously disrespectful way in which we were accustomed. This most certainly was not the time for any of that.

But, simply as a point to consider until then, I felt compelled to mention the fact that the awarding of the money to the big winners did present one small problem of sorts, because Jack was the winner of the "Biggest Fish" award, which carried with it a monetary value. I suggested that, after clearing things with Jack's wife and family, we take Jack's share of the pot and put his winnings toward the purchase of a permanent, memorial trophy; the STIFFS fund could supply the balance. I proposed that we all "think about it," and that everyone should have a hand in designing an impressive trophy. It should allow space for a small plaque to be added each year listing the new winner and winning fly—our mascot fly for a year—The World's Most Perfect Trout Fly. I couldn't imagine Jack's wife not being completely support-ive and honored by the STIFFS paying such homage to her husband.

Jack's special night continued. We spun yarns and laughed at anec-dotes about Jack, a tribute that could never have taken place while he was alive. That big fish also appeared, at least on the surface, to have given rise to a new respect for Jack, and I planned on keeping it that way, even if he would never have the opportunity to appreciate it.

It was too late for Bill and me to sit and talk, so we committed to a powwow the next night. As I stepped out onto the porch, I wasn't even sure what I would share with my best friend. I turned at the top of the steps and, as I often did, glanced back at the empty rockers.

"Thanks," I said softly, only loud enough for a spirit to hear.

Chapter 34

"There isn't one person I know of who isn't damn glad to see the back end of this week," Bill sighed when he came into the library. "Here—this will do you more good, and do it a whole lot faster than beer," he said, handing me a scotch.

"Can't argue with that logic. We haven't had a chance to talk this week," I started, once Bill had settled into his chair, "though I'd be hard-pressed to remember a time when it wasn't more sorely needed. Anyway, before we get too involved in other things, I want to thank you again, and tell you that your friendship was never more appreciated than when you offered to speak to Cathy on Sunday night, after everything happened. As selfish as this may sound, that task was one of the first things that crossed my mind when I couldn't revive Jack—not the unbelievable realization that he'd just died while we were talking, but having to face his wife and kids, trying to explain what happened. It made me sick to my stomach."

"Cathy is a fine woman," Bill said. "I've known her since she was a teenager, right after her parents moved up here from Pennsylvania. It just seemed like the proper thing for me to do. You and Jack were not the best of friends, and I'll be honest with you—I never could figure out what she saw in Jack. They seemed such different personalities, her quiet and sweet, and him loud and . . ." Bill saw no need to finish that thought. "But then again, I'm sure most people couldn't understand what Sarah saw in me, either."

"Well, it's important to me that you know just how much I appreciate your gesture, that's all," I said, reaching over to firmly grab Bill's arm, resting on the edge of his chair, the way friendship is often expressed when words aren't enough. "That's all," I repeated.

"You're welcome. Now, *that's* all," he said, patting his hand on top on mine.

Maybe because the night was just getting started, or maybe because neither of us knew where to go from here, we just sat in silence for the next minute or so, thinking, not thinking—I'm not sure which.

"Jack Windermere with the biggest fish . . . That's pretty unbelievable, isn't it?" Bill finally spoke.

I wasn't sure if his "isn't it?" was rhetorical, but I believe that Bill knew I had something more to say about Jack's fish, and about that "unbelievable" happening. I had yet to make a deal with my conscience. Nobody could keep a secret better than me, but for the last few days I had been debating whether or not Jack's actions were deserving of secret status—at least, between best friends. On the other hand, I rationalized that nothing positive could be gained at this stage by revealing the truth. I had already committed to preserving the fable, and a faultless Jack, by telling the story of Sunday evening the way I did. I never said he'd caught the fish with his Probe; however, I'd insinuated Jack to folk-hero status simply by not declaring that he hadn't. Ever since I'd suggested we name our contest trophy after Jack, I knew Bill had sensed something was more than a little fishy.

"Yeah . . . about Jack's fish," I said.

Bill, with a discerning little smile, looked over at me. "Something to say?"

For my own peace of mind, Bill willingly committed to secrecy what I was about to tell him, then I immediately apologized for asking him to do so.

"Continue," he said.

I started at the very beginning, all the way back to Friday night. I told Bill what he already knew—that Jack and I had been at odds even before the first cast was made. I rehashed our squabbles over the use and misuse of time, and our thinly disguised attempts to disrupt and intimidate and otherwise muddle the waters of our interactions. I told how my teammate had accused me of not fishing with a dry fly when a trout took my momentarily submerged fly. I detailed how Jack had indicted me for cheating when I'd caught a trout with a sparkle Caddis, charging that a few strands of crystal flash in the wing made that fly different from the Caddis pattern I'd chosen at the start of the Contest. Each session, each turn, created new challenges, and any attempt at a strategy was confronted with accusations of deceit and Machiavellian schemes.

"It was such a pleasant time," I commented sarcastically. "I preferred to have Jack start an evening session, and each time he would invariably go out of his way to turn the tables. I wanted to go second because the later I got to the water, the better my chances were of catching a fish, as long as it was different water, and not water Jack had just hammered. Jack wanted to go second simply because I wanted him to go first. That's what I was up against every miserable minute we were together.

"When he went first and caught a fish or two, he would be his usual smug self, making smart-ass comments in an attempt to rattle me. But all he did was make me focus and try even harder to dash any hope he might have had of success. I went out of my way to land extra fish to put in my column, just to bury him further behind and to watch him fume. I wanted him so deep in the hole that he couldn't see light when he looked up. I know I've already told you most of this, but I need to set the scene here.

"So, anyway, the more time we spent together, the harder I tried to extend my lead. By the end of the Sunday-morning session it was getting unbearably humiliating for him. I suppose I should have taken a more sympathetic path, but I couldn't seem to bring myself to that level of compassion; he just wouldn't stop provoking me.

"Then, on Sunday evening, things seemed to change drastically. I had decided, even before heading out, to honestly try to ignore him— to just let him piss in the wind—and instead, think about enjoying the opportunity to win this contest. After all, at that point it was mine to lose, and I planned on not letting Jack disrupt things enough to influence me. But almost right away he was acting very . . . different— quiet, focused, far less combative. I thought that maybe all the praying he did—even while he was fishing, I must point out—had enlightened him. I don't know, possibly he'd decided to take a less-confrontational approach during the last of our Contest. I know, I know . . . I'm rambling. Bear with me.

"I had already landed a beautiful fifteen-inch brown, in my only turn so far in that session, to establish a bigger fish—at least between us. So now, even that had become a more difficult goal for him to reach. We also know that there are bigger trout swimming around here; Andy had that sixteen-plus fish from Friday, and we all know that the next big fish is merely a cast away. I was still hoping to top Andy with a well-executed cast or two at the ledges when we got there.

"There were, however, a couple of things that I'd failed to take into account: First, Jack also knew a big fish could be caught at any time; and second, just by looking at him, I should have known that I'd humiliated Jack to the point where he needed to do something to redeem himself—something drastic, if necessary, not only to prove something to me and the rest of the STIFFS, but to himself as well.

I also noticed that he looked terrible; pale and pasty, breathing hard, moving slow."

I thought I might be babbling through too much armchair analysis and too much history, but Bill knew I had to tell this my way, so he sat in silence, listening to me vent. He even went and refreshed our drinks.

"So where were we?" he said, handing me a fresh Glenmorangie.

"Jack was humiliated; he was acting strange, and he looked like shit warmed over," I said.

"Oh, yeah. Continue."

"So, Jack began fishing like he truly wanted to prove himself. He started taking water temperatures, changing flies frequently, often after only a half-dozen casts. He also began turning rocks over to check for insects—and that should have tipped me off. We were in a one-fly contest; what difference would available insect life have made to him? I gave him the benefit of the doubt, thinking maybe he was trying to garner some insight about size, or possibly fishing a slight variation of his Probe. I really was trying to put a constructive spin on his actions.

"But, as was usually the case when I attempted to see Jack in a positive light, I was wrong again. He wanted—maybe *needed* is more accurate—desperately to catch a big fish, and his plan to do that, and thus reclaim his dignity, was to cheat. Jack Windermere really did catch that magnificent trout, but it didn't count. All this rock turning was merely to harvest some caddis worms from their casings. He cheated."

Bill's reaction was predictable; he said nothing. I could see him shake his head and purse his lips, half closing his eyes into a condemning frown of disapproval and disappointment at the actions of a man he had called a friend.

"When we reached the Trench, a couple of runs above the ledges, one of his fly changes was to a scud hook so he could fish with a live caddis worm, and because of his behavior, I now believe his success earlier in the session was the result of the same tactic. Well, I guess you pretty much know the rest of this tale. He hooked this impressive brown and fought it to the pool below us. He really struggled to keep up with the fish. I don't think I'd ever seen him so intense, so overwhelmed. He needed to land that fish.

"As you know, our rules stated that he had to net the fish to make it legal, and I reminded him of that. So, he made an attempt to do it himself. He screwed that up royally and turned it into quite an adventure. The fish bolted away, but miraculously it remained hooked—I have no idea how. Then I did something that surprised even me. After that near fiasco, I was so impressed with the size and beauty of that fish that I too wanted to see it landed, just so I could touch it and appreciate it up close. It was then that I offered to net the fish for him, promising not to tell anyone. He could say that he'd netted it and claim the trout in the Contest.

"Believe it or not, he questioned my motives. However, the thought of losing that fish was too much for him to bear, so he reluctantly agreed. I landed the fish for Jack, but when I tried to unhook it, as the Contest rules stated I must, he did everything in his power to keep me from doing so, nearly knocking me over to grab the net, and even suggesting that we take his picture with the fish still hooked, just in case it regained its strength and tried to escape, so we wouldn't lose it.

"And then suddenly, Jack stopped fighting and just sat there in the river. He leaned back, propped up by his elbows in the shallows, his waders slowly filling with water. He just gave up. I've thought a lot about what happened over the past few days, and, looking back, I think maybe, if I'd been a little more discerning, a little more human and less antagonistic, Jack wouldn't have died. It's possible that the intense battle with that fish and the realization that he was about to be discovered—well, maybe that blast of adrenaline shocked his heart. Maybe that fish and I killed Jack."

"That, my friend, is quite a story," Bill said. "Did you ever take the picture?"

"No, and what I told the STIFFS the other night was true—the fish was never measured, but not because it got away. It was because I was so enraged with Jack that I simply revived it and released it."

"That truly is an amazing story," Bill said, continuing to shake his head slowly in disbelief. "You know, while Andy and I were taking a break one morning and discussing how the Contest was going, we both commented on how Jack looked physically unwell, and pathetically out of shape. When I talked with Cathy after the wake, she told me Jack had indeed been feeling poorly as of late. She'd tried to convince him not to participate in this 'foolishness,' as she called it, knowing how involved he always got in this sort of thing.

"I don't know if you remember, or even if you were living here then, but Jack had a heart attack years back that nearly killed him. I'd venture to guess that if fishing hadn't done him in, then mowing the lawn or a friendly game of golf would have. I don't think Jack knew how to relax and enjoy something simply for what it was. For Jack, life was a competition, whether he was trying a case in court or attempting to raise more money than the next guy for the church, or merely golfing with his friends. Jack needed to be first. He needed to win . . . or die trying."

It appeared to me that Bill had his friend pegged, although having had that intimate talk with Jack, I had a slightly different interpretation of the man's actions.

"Let me tell you something that Jack told me," I responded. "His intense competitive drive was not always a desire to win, but rather a desire not to lose; he truly lived that adage. His fear of losing trumped the joy of winning. That sure would take a lot of the fun out of most things, wouldn't it?"

"For most of us," Bill answered. "That fear of losing can also manifest itself as merely keeping your fellow competitor from winning.

How's that for playing Freud? I saw Jack do that very thing by disrupting a friendly little cribbage tournament I had here at the inn years ago. I won't go into details, but once he knew that he wasn't going to win, he saw to it that no one else would, either, simply by claiming that one of the players, old Ralph Weston, was misdealing. Well, that pretty much put an end to our card playing. And now with our trout-fly competition, he decided that he needed to cheat. Funny how things happen."

"He knew he had no chance of winning our contest," I continued, "but once he got caught doing what he did, he claimed he was only trying to keep from being further humiliated by catching the biggest fish."

"Everything he did seemed to come back to him. It was never the actual event that was important—it was how it affected Jack. But aren't we all guilty of doing much the same thing?" Bill asked.

"No, I don't believe so," I quickly answered. " 'Is it good for me' functions on many levels, the most important, I suppose, being the perception that the good is inherently a universal good—a moral good. The belief that what you are doing for yourself is also good for others—certainly not for everyone, and not all the time, but good for others most of the time. Your 'good' should also do no harm."

"And you're able to determine what that is?" Bill questioned.

I laughed. "Yes, I am that aware. For example, have I ever hurt you? When we're out fishing, am I not considerate of your needs and desires out there? Don't I often offer you first chance at the best water? Have you ever witnessed me annoying or destroying anything, or anyone, for the pure enjoyment of it?" I asked, attempting an amusing interlude.

"Yes," Bill immediately shot back.

"Not counting any situation that involved Jack Windermere."

"Then, no." Bill grinned.

My injection of a little humor into our otherwise serious discussion of Jack and his actions was indication enough that it was time to move our powwow along. But before I was comfortable letting our observations about Jack fade into this night, I was compelled to make one last comment, something that had been eating at me since Sunday night.

"Of all the things that Jack said, I think what troubles me most is something he didn't say. Even as he was trying to explain what he'd done, and why he did it, he never found it necessary to apologize. He never said he was sorry for his actions, or acknowledged that they were wrong. Rather, he seemed much more concerned with trying to justify them. I wish I could believe that he died before he'd had a chance to say he was sorry—not just that he'd made a mistake, but that what he did was wrong."

Bill didn't say a word, just drank his scotch. We both knew we were far from finished with the ghost of Jack Windermere. After a brief silence, it was Bill who set the direction of the evening's course.

"Rick's Wreck—the best damn trout fly in the world," he laughed. "I'm surprised. I guess that's why you play the game."

"I'm glad it was Rick," I said.

"You're the reason it was Rick," Bill replied.

"I think Jack's the reason it was Rick," I responded. "Do you know, you and I haven't discussed the Contest at all since Jack's death; how did things settle out between you and Andy? I don't owe that old fart a beer, do I?"

"No, sir," Bill said proudly. "He owes you—and make sure you collect it here."

"What happened with you two?" I asked. "If I'm getting a beer, you must have finally topped him. And what about all those missed fish of yours he kept complaining about?"

"Hmm . . . where do you want me to start?" Bill asked, squinting his eyes in a manufactured, pensive look.

"Start with what happened; I'm sure those missed fish will show up at some point."

"For us, it often became quite entertaining—at least for me. Andy would pretend to be pissed off every time my leg started acting up and I'd want to slow things down. He would get just as tired as I was, but since I'd be the one to suggest we ease up a bit, he would immediately call me an old cripple, and then push himself a little harder. It really became quite amusing, especially when he'd take the lead in the Contest. We swapped the lead several times as we plugged along. I honestly didn't care much about who was ahead, but it was fun watching his frustration and listening to him piss and moan when he was behind.

"He started calling me William the Tortoise. He would even accuse me of purposely crawling to the next run if it was his turn and he was trailing in the Contest. It was all in good humor—I think—but when it came down to the end, I got serious for a few hours and took a couple nice fish to retain the short lead I had at the time. It was, I will admit, rather rewarding beating my friend, since he seemed to be trying so hard to keep it from happening. I never did catch a bigger fish than his seventeen-incher—oops, I mean sixteen-and-a-half-incher."

"You should have used a caddis worm," I said.

"I wish I'd thought of that," Bill said, laughing. He offered to refresh our drinks again. It had not gone without my notice that he'd completely ignored the missed-fish controversy. My friend had danced around the topic every time it came up, right from the very beginning on Friday night, indicating that there was more to it than merely missed fish.

"Boy, Andy sure didn't like being second," Bill said, handing me another ample drink and repositioning himself in his chair. "He's always competitive, as you know, offering silly, little streamside wagers to liven things up, but he was noticeably different during this contest. He was often more serious, not as much fun."

"I'd be willing to wager that after you missed a few fish early on, and he suspected you were doing it on purpose to annoy him, you found it entertaining to keep doing it," I commented, determined to get to the bottom of this. "Correct me if I'm wrong, but I'll bet you enjoyed provoking him—in an affably sadistic sort of way, of course."

Bill just chuckled under his breath as he exhaled. Our third scotch was making the idea of a true confession much easier for him. He simply started talking, as if he knew all along that he would, needlessly swearing me to secrecy as I had done with him earlier.

"Like you, I was not an advocate of this contest," Bill said. "The more I thought about it, the less enthused I became with the whole idea. I mean, how crazy is the concept of a perfect fly—or a perfect anything? So anyway, I was thinking about those Sam Tippett journal entries, where he wrote his thoughts about the perfect time on the river, and I realized how far it was from what we were about to embark on in the name of seeking the same thing—perfection. I was merely thinking of what Sam had said—no specific intentions, mind you—just how purely elegant and innocent his idea was.

"I was sitting alone in the library, looking over the exquisite Tippett's Crossings you'd brought me, and I thought, What the hell? I didn't give a shit about this contest. I didn't give a flying caribou nut if Andy caught more fish, or bigger fish, than I did. I certainly didn't have a damn thing to prove to him or anybody else when it came to fishing this river." Bill looked over at me with a sly smile and said, "So I cut the hooks off a couple of your flies."

"You missed all those fish on purpose," I said, surprised . . . yet somehow, not. It was just the kind of thing Bill would do if he felt like it.

"I choose to think of it as missing them by design," Bill said. "It was actually quite . . . inspiriting, if I may borrow that wonderful word from one of your essays."

"You may. And I'll bet you know exactly how many fish you missed with your hookless flies."

"I do; eleven."

"So, what we have here is a competition where one man cheats to catch fish and another man goes out of his way *not* to catch them," I said.

"I suppose that's true. However, we both know it's never that simple. Reasons motivate actions, and it appears that you, Benedict Salem, are the only person who will ever know the reasons why both of those things happened . . . and you have a self-imposed silence for one and the commitment to secrecy for the other." Bill glanced over at me with an impish little smile. "How will you ever be able to live with yourself?"

Suddenly, things appeared in a new light. Bill had just put the absurdity of all this in perspective. How would I be able to live with what I knew? I knew nothing—at least, nothing of any importance to anyone else. This contest may have been born to find the perfect trout fly in our little world, but when it was over, it revealed far more about each of us as men—as human beings. Ultimately, the first Jack Windermere Trophy was a prize that did more to expose the imperfections in men than it did to define what constitutes true perfection, in anything.

How diverse and seemingly unrelated are the paths people take in their pursuit to discover something. Once our Contest started, it truly became more about the men competing in it than about trout or trout flies or any noble quest for perfection. How small and corrupt and ignoble a world can become when one loses sight of one's intentions, and how they are pursued.

How, indeed, would I ever be able to live with what I knew?

Epilogue

The Jack Windermere Trophy holds a place of distinction on a small, well-lit shelf behind the bar in the Winged Frog at the Crossing House. I will humbly mention here that the last plaque added to the Jack Windermere World's Most Perfect Trout Fly Trophy was inscribed with BENEDICT SALEM and BROWN DEERHAIR CADDIS. Whether there were other such inscriptions in the past is of little consequence. All that really matters is that for the moment, for this moment in time, the brown Deerhair Caddis is the "Perfect Trout Fly."

One other item of significance that I think worthy of mention is that both our Crossing House river and Day Brook have been improved upon and enriched because of the combined efforts of the STIFFS and the newly initiated Ecology Club at Mike Hartland's High School.

Our rules have been revised and tweaked many times, and we seem to have finally arrived at a condition as impartial as is humanly possible with fly fishers responsible for defining exactly what constitutes just behavior and tolerable actions. *Fair and equitable* was far more difficult to determine than *perfect*, primarily because by their very need to be part of any equation, *fair and equitable* involves other people. On the other hand, *perfect*, by any definition, is a personal prescription of the ideal—a personal truth, as Sam Tippett so eloquently tried to explain.

Sometimes we as humans feel a compulsion to overemphasize our point of view—a need to be understood, and a selfish desire to have our opinions validated. We want our beliefs to be perceived as just as important to everyone else as they are to us. However, it is one of life's great lessons—hopefully one that most of us will learn at some point in our travels—that this is rarely ever the case. Our prejudices, which ultimately lead to our perceptions of perfection, are dogmas sermonized at the church of "Me." In retrospect, trying to get others to join our own little congregation and bow down before the angling gods venerated at our own private chapel on the stream is where our original Contest lost its way. Now, we honor each year's winner in the proper spirit of the endeavor, even if we don't agree with, or we refuse to accept, the reality of the results.

After all this time, the essay that I alluded to while telling this story remains unfinished. Despite a dozen serious attempts, I have never found the words to explain what, as I perceived it, took place in the three days of that first Contest—the unreasonable notion of competing to prove an unprovable concept. Like sections of Sam Tippett's journals, maybe it is just an opinion—an observation or perception—that should be kept private. The only part that rang with undeniable truth was the opening paragraph:

> It's not difficult to understand why individuals with a mutual interest have a desire to assemble in an honest attempt to share in that pleasure. The camaraderie and common cause create friendships that might not—very often, could not—function on any other level or in any other world. However, the diverse personalities that can be charmed by the same pursuit can sometimes be the root cause of a certain amount of . . . I guess what would most accurately be described as tension within that group.

I still carry the secret of what really happened that day, cloaking the truth entangled in Jack's death. After reflecting on what it means to pursue an ideal, and sorting through the debris left in the wake of such a quest, I have come to believe a couple of things: We look for perfection in the things that are most significant to us. Given that fact, no matter how hard we search, in the real world, true perfection can only be experienced in moments.

Maybe that's why I've found my passion in fly fishing.

It is while fishing that I find the opportunity to glimpse perfection: a perfect cast, a perfect morning, and yes, at times, even the insight to understand the perfect design of an insect's wings. I have also come to believe there is something revealing in the desire to understand perfection and in caring enough to pursue it. It may be that the true beauty of perfection lies in the myth—the belief and the hope that such a thing actually exists.

There are also certain moments when I rejoice in the irrefutable beauty of life and its serendipity. I offer this as evidence: Lucy and I will celebrate our first anniversary by dining in the Castle terrace at the Crossing House, and then sharing drinks with friends in the Winged Frog.

How perfect is that?

About the Author

James Hurley is a writer, visual artist, and musician living in Massachusetts. His articles, essays, and sketches have appeared in numerous publications throughout New England, as well as several national magazines, including *Fly Fishing* and *Salmon Trout Steelheader*. His first book is an historical novel, entitled *Spirit of the Sycamore*, and is set in the independent Republic of Vermont during the time of the American Revolution.

Hurley is also a professional musician. He played and taught guitar and other fretted instruments for thirty-seven years and was the classical guitar teacher at the Williston-Northampton School in Easthampton. A self-taught visual artist, his successful watercolor series "Trout with Flies" combines his passion for art and his love of fly fishing. The images show in many galleries, and some have been reproduced onto a successful line of casual clothing. When Hurley is not fishing, making music, or painting, he is hard at work on his next novel.